The Full Moon

A Novel

David Neth

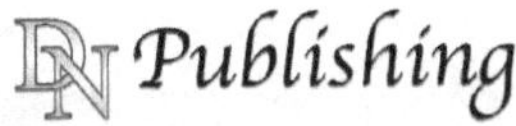
Publishing

The Full Moon
Copyright © 2016 by David Neth
East Pembroke, NY
www.davidnethbooks.com

Subscribe to the author's newsletter for updates and exclusive content:
tinyurl.com/nkkxenq

Publisher: David Neth
Copyediting: Tammy Salyer of Inspired Ink Editing
Proofreading: John Ognibene
Cover Design: kpgs.designs@gmail.com

ISBN 978-0-9905177-2-6
First edition

Follow the author at:
www.facebook.com/davidnethbooks
www.twitter.com/davidnethbooks
www.instagram.com/dneth13

To my mama,
just because I love you.

Chapter One

"Hold the elevator!" Kathy raced through the lobby with her bag slung over her shoulder. She was trying not to trip in her heels.

The men and women in the crowded elevator ignored her, pretending to not see her racing through the lobby like a madwoman. Luckily, a man held out his hand in between the doors just as they were about to close. He was wearing a black suit that fit him perfectly. Kathy was surprised. It was a rare sight to see a man dressed so nicely. But then, she had never really gone to an office building like this before. Her prior experiences with men were the try-too-hard Abercrombie type. And she was definitely over those guys.

She was glad that she had at least one good suit of her own. It wasn't exactly a suit, but the gray between the jacket and the skirt matched so perfectly that nobody noticed. She checked out the other women in the elevator with her and judged how much they spent on their outfits. More money than she had, certainly.

"Thank you!" Kathy smiled and repositioned the bag on her shoulder. She hit the button for the fifth floor and squeezed in next to the man.

"Of course. I never mind sharing an elevator with a pretty lady like yourself." He smiled.

Kathy rolled her eyes and noticed how many other people did the same. He was certainly trying to charm her, but she would've been lying if she said it didn't help. Especially when she was already stressing out. She smiled at him briefly and then fixed her eyes on the display above the elevator doors that read which floor they were on. With the amount of people on the elevator, it was no surprise that it stopped at every floor. She grumbled at the people who got off on the second floor. Couldn't they take the stairs? The doors opened on the fourth floor and the man stepped out.

"I hope you have a wonderful day," he said as he exited the elevator.

Kathy smiled and muttered, "You too."

Soon she stepped out onto the fifth floor and searched for Johnson & Cramer, Inc.

The hallway was bland, nothing like the beautiful lobby on the first floor, with cream walls and no signs directing where each business was located. She stepped away from the elevator and decided to take a left, searching for the correct office. She reached the end of the hall and still hadn't found it so she turned, passed the elevator again, and went in the opposite direction, finally finding the place.

There wasn't anyone at the front desk, so she tapped the little bell on the counter and waited. Soon a man in a loose-fitting gray suit walked out of his office with a to-go cup of coffee from the café downstairs. His blazer gaped open and unbuttoned and his belly hung over his belt.

"You here for the interview?"

Kathy extended her hand with a smile—one she'd practiced with her sister the night before—and said, "Yes. I'm Kathy Walker. So nice to meet you. Are you Mr. Johnson or Mr. Cramer?"

The man chuckled. "No, they're both dead." Her face flushed with embarrassment, but she smiled and tried to play it off. The man shook Kathy's hand and then took a sip of his coffee. "I'm Richard Burke. I'm the sales manager. Why don't you come in my office and we can chat?"

Kathy nodded and followed him.

"Have a seat," he offered with an extended hand as he looped around to his seat behind his desk. Papers littered it, except for the area on the corner of the desk to his left where his computer sat. "I had a chance to take a look at your résumé." He sighed. "Honestly, I was a little underwhelmed. You have very little job experience. My concern is that if I hired you to be my assistant, you wouldn't be able to keep up with the work."

Kathy's stomach lurched. This guy cut right to the chase. "Yeah, I...um...well, I have been out of work for a bit, helping my sister raise her kids. She has two boys." Since Samantha's husband left her last month, she had been her sister's support at home. But now that Steven's paycheck wasn't coming in, Kathy needed to chip in financially, too.

Richard looked down at his copy of her résumé.

Her last job had been at the gas station. She worked the overnights and saw her fair share of weirdos. "Well, officially," she added as he scanned her résumé. "In that time I've been working under-the-table a bit."

Richard leaned back in his chair and rocked back and forth, his right leg crossed over his left. He balanced his coffee on his bent knee and held the foot resting on his knee with his free hand. "Yeah? What kind of work was that?"

Kathy hesitated. "I was working at a hotel downtown, occasionally."

"Front desk?" There was optimism in his voice.

"Um…actually, more in the entertainment…business." She saw his eyebrows scrunch together in confusion and pressed on. "They hired me as a psychic. Actually, in that position I was able to learn some great communication and customer service skills that I think would be useful to me at a job like this." She was hoping she could spin her desperate stint at the hotel into something positive.

Richard smiled. "Miss Walker, I appreciate your enthusiasm for this position, but I'm afraid you aren't qualified enough. I have interviews lined up with other applicants with years of experience working in a secretarial position who would make excellent assistants. I'm sorry, but I don't think this is going to work out."

The Full Moon

Kathy gave him a curt smile and reached for her bag on the side of her chair. "Well, I appreciate you taking the time to meet with me. Good luck filling the position."

"Well, hold on a minute, Miss Walker," Richard said. He stood and walked to the door, closing it. "I believe I could free up some room on the payroll, if you'd be willing to do some… extracurricular work." He stepped closer to her and reached for her hand.

She backed away from him until she was up against the wall.

"You'd have the same salary, benefits, everything. I'm sure I could find something around here for you to do." He placed his hand on her hip and moved closer.

She put her hands on his chest and pushed him back. "Mr. Burke, I may be unqualified for this position, but I'm not stupid. I'm not going to be your office whore so you can feel like a man."

"Whoa, sweetie—"

"*Don't* call me 'sweetie.'" She moved to exit, but he grabbed her arm. "Let go of me, Mr. Burke."

"I'm sure we can sort something out," he pushed.

Kathy whipped her arm around, breaking free of his hold. She held up her other hand, and he stopped moving, frozen in place. With a deep breath, she contemplated kicking him to prove her point but decided against it.

Instead, she opened the door and exited his office. One of the insurance agents by the front desk asked how the interview went.

"Your boss is a pervert," Kathy stated. She repositioned her bag, hooked her thumb on the strap, and walked to the elevator.

On her way down, the elevator stopped once more on the fourth floor and the man in the black suit stepped in.

"You know you can't live in the elevator, right?"

Kathy rolled her eyes and ignored him.

"Bad day?"

She nodded.

"Care to unload it on a complete stranger over lunch?"

She looked up at him. "Right now? Don't you have to work?" She had only been at the interview for fifteen minutes, max. Didn't this guy have anything better to do than ride the elevator all day?

He shrugged. "Yeah. Unless you have other plans."

Kathy wanted to say no, but she was not one to believe in co-incidences. This was the second random encounter with this man today. It had to mean something. "Sure, all right."

"Yeah? Do you have a preference on a place to go? You seem like an easy-to-please girl."

Sidestepping his comment, Kathy suggested the café downstairs.

"Sounds good to me." He held out his hand. "I'm Will, by the way."

"Kathy." His grip was firm and his smile was charming, but she was sure this would be the last she saw of him. She had no intention of ever showing her face in this office building again.

They ordered at the counter, and the woman who helped them already had Will's dish ready to go when they arrived.

"I called from upstairs. This is my usual go-to place for lunch," he explained.

"Oh. Did you want to go somewhere else?" Kathy asked.

"No, I like it here."

After Kathy ordered, they took a seat at a table by the window.

"So do you care to spill about your lousy, horrible, no good, rotten day, or do you want me to help you forget about it?" Will asked.

Kathy smiled, stirring her spoon in her soup. "I had a job interview for an assistant position at Johnson & Cramer...basically a glorified secretary."

"I'm guessing it didn't go well?" Will took a bite of his wrap.

"Besides the fact that I have no relevant job experience and that I've essentially been unemployed for the last six years, the guy was a real dick," Kathy blurted. She sat back and took a deep breath. "Sorry."

Will held up his hands in a surrender gesture and said, "I know. Bad day."

"And now I have to go home and tell my sister that I screwed this up," she continued. She absently stirred her spoon in her soup. Being the hotel psychic wasn't really a lucrative job, but it helped. Now that the hotel was under new management, Kathy had been the first to go. Samantha had been nagging her since then to find another job.

"You're supposed to eat it," Will joked, indicating her soup. Kathy cracked a smile and let go of her spoon. "Look on the bright side: you were still able to walk out of there with your head held high. And hey, you still have your *incredibly* good looks."

"Apparently that's all I'm good for." She turned her attention out the window at the crowd walking on the sidewalk. They had jobs and families and places to be. For a moment, Kathy envied them.

Will wiped his hands and looked at her. "That's not what I meant…"

"I know. But that's what Richard Burke was looking for. Some office fun," Kathy said. "I'm sorry. I shouldn't be telling you all this. You work in the same building as him."

"Richard Burke?"

Kathy nodded.

"That man is a snake! His last secretary left after suing him for sexual harassment! If I knew you were going there, I would've warned you!" He tossed his napkin on the table. "I'm going to straighten him out."

"No! I already took care of it." She wondered if her magic still had its hold on him. She didn't want Will walking in on a magically frozen Burke. Even if she planned on never seeing him again.

"You're right." Will relaxed. "You don't need anyone to fight your battles for you. You certainly look like you can take care of yourself. But please, eat."

Kathy smiled and brought a spoonful to her mouth. Her first bite to eat since breakfast. "Wow, this is good!"

He smiled. "Right? That's why it's my daily favorite."

She ate a bit more and asked, "So where do you work?"

"I actually am in charge of a small law firm up on the fourth floor. William Brown Attorneys."

"Wow! That's incredible!"

"Yeah, it's pretty nice being my own boss and all. Right now it's just me and another lawyer friend of mine, so a lot of the house-keeping stuff like finances, phone calls, meetings, they're all done by me. Well, pretty much."

"Are you looking for a secretary?" Kathy smiled.

"Do you know someone?"

"Maybe." Kathy broke up some crackers in what was left of her soup.

"I know who you're talking about. I heard she's completely unqualified." He smiled.

"Too soon!" Kathy laughed and tossed a bit of her cracker at him.

He put his hands up in another surrender gesture and said, "I'm kidding. But really, I would love to hire you, but the money just isn't there yet. Hopefully soon. I'll definitely keep my eyes open for you, though."

"How are you going to reach me if you find something?" Kathy took a spoonful of the rest of her soup. As thick as he was laying it on, she was surprised he hadn't weaseled her number out of her sooner.

"I was hoping this would be a sly way to get your number."

"You think it's that easy, huh?" Kathy laughed.

"Well, I did buy you lunch," Will prodded, flashing a smile. "And I've been a shoulder to cry on in this devastating time of your life."

Kathy rolled her eyes again. "Oh, what a gentleman. Do you have a pen?"

"Of course." He opened his jacket and pulled a gold ball-point pen out of the inside pocket. It had the name of his business branded on the side.

"You can't afford a secretary, but you can buy novelty pens?" Kathy scribbled her name and number on a fresh napkin. She couldn't believe she was doing this. The last time she'd given a guy a number like this she had been drunk. She'd needed to change her number in order to get him and his buddies to stop calling.

"It's called *branding*. Some expenses are worth it," Will explained. "Plus, I can write it off."

Kathy smiled and slid the napkin over to him. "Don't give this to your college buddies for a late-night booty call. I have caller ID."

Will folded it and placed it in the pocket inside his jacket. He placed his hand over it and declared, "I will protect this to the death."

Kathy laughed. Her day was turning out to be better than where it was originally heading.

Will glanced at his watch. "Oooh, I have to go. I have a meeting with a client in half an hour and I haven't prepared for it yet. Can I walk you to your car?"

Kathy cringed. Her best self was not coming across. "I don't have a car, actually. You could walk me to the bus station, but it's about three blocks away."

"Where do you live?"

"Just on the edge of the city on Arlington. Not exactly easy walking, especially in these shoes." Kathy stuck out her foot so Will could see the artificial height she was walking on.

"I see that." He stood and offered his hand to help her up. "I will walk you to the bus stop, but I'm afraid I won't be able to wait with you."

Kathy took his hand and stood. For a moment they were nearly pressed up against each other until Will took a step back. "Won't you be late for your meeting?"

"I'm my own boss, remember? I think it's worth it. I want to make sure your day only gets better from here."

"You're really working it, huh?" Kathy said, leading him out of the café and in the direction of the bus stop.

"Is it working?"

"Maybe you should try that number to find out," Kathy suggested. They crossed the intersection and she reached for her ear. "I think I lost an earring."

Will looked around the sidewalk. "I'll check the other side."

She grabbed his arm to stop him and said, "It's not a big deal. I have more."

When they reached the bus stop, they both hesitated, unsure how to properly say good-bye.

"Thank you for lunch."

"It was my pleasure," Will said. "Good luck on your job search, and I will definitely be keeping my eye open for you."

Will moved to kiss her cheek and ran into Kathy's extended hand. They laughed and settled on a wave.

Kathy watched as Will walked back to the office building. She couldn't help but smile. All things considered, it was a very good day.

Chapter Two

Kathy gulped down a glass of water after her morning run. She had taken her nephews to school and had already thrown in a load of laundry. Her goal for the day was to set up a couple more job interviews. Her sister, Samantha, had helped her tweak her résumé to make it look more professional. Kathy hoped the changes would do the trick. She also hoped that she never met another interviewer like Richard Burke, but she knew that was likely a fantasy.

She grabbed a hand towel from the stove and wiped away the sweat beading up on her forehead. She had just kicked off her sneakers when the doorbell rang.

Kathy peered through the stained glass on the front door, trying to make out who it was. It was not unusual to get unexpected or uninvited guests. She relaxed a bit when she saw a suit coat and tie. Anything that was looking to kill her or her family was not usually dressed so nicely.

"Good morning." It was Will. Kathy flashed him a smile and then realized that she looked like a mess. A complete opposite of what she'd looked like the last time she'd seen him. Instead of a gray pinstripe suit coat and skirt, she wore a pink tank top and black shorts. Her hair was matted with sweat, and she was sure she stank, too.

"Hi," Kathy responded, a little confused. "How do you know where I live?"

"You told me Arlington, remember?"

She ran her hand along the top of her head, hoping to smooth out a few escaped hairs from her ponytail. It still didn't make sense. She had only met Will once and here he was on her doorstep.

Finally, Will sighed. "Okay, I cheated. I asked a neighbor. Told her you were a friend of mine from college."

Kathy pointed to the house across the street. "Mrs. Kors?" Kathy's busybody neighbor was always looking for reasons to check in or get the latest gossip. As a retired woman in her 70s, she frequently binged on the latest scoop.

"The short old woman across the street?" He tossed a thumb behind him. "She seemed sweet."

"That's the one." She folded her arms across her chest and asked, "So…what are you doing here?"

"Well I bought you lunch last week, I just figured it was your turn to return the favor." He flashed another charming smile. Kathy cocked an eyebrow. "I'm kidding, unless you're offering." He paused to see if she would bite. When she didn't, he continued, "What I came here for was to return this." He held out his hand. Sitting in the middle of his palm was the earring Kathy had lost the day of her interview.

"Where'd you find it?" She scooped it up and studied it, making sure it was the same one.

"One of the girls at the café found it. They thought it might belong to you since it was at my usual seat," Will explained.

"Well, it was very nice of you to return it. Thank you," Kathy said. She gripped the door and made to close it, but Will's voice stopped her.

"Would you like to go to dinner sometime?"

Kathy stopped and looked at him before answering. Her knee-jerk reaction was to say no. She knew she wasn't exactly a catch. Unemployed and living with her sister, who was a single mother of two. The only thing going for her was her looks, and she knew that whenever a guy spontaneously asked her out, he was rarely looking for a meaningful relationship. However, the more she looked at Will, the more she found herself forgetting all her previous experience with men.

"On a date?"

Will tilted his head sideways and nodded shyly. "I was hoping."

They considered each other for a moment. A crash from the kitchen broke Kathy's trance. She knew her sister wouldn't be home all day, and it was too early for the boys.

"Um…sure, yeah, I will." She looked back into the house and then back at Will. She needed to get rid of him, fast. The noise was likely an attack, and she didn't want Will caught in the crossfire, nor did she want her secret exposed.

"Is everything all right?" He stepped forward, but Kathy pushed him away.

"Yeah, it's fine. Look, you have my number, so call me and we'll set something up." She closed the door farther and farther as she spoke. "Bye!"

Once the door was shut, she raced to the kitchen. She saw a puddle of water by the sink but no sign of an intruder. Grabbing a knife, she crept through the house. She stopped when she stepped in another puddle of water in the living room, which soaked into her socks. Looking around on the floor for a trail of water to indicate where the trespasser was, she tensed up when she felt a drop of water on her neck. She looked up and gasped.

A slimy fishlike creature perched upside down on the vaulted ceiling. Covered in scales and fins lining the middle of his head and down his back, he bared his razor-sharp teeth and hissed when Kathy spotted him. His long claws dug into the wall, holding him in place.

After a moment of hesitation, he lunged at Kathy. She slipped on the puddle as she tried to escape and fell to the ground. The creature caught her ankle in his slimy grasp and pulled her toward him. Kathy managed to grab on to the front parlor door frame and used her other foot to swing around and kick the beast in the face.

Back on her feet, she snatched up the knife and drove it into the creature's chest. Despite being impaled, the creature let out a roar and swatted at Kathy, scratching her arm and drawing blood.

She scrambled up the stairs and to her bedroom, slamming the door behind her. She searched for something she could use to contain him or slow him down.

Kicking open the door, the creature hissed once again at Kathy before stepping into the room. Out of options, she nabbed her hair dryer, and firing it up to full blast, she pointed it at the creature. He sent out another hiss and jumped out of the hallway window and down to the yard. Kathy watched as he jumped over the fence and down the street. She swore to herself, knowing there was no way she would be able to catch him on her own.

* * *

"I'm home!" Samantha announced as she walked through the front door.

"We're in the kitchen!" Kathy called. She was pulling a pan out of the oven. "And dinner's ready!" It was a chicken left over from another meal that Samantha had made a few weeks before. All Kathy needed to do was pull it out of the freezer and stick it in the oven.

"Oooh, perfect timing!" Samantha hooked her keys by the door and kissed each of her boys on the head. They were at the kitchen table doing homework. Sixteen-year-old Josh, Samantha's oldest, was the main reason his brother, Chris, who was fourteen, finished any of his homework at all. "How was your day, boys?"

"Good," they droned.

Once the table was cleared of textbooks and notebooks, Kathy, Samantha, and the boys sat down for dinner.

"Any luck with your job hunt?" Samantha asked her sister. She cut into her chicken and took a bite.

"Y'know, I started the day off great. Very productive, but some things happened and it just didn't turn out," Kathy said. She knew Samantha didn't like to talk about demonic attacks too much in front of the boys. The attacks were inevitable, but Samantha wanted her children to be as normal as possible without being scarred by whatever was hiding in their closets.

Kathy thought the whole idea was stupid. The boys would need to know how to use their magic to protect themselves eventually. It was only a matter of time before they were targeted. But they were Samantha's kids, so Kathy tried to keep talk of demonic activity to a minimum.

As a result, the sisters often used ridiculous excuses to evade any magic talk. Kathy was sure the boys didn't buy it, though. Josh and Chris were young, not stupid. They were smarter than Samantha sometimes gave them credit for.

"I noticed the laundry didn't get done," Samantha pressed.

"But I mopped the floor," Kathy countered.

"And she made dinner," Josh added. The sisters bickered a lot, especially now that Kathy wasn't bringing in any money. Josh remembered how much arguing there was in the house when his dad was still around. So now he always tried to calm the storm before it turned into something bigger.

Hearing her son's tone, Samantha gave in. "Yes, you're right. Thank you, Kathy." She turned to her youngest son and asked, "Did you finish your homework?"

"I just have a couple of math problems left, but they shouldn't take me long," Chris said. He attempted to shove a giant spoonful of mashed potatoes in his mouth.

"Smaller bites, Chris, c'mon," Samantha said. She thought back to the days when their father had been there to help her out. It made her sad to think that Steven could so easily abandon his family. His children.

When dinner was over, Samantha and Kathy started on the dishes as the boys finished their homework.

"There was an attack today," Kathy whispered to her sister. "And I didn't get him."

Samantha put down the plate she was drying and turned to Josh and Chris.

"Boys, would you mind finishing upstairs in your room? Your aunt and I need to discuss some stuff," Samantha said.

"Are you going to talk about magic? I want to help!" Chris loved magic, despite not having any active powers of his own.

Samantha tried not to lie to the boys, so it was difficult for her to respond truthfully when they asked her outright about magic. "Yes, we are. But right now I need you to finish your homework." She smiled at him. "We'll come to you guys if we need help."

The Full Moon

Chris sighed and left the room with Josh. Samantha knew the boys—especially Chris—were anxious to be in the midst of the action, but it would be too soon before they were. She wanted to protect them as long as she could, but she also needed to prepare them for any attack that might happen if she or Kathy wasn't around. Now that they were getting older, it was getting harder and harder to keep them in someone's company for their protection.

Once the boys were gone, Samantha pressed Kathy for more details. Her sister dried her hands and pulled the magic book out from the pantry.

"I was looking through it when the boys came home," Kathy explained. "I really don't think we should hide it from them this much. They should know that at any minute we could be attacked."

"I don't want them to be terrified their whole lives. They're just kids," Samantha said.

"They're teenagers, they're not helpless," Kathy countered. She flipped to a page in the book. "Anyway, this is the guy who attacked me."

"Vepar?"

Kathy nodded and pointed to a warning in the entry. "This scared me."

Samantha read from the book: "'If his blood mixes with anyone else's, they too will become a creature like him.' Did he bleed on you?"

Kathy shook her head. "No, but he scratched me pretty

good." She showed off her wounded arm. "His blood didn't mix with mine, but I got some of his slime in there. I thought that might add to the mutation process, but I think I'm good."

"Why didn't you call me?" Samantha gripped her sister's elbow and examined her arm. "What would've happened if the boys came home and you were some fish-mutant?"

"Plus side? I'm not. And the book has a potion that'll help kill him," Kathy said.

"Okay." Samantha let go of Kathy's arm and looked at the entry in the book. "So do you have anything of his that we can track him with?"

Kathy bit her lip. "No. I didn't think of it. I mopped up the mess so the boys wouldn't see, and that was all he had leftover. But he freaked out when I shot my hair dryer at him, so I'm guessing he can't stay out of the water that long."

"Kathy! It's going to be impossible to find him!"

"Why? I just figured he'd be in the lake. We head out to Presque Isle and look for him. Simple as that. He'll probably want to stay away from people, so a beach in April is perfect."

Samantha tucked her dark hair behind both of her ears and crossed her arms. The same stance she took whenever the boys were making poor arguments to get out of housework and she was getting frustrated with them. Kathy didn't appreciate Samantha treating her like one of the kids.

"Think about it, Kathy. Do you know how many people in Erie have a swimming pool? By April they still have them closed, which means they're not using them. Not to mention that it rains a lot this time of year, so he could probably rehydrate himself without entering a large body of water. And what about if he hurts someone before we can find him?"

Kathy held up her hands. "All very good points. But look, I actually saw this thing with my own eyes. He's not that intelligent. Someone sent him. He's not going to hurt anybody unless whoever is in charge of him orders him to do it. Since he came here looking for me, I'm most likely the target."

Samantha sighed and leaned back on the counter. "Okay. But I still think it's a good idea to equip every one of us—including the boys—with this potion so that, just in case you're not the sole target, we are all protected."

Kathy smirked. "You're going to corrupt the minds of your tiny children? How will they survive!?" She laughed and Samantha shot her a look.

"Finish the dishes. I'll start heating water."

They began preparing the potion, dropping in the various ingredients the book called for. They only had to substitute a few, but Samantha was very confident in her potion-making abilities and knew the substitutions wouldn't be a problem.

"So why do you think you're the target?" Samantha asked. She was waiting for the potion to thicken before adding the next ingredient.

Kathy shrugged and continued with the dishes. "I don't know. Maybe it's the whole family? I was just the only one home. I know several people are dying to get their hands on the book. Or it could be our powers. You never know with these things."

"True. Which is why we need to be extra careful. We don't know enough about this guy," Samantha said.

"Yeah, but I don't think we should put our lives on hold just because we get attacked." Kathy set a dish in the drying rack. "We should still go to work, go shopping, go on dates, see friends… you know…"

Samantha raised her eyebrows and smiled. "Do you have something you want to tell me?"

She could always tell when Kathy was seeing someone new. She acted like a teenager every time she was about to go on a first date. Still, it had been a while since Kathy was this lovesick. She began giving up on men once she saw the pain Steven had inflicted on Samantha when he left. Samantha was glad to see that Kathy was getting over her fear of getting hurt like she did.

Kathy shrugged. "Last week when I was at that crappy job interview, this guy I met in the elevator asked me to lunch—"

"You meet guys in the most random places!"

"I wasn't putting out! It was just lunch!" Kathy was smiling. A week had passed since she'd first met Will Brown, and she barely thought of him. Now she couldn't help smiling whenever she did. "Anyway, he showed up this morning and asked me out."

"House call?"

"I lost an earring." Kathy knew what her sister was implying.

Samantha smiled and added the next ingredient. "All right, this thing is just about done. Let me go warn the boys."

"They'll be fine, Sammy. Don't worry about it too much."

CHAPTER THREE

Kathy's phone buzzed on the table for the third time that morning.

"Are you ever going to answer that?" Chris asked. He was lifting the bowl of sugary milk leftover from his cereal to his mouth.

Kathy silenced her phone. "I know what he's calling for, and I don't have an answer yet."

"Is it your lawyer?" Samantha was spreading butter on a bagel.

Kathy rolled her eyes and smiled. "He's not *mine*. But yeah, it's him."

"Have you gone out yet?" Samantha asked.

Kathy shook her head. "Not yet."

Josh held a piece of toast between his teeth and slid his books into his backpack. When his hand was free, he took a bite and asked, "What are you waiting for?"

"With Vepar attacking at any minute, I don't want to risk bringing someone home and exposing our secret. Or accidentally getting him killed," Kathy explained. Samantha shot her a look so she added, "Not that anyone's dying. We just have to be careful, that's all."

Samantha was eager to change the subject. "Do you boys have your potions?"

Chris waved it in the air. "Got it!" He slipped it into his pocket.

"Don't get it taken away this time, okay? I used the last of the mugwort in that batch." The last time the boys had needed to take a potion to school, Chris kept playing with it in class and it had been confiscated by the teacher. That had been a tough one to explain.

"All right, get your things." She shot a glance at the clock. "Oooh, I didn't realize it was so late already. We need to go." She popped the last bite of her bagel in her mouth, wiped her hands on her napkin, and rushed out the door with Josh and Chris in tow.

When her sister and her nephews shuffled out of the house, Kathy stood from her seat to tackle the dishes. Just as she filled the sink, her phone rang again.

It was Will. Again. She stared at it for a moment, deciding whether or not she should answer it. She wanted to go out with him, but she didn't know how to tell him that she was putting off their date on account of his safety. She didn't want to give him the impression that she was blowing him off. After going back and forth in her mind, she finally dried her hands and answered at the last second.

"I'm so sorry I haven't gotten back to you," Kathy started before he could say anything.

"Are you even still interested? I asked you out a week ago, and I haven't spoken to you since. I thought I might've had the wrong number." His deep, warm voice was a very nice sound to hear that early in the morning. Kathy couldn't help but smile and wonder what was wrong with her.

She cringed and tried to keep a casual tone. "Yeah, sorry. It's been a crazy week. But my nights are basically free the rest of this week." As long as Samantha was home to watch the boys, she wouldn't have to worry too much about an attack from Vepar. Her sister would definitely call if something happened. They each had the potion, so all that they needed to do was wait it out. There hadn't been any strange reports, so obviously Vepar wasn't on a killing spree.

"How's tonight?"

"Tonight?" Her voice betrayed her with a squeak. She cleared it and said, "Um…yeah, that could work."

"I hope you're in the mood for seafood. There's this great restaurant at the hotel on the bay," Will said.

Kathy's mind snapped to her intermittent stints as the hotel psychic. She knew that hotel—and that restaurant—very well. Showing her face there would be embarrassing, but she didn't want to tell him no again. "Perfect."

"Great! I'll pick you up at six?"

"You already know where I live, so sounds good."

* * *

As Will and Kathy walked into the hotel, he apologized for having to park so far away. There was an event at the convention center on the next pier over, taking up all the area parking. They'd managed to find street parking but still ended up walking six blocks.

"Will, it's fine. It's not your fault." She wore a sleeveless red satin dress with black heels. By the time they reached the hotel, her feet were happy to be resting. They were certainly not hiking shoes.

Will ordered for the two of them. Kathy didn't hear what it was he ordered—for dinner or for wine. When he saw her concerned face, he said, "You'll like it. Trust me."

She smiled and took a sip of her water. "So, how's the practice?"

"Good, actually. I signed another client just today. Her case doesn't seem to be too hard, but I guess we'll see what the defense has when we get to court," he said. "How's the job hunt?"

"Horrible." She took another sip of her water nervously. The fancy hotel with seafood and wine, it was not her typical style. These weren't her type of people. She felt like a fake for trying to be like them. She usually set up in the front lobby, dressed in her most festive psychic attire and asking folks if they'd like to know their future. She set her glass on the table and took a deep breath.

"Have you heard of any openings for me?"

"You see, I realized later that I don't know much about you," he said with a smile. "I'd like to change that."

Kathy looked him in the eyes. She liked him. He had potential, that much she knew, but she wanted to be sure he understood just what he was getting into. From what she could tell, Will was used to elegant seafood dinners. The piano playing softly in the corner didn't strike him as too much. Kathy was used to heating up ramen in the microwave and watching TV while slurping up her noodles on the couch. She needed to set the record straight before either of them got in too deep. "Actually, my last job was at this hotel."

"Oh, really? Front desk?"

She smiled briefly and said, "Hotel psychic. I wasn't exactly on the payroll, but they let me set up a table. I made decent money, too. But then the hotel staff thought I was taking away customers from their other services and they asked me to leave." Waiting for his reaction, she took another sip of water and asked, "Your thoughts?"

He seemed confused, but not scared like Kathy expected. He smoothed out the cloth napkin on his lap. "Can't say I've ever heard that one before. It's interesting."

"Most people thought I was nuts. Especially since I didn't have a car, so I took the bus. To most of the city I was the crazy psychic lady. I'm surprised you've never heard of me." That was a lie. People on the bus definitely gave her quizzical looks, but she didn't have the reputation. At least, not to her knowledge.

"What was your niche? Tarot cards, palm readings, crystal balls?"

Kathy smiled. No one who didn't have at least a little knowledge about mediums ever asked about her niche. He was more interesting than she'd given him credit for. But there was still more left to tell—a lot more. If only he knew just how divine she was.

"I've never done tarot cards. I couldn't tell you how to read them. And if a psychic has a crystal ball at her table, run. She's a scammer. I mostly did palm readings. Occasionally, I did tea leaves as well, but the hotel didn't really like it when I brought in a dump bucket for the water."

"Could you read my palm?" He offered his hand, and she took it before she realized what she'd just agreed to. A lot of times she had an actual vision—an extension of her time specialty as a witch. She wondered if she would be able to see his future on command. Sometimes it was difficult to determine the difference between the reading and her feelings.

She forced herself to look down at his hand. Tracing some of the wrinkles in his palm, she shared her findings. "Well, I see lots of stress…likely from your start-up. Conflict…passion…oh, but then here's success." She pointed a finger to a spot on his palm. "See that line? That's what's to come. This over here," she moved her finger, "that's what is."

"Can you see what was?" He looked up at her, and she realized they had been leaning closer to each other.

She sat back and reached for her water again. She opened her mouth to respond but was interrupted by the waitress bringing over the wine. Kathy breathed a sigh of relief. They were only twenty minutes into their first date and she was already searching his palms, hoping to see their futures connected. She needed to cool down.

"What do you think?" Will held up his wineglass.

Kathy took a sip and considered for a moment. It was rich. Full bodied with a hint of strawberry. She didn't know much about wine, but she knew this was good. "Very nice."

"It's only half as good as the food." He brought the glass to his lips but pulled it away before taking a sip. He raised it in front of him instead. "To a wonderful evening with a beautiful woman. How did I get so lucky?"

"Don't get too excited about that success in your future." She raised her glass and clinked it with his before taking another sip.

* * *

After dinner, the two walked hand-in-hand to the end of the pier. The evening had gone perfectly. Kathy hadn't enjoyed a date so much in a while. She could already tell that things were different with Will.

The full moon was out, reflecting off Lake Erie and illuminating the sky. The glow from the city lights helped brighten the sky as well.

"It's beautiful," Kathy said. She rested her head against his arm.

"I like to come out here every so often just for the view. Presque Isle has an even better view, but—"

"I think this is perfect." She looked up at him and reached up on her toes to meet his lips. Kathy knew from his kiss that falling for him was a good thing—a great thing.

Prior to meeting Will, she'd felt completely burnt out from all the stress in her life: making a living with no skills an employer would be interested in, helping her sister raise Josh and Chris, and keeping up with her supernatural responsibilities was a bit too much at times. But standing out on the edge of the pier with Will completely erased all that, and for the first time in a long time, she was carelessly happy. All her subconscious thoughts were gone, and she was entirely in the moment.

The two were so consumed with each other that they didn't hear the splashing of the water. It wasn't until Kathy felt a slimy hand on her leg that her attention was brought back to reality.

She landed with a thud on the pier as something pulled her into the water. The water was up to her waist by the time Will had hold of both of her arms and pulled her up. The splash of the water hid the creature from sight, which Kathy was grateful for. She didn't want Will to see. She might be able to still pass this off as her being clumsy.

Once she was safely on deck, Will asked if she was all right. She barely had time to nod before Vepar lunged from the water and landed on the edge of the pier. He hissed at the couple, spraying them with water and slime.

Kathy put her hands up and froze both Vepar and Will. She needed to act quickly. She knew there would likely have been people in the hotel or farther down the pier who had seen or heard the commotion. She searched for her purse that held the potion to kill the water creature, but she couldn't find it. She must've dropped it in the water when he first pulled her in.

She needed to get Will away safely without exposing who she was. If that was even still possible. She could easily have unfrozen him and ran, but then she would be facing twenty questions about what happened. She wasn't ready for that conversation with him yet.

Before she could think of anything, her magic wore off and both Will and Vepar unfroze. The creature swiped at Will with his claws, tearing his blazer. Kathy pulled off her shoes and drove a heel into the creature's back. She saw the point of the knife she'd stabbed him with the week before and knew it wouldn't stop him. He turned and pushed her. Landing on the edge of the pier, she moved to get up, but when she shifted her weight she lost her balance and began to topple into the dark water. She gripped the bollard on the edge of the pier to keep herself from falling in.

Looking up at Will, she saw him charge Vepar, and a large sword appeared in his hands. Swinging it sideways, he tore through the creature's flesh and its head dropped to the dock. He kept swinging until pieces of Vepar scattered across the end of the pier. When he was done, he stood and admired his work, huffing and puffing. Kathy could see blood sprayed across his face in the moonlight. The sword in his hand disappeared, and he reached down to help lift Kathy back onto the dock.

He looked at her and said, "Grab the other end of the net over there and help me round up the body before anyone sees."

Chapter Four

"What the hell was that?" Kathy pointed at the parts of Vepar that Will was stacking in a small pile at the end of the pier.

"Keep your voice down." Will shot an anxious glance back at the hotel. "You're going to draw attention." He chucked a piece of the creature's leg onto the pile.

"What, are you some kind of…wizard or something? A witch?" She knew she hadn't imagined Will conjuring the sword. He was hiding something, just as she was.

"Kathy, I'll explain later. Right now we need to dispose of the body before anyone sees."

He held her hands in his. She looked up and saw Vepar's blood splattered across his face. She nodded slowly and reached for the net at the edge of the pier. "Careful. His venom is still pretty potent."

The Full Moon

"What about the blood on your face?"

He brushed it off with his sleeve. "I'll be fine."

They spread the net out on the deck and tossed the body pieces in the center.

After they managed to scoop up all the pieces, Will said, "Stay here. I'll bring the car up."

Kathy nodded and watched as he jogged down the pier.

She examined herself. Her dress had been ripped at the ends by Vepar's claws. There was another tear by her knees. She must have scraped it when Will was pulling her out of the water because there was a faint trickle of blood that blended in with her red dress.

She tried to straighten out her hair. It had been pulled back in a bun, but during the attack most of it managed to slip out. She tried to correct it before giving up and letting it all fall on her shoulders.

Headlights blinded her from down the pier, and she stood in front of the net just in case it wasn't Will. A man stepped out, and the car continued to sit idle with the engine still running. The lights illuminated Kathy.

She still couldn't make out who it was until Will jogged up. "Let's try to get him in the trunk. I think I know of a place where we can dump him." Kathy nodded and helped Will pull in the corners of the net. The body was soaked and heavier than they expected.

Will rested with his hands on his knees after they managed to bring the net to the back of the car. He let out a breath and said, "I'm going to try to lift him. You help push him into the trunk. Remember, don't let his blood touch yours."

Pulling up her dress, she bent her knees to get under the net when Will lifted it. He counted to three and yanked it up. Kathy pushed the bulk of it toward the trunk and helped Will squeeze in the parts that wouldn't fit.

"It's not going to work," Kathy complained. "He's too big for the trunk."

"It has to fit." Will shoved and cracked some of Vepar's bones, which sent chills down Kathy's back. Finally, he slammed the trunk down. "There. It fits."

He wiped his hands on his pants. He was a worse mess than Kathy was. Her clothes were mostly ripped and torn, but Will was splattered in blood. His white dress shirt looked almost completely red now.

"What are we going to do with the body?" Kathy tried to keep her voice even. She didn't want Will to know how scared she was. She knew she could be walking right to her death with him.

He clenched his jaw and watched as some people began to exit the hotel. "Get in the car."

Kathy sat quietly as Will raced down State Street. Either this man was a homicidal killer, or he was somehow magical. She now doubted whether she had actually seen him conjure the sword. It could have been something her imagination had filled in. But no, he didn't have the sword beforehand and he didn't have it now. Yet the body was still cut into pieces. He had definitely done something.

Will turned onto Highway 79 going south and raced out of the city.

The Full Moon

"Where are we going?" Kathy's voice was tiny in the tension-filled car. She felt like a fool for falling for him so fast and having it all turn bad in such a short time.

"We need to dump the body. Preferably somewhere away from water."

"Do you have an idea of where?"

Will nodded. "Farmland. We'll have to find one that isn't being used this season."

"You've done this before?"

Will looked over at Kathy. "You don't have to be afraid of me. I'm not going to hurt you."

She didn't answer. Didn't even look at him. She kept her eyes on the road as they raced away from the city. As guilty as criminals.

"I know you're a witch," Will said.

"So shouldn't *you* be the one afraid of *me*?"

"I've dealt with witches my whole life. None of them were nearly as…captivating as you."

Kathy rolled her eyes, yet still flashed a smile. "Okay, so I'm a witch. What are you?"

He kept his eyes on the road. "I have…powers, yes."

"I know. The dead guy in the trunk told me. But what are you? Are you a witch?" She needed to know what type of magic he possessed, that way she could figure out his limitations. She never saw him brandish a wand, so he definitely wasn't a wizard. She didn't remember him speaking any charms or spells, so he likely wasn't a sorcerer—although if he was and he didn't use a charm, his magic was highly advanced and she was in trouble. He had to be a witch.

Will shook his head. "I'm not a witch."

Kathy crossed her arms and faced forward again.

"It doesn't really matter what I am. At least not now." He tried to reach over and rest a hand on her knee, but she crossed her legs and pulled away from him. Placing his hand back on the steering wheel, he continued, "We have a job to finish. It's been a weird night. We both need to sleep on it and figure this all out in the morning."

Five minutes later, Will took an exit and drove down a dark rural road. Besides the glow from the headlights, the only light came from the full moon.

"Keep your eye out for a possible spot. It needs to be away from water, otherwise he could re-form himself," Will said.

"So he doesn't ever die?"

"Not as long as there is still a drop of water in his body," Will explained. "We'll bury the pieces separately to help dry him out faster. Once his body is completely dried, he's never coming back."

Kathy wondered how he knew so much. She had an entry on Vepar in her magic book, but she still didn't know the details about how to kill him. Besides the potion.

Will turned off his lights and pulled onto a farmer's path through an empty field.

"Farmers tend to rotate fields whenever the nutrients in the ground are used up. This field must've been vacant this season," Will explained. "That means it should be pretty dry."

The car rocked back and forth as they slowly worked their way farther down the uneven path deeper into the field. Kathy could hear Vepar's body thrashing around in the trunk.

About halfway in, Will stopped the car and said, "This looks like a good place."

Barefoot, Kathy stepped out of the car and walked to the trunk.

"Where are your—oh, yeah." She had left the one shoe at the pier, the other was still lodged in Vepar's back.

Will popped the trunk. "Same thing as before. Ready?"

Grabbing hold of the net, Will and Kathy pulled hard. The body moved slightly but remained snug inside the trunk. Kathy slipped in the dirt and fell to the ground, but she popped up and kept trying to free the net.

Eventually, they worked the net out of the trunk, and the body plopped onto the ground.

Kathy looked up at Will and asked, "Do you have a shovel?"

He held out his hand and conjured one.

"Oh, right. Are you going to need help?"

He pulled off his torn blazer and rolled up the sleeves of his bloody dress shirt. "I'm not going to make you dig. Especially without shoes. Have a seat."

Will went to work on the first hole. He measured halfway down the shovel and deemed it deep enough to hold Vepar's body. He counted eight steps away and started on the second hole. Kathy sat in the passenger seat and watched. Once six holes were dug, he wiped the sweat from his brow and asked, "Would you mind helping me distribute the body parts?"

"Every other date I've been on usually ended with a kiss at the door." She stood and reached inside the net for a slimy dismembered limb.

"The night's not over yet." Will smiled. He had his hands on his hips and breathed heavily. "Besides, this is a date you'll never forget."

"And some people say romance is dead." She couldn't help but smile. The attack wasn't Will's fault, and at this point there was nothing left to do but laugh at the absurdity of it all. She had been in other strange predicaments because of her supernatural legacy and felt sure this wasn't going to be her last.

Just as she dropped a piece into the dirt, Will spun her around and kissed her. "See, now it's romantic."

She smiled at him until she realized they were standing beside a cut-up corpse, and she snapped back to reality. "Um…where are we putting the…uh, big piece?" She pointed to the net below her.

Wiping away some more sweat, Will pointed to a large hole to his left. "I think the one over here is deeper, so we're probably better off putting the torso there. We should probably keep the head away from it, though."

Kathy nodded and opened up the net. "It's like Santa's bag on Christmas morning." She reached in and grabbed an arm and tossed it in a nearby hole.

Once the limbs were scattered, they both moved the torso to the deepest hole.

"It looks pretty dried out already. Shouldn't take much more," Will noted. "I'll finish up here."

He looked exhausted and Kathy wanted to help him, but there was no way she could do that without shoes. She wondered if Will could conjure some for her. She decided against asking and turned to return to the car.

"Wait! Here." Will reached into the hole the torso was in and pulled out Kathy's heel and the kitchen knife she had stabbed Vepar with, then handed them to her. "I believe these belong to you."

She took them without thinking and threw them by her feet in the car. Both would likely end up in the garbage when she got home. Especially since she'd left her matching shoe somewhere on the pier on the lake.

After Will finished filling in the holes, the shovel disappeared from Will's hand and he returned to the driver's seat. "I think we're good."

"We don't need to say a spell or anything to make sure he's really dead?" Despite the work they put into it, everything seemed too easy.

"You witches and your spells." Will laughed. "No, this is definitely the end of the road for him." He started the car and headed back down the path toward the road.

They chatted on the way back to Kathy's house, avoiding the topic of body disposals. The darkness of the night hid their bloodstained clothes and unkempt appearance.

Back at Kathy's house, Will walked her to the door.

"I'm sorry tonight didn't turn out the way you expected it to," he said.

Kathy smiled. "It was certainly memorable. But not something I want to repeat. I think our next date should be quieter."

"Yeah? What did you have in mind for the next one?"

"Anything that doesn't involve killing a human piranha and

burying the body. That would be nice." They both laughed, and when she smiled up at Will, he leaned down and kissed her.

"Call me when you're ready for date two," he said and walked back to the car.

* * *

Samantha, wearing a white T-shirt and flannel pajama bottoms, was sitting in the kitchen reading the newspaper and drinking tea when her sister walked in. Kathy tossed the bloody kitchen knife and her shoe on the table.

"What happened to you!?" Samantha nearly spit out her tea at the sight of her sister.

"I had one of the weirdest nights of my life," Kathy said, plopping onto the barstool next to her sister and leaning on her hand. She could feel the dried slime in her hair. "What are you still doing up?" She glanced at the clock and saw that it was almost one in the morning.

"The boys and I had a movie night and I was just cleaning up," Samantha said. "What did you do?" She reached for the hole in her sister's dress. "You're bleeding!"

"Oh, that's just a scratch."

Samantha looked her sister over and inspected the scratch on her knee. "Kathy, this is bad. Did he hurt you?" She got up, ran a dish towel under the faucet, and started dabbing at Kathy's face, wiping up the slime. "What happened?"

"Well, dinner was…eh, okay. Nice, but basically uneventful," Kathy said, diving into her story. "But then we were on the pier by the Bicentennial Tower, and Vepar grabbed me and nearly pulled me into the water."

"Vepar attacked?" Samantha nearly shouted.

"Yeah, but apparently Will is somehow supernatural—I'm not quite sure exactly what he is, but he's the one who killed Vepar."

Samantha put up her hand to stop Kathy and closed her eyes for a moment. "Wait, wait, wait! Will is supernatural?"

Kathy nodded. "Guess so."

"And he killed Vepar?"

"Yes."

"Well, what is he exactly? A witch? Seer? Brute? What, Kathy?"

Kathy raised an eyebrow. "Cool it, Sammy! He didn't say. But he saved me tonight. Let's be grateful for that right now."

"I just think it's a little suspicious that this guy just happens to be magical. What did he say when you told him you're a witch?"

Kathy thought for a minute. "He actually didn't have much to say."

"He knew already. Kathy, this guy could be dangerous."

"Yes, Sammy," Kathy droned.

"So how did Will kill Vepar?"

"Chopped him up." Kathy smiled and reminisced about the incredible night she'd had, despite all the complications. "We buried him in some random farm field outside the city."

"Kathy, do you understand how crazy you sound?" Samantha gave up with tending to her sister and retook her seat. "You're not going out with him again, are you?"

"Probably."

Samantha sighed. She wanted to forbid her sister from seeing him, but Kathy was right: Will had saved her. Of course, Will was also the reason Kathy had been on the pier to begin with.

"Just be careful," Samantha warned.

"Always."

"Find out what he is. Sooner than later."

"Before I get too serious with him, he's going to have to tell me what he is," Kathy said. "Don't worry! I'm not going to go off on the crazy train over some guy."

"Good." Samantha finished her tea and deposited the mug in the sink. "Now, get these things off the table."

"What are you going to tell the boys?"

Samantha hadn't thought about that. "Um…I guess just say that you were attacked and you managed to take care of it. They don't need to know the details."

Kathy nodded. "Got it." She had to agree with her sister on this one. The boys didn't need to know what her night had entailed.

Chapter Five

Kathy often found herself dreaming of Will now. Not in the sappy happily-ever-after way, but whenever she dreamed lately, he was usually there in some way. She dreamed either of their first date or introducing him to her family—she was already stressing out about how Samantha would react to him; Kathy knew her sister had already formed an opinion of him.

This night's dream was different. It was vivid, and Kathy felt as if she were standing right next to Will, only everyone in her dream couldn't see her. Or at least they didn't acknowledge her.

A woman with long, silky black hair arrived. Black lipstick adorned her lips, and her skin was as white as a ghost's, almost glowing. She wore long, sweeping red robes that dragged on the ground and swung in the breeze as she turned.

Next to the woman stood Vepar at attention, with his arms

behind his back and his eyes locked forward.

They were standing on a beach, the wind rippling through the robes of the woman with black hair. Kathy could feel the chill herself but still couldn't place where they were. Water washed up and licked at Vepar's feet, keeping him wet.

The woman spoke to Vepar, but Kathy couldn't hear the words. She looked authoritative, and by the way Vepar responded—a curt head nod before splashing into the water and disappearing out of sight—she must have been.

After Vepar was gone, Will began speaking to the woman. At first he looked obedient to her as well until their discussion escalated into an argument, and they began shouting at each other. Still, Kathy couldn't hear a word they were saying, yet the sound of the wind along the cold beach rang in her ears.

The cold intensified, although Kathy began to sweat and shake. In an instant she sat straight up in her bed, her clothes and the sheets soaked from her sweat, the scene at the beach just a memory.

This wasn't just a regular dream. This was a vision. Will was involved with the woman who'd sent Vepar to attack, and Kathy needed to find out what he was up to.

* * *

Kathy burst through the door of Will's office later that morning. She hadn't been able to sleep since she woke up from the vision and had spent her morning going for a run and cooking breakfast for her family—anything she could do to stop herself from creating more what-if scenarios in her head. She was trying to talk herself out of going to Will's office today, but the more quiet time she had to herself, the more she realized she wasn't going to be able to leave it alone.

"I need to talk to you."

Will looked up from his computer. "Good morning!" He smiled at her, but it faded when he saw her stern look. "What's the matter?"

Kathy closed the door and sat in the chair across from him. She pulled it closer and rested her hands on his desk. "As a witch, my specialty is time. A part of that specialty is the ability to have visions. Of the future, mostly, but sometimes the past as well. Sometimes I don't even have to be present in the vision for me to see it."

"Honey, I don't mean to rush you, but I have a meeting in about fifteen minutes." He reached across for her hands, but she pulled them away.

"I want to know why you were talking to the woman who ordered Vepar to attack."

Will gaped at her. "What woman?"

She shook her head. "Don't play stupid, Will! Dark hair, dramatic wardrobe. You guys were on the beach with Vepar."

"How do you know she's the one who sent him?" He didn't deny it, and that scared her.

She tried to maintain control of the conversation. "Does it really matter?" She leaned on the armrest and clasped her hands in her lap. "Either way she's demonic, right?"

Will nodded. "Yes, but it's not what it looks like."

"I sent my nephews to school with a deadly potion to kill a creature you knew was coming!"

"Keep your voice down," Will demanded. He took a breath and softened his tone. "If I wanted to hurt you or your family, why would I kill Vepar myself?" Kathy dropped her eyes to the floor. He had a point. "I hadn't met you yet when Vepar was first given his orders," he finished.

Kathy shifted her glance to the window behind Will. Across the street in the next building a woman with a baby carrier climbed the stairs.

She took a moment to think about what he said. She didn't believe that everything was so coincidental with the way things played out on their date. It didn't completely add up. Maybe it was just Samantha's doubts creeping into her head, but she was bound to get the whole story.

She shifted her stare back to Will. "What about the pier?"

"What about the pier?" He was getting annoyed.

"You're telling me that it was just a coincidence that you brought me to the edge of the pier and that's when Vepar decided to attack? Maybe you killed him so you could play hero?"

Will stood and walked over to Kathy. He sat on the edge of his desk and crossed his arms. "I promise you, I do not want to hurt you. I'll explain everything to you over dinner tomorrow night." He looked at her for a moment before continuing. "I'm not trying to sweep this under the rug, but my client will be here any minute."

THE FULL MOON

She didn't want to believe him so easily. Everything she knew and everything her gut told her was to run and put as much distance between them as possible. But the man had a right to explain himself. She would decide then.

He leaned down to kiss her, but Kathy backed away. "Not until I hear your explanation."

He smiled and reached behind him on his desk and handed her a piece of paper. "It's not a secretarial position at an insurance agency, but it's a job."

She took the paper and looked it over. It was a job posting for a day care center. They were looking for an assistant. She wanted to keep a level head with Will until she heard his side, but she couldn't hold back the smile that erupted on her face.

"You said you've been raising your nephews since they were little," Will said. "I thought it might be something you'd enjoy."

It wasn't a terrible idea, and according to the posting, it was full time. Samantha would be thrilled.

Will pointed to the bottom of the page. "They're having open interviews today. I'd suggest stopping by."

* * *

Samantha pulled into the driveway just as Kathy approached on the sidewalk from the bus stop a few blocks away.

Noting Kathy's pinstripe "suit," Samantha asked, "Did you have an interview?" She slipped her bag over her shoulder. It was filled with work she had brought home.

"Yep!" Kathy beamed.

Her sister smiled. "Ooh, where?"

"The day care on Pittsburgh Ave."

Samantha furrowed her brow. "Day care?"

"It's full time! And at least I'll be able to help with the bills and stuff. I know the boys have been complaining that you took away cable," Kathy said. They had walked around to the back door of the kitchen where Josh was at the table, working on homework.

"I didn't take it away! It was either cable or heat." Samantha hung her keys on the hook and asked her son, "How was your day, sweetie?"

"Good. I'm almost done with my homework, but I have to be back at school by six to help set up for the art fair."

Samantha shot a glance at the clock over the stove. "Crap! Is that tonight? I'm sorry, honey, I have a ton of work. I don't know—"

"I got it, Sammy. Don't worry about it," Kathy said, plopping herself in the chair next to Josh and kicking off her heels. "If I do get this job, I am saving for a car. This walking to the bus thing is getting old."

"You got a job?" Josh asked. He tapped the end of his pencil against his paper.

"Maybe. We'll see."

Samantha reached for a glass from the cupboard and filled it with water. "You know, you never told me you had an interview."

"It was sort of a last-minute thing. Will told me about it, actually."

THE FULL MOON

"Oh. Will," Samantha mumbled into her glass. After she took a sip, she asked, "He called you to tell you about this job?"

Kathy bit her bottom lip. "Not exactly. I went to talk to him about something…I'll tell you later."

Josh was scribbling in his notebook. He didn't look up when he said, "I get it. I'll be gone in forty-five minutes."

* * *

As Kathy got out of Samantha's car after dropping Josh off at school, she stopped when a police car pulled in behind her. She walked over to the car as the policeman stepped out. He had a receding hairline but otherwise looked young and fit. He was holding a manila envelope.

"Kathy Walker?"

She nodded.

"I'm Officer Hank Warner."

Kathy noted how he kept one hand on the folder and the other hooked on his belt.

"If you don't mind, I'd like to ask you some questions about the night of April 25."

It took a minute for Kathy to connect the date with the day of the week and then she remembered that the twenty-fifth was the night she and Will had killed Vepar. She tensed and knew Officer Warner picked up on it.

"Uh…sure, that's fine, yeah," Kathy said, her mouth suddenly dry.

Refusing to speak to him would be like confessing. But she

51

wondered if she should wait for Will because he was a lawyer. He would know what to say so they wouldn't be incriminated. Although, if anyone had spotted him at the scene, then that wouldn't help her case either. She couldn't be represented by a man who had been covered in more blood than she was that night.

"Do you have any idea where you were that night?"

She didn't know if she should lie or not. Will had paid in cash, so they couldn't trace his credit card, but surely the two of them had been picked up on a security camera somewhere in the hotel. She just hoped there weren't any cameras outside the hotel and that everything relied on eyewitnesses—which could be magically swayed.

"I had a date that night." She stopped herself from continuing. All she needed to do was answer his questions and not volunteer information that wasn't necessary. She really wanted to freeze Officer Warner and call Will for advice, but she decided against it.

"Who was your date?"

"Some guy I just started seeing. He tried to impress me with his wallet." She wanted to downplay it, but she knew she wasn't coming across as aloofly as she wanted.

"Where'd you go?"

"The hotel by the pier. The Sheraton, I believe."

He nodded and shifted through the contents of the folder without showing her. "Fancy place. What were you wearing?"

"Can I ask what this is about?" She realized that she forgot to ask that. An innocent person would've asked that first.

THE FULL MOON

"We have a couple of eyewitnesses saying they saw a skirmish on the pier that night. They placed a woman," he pulled a sheet out of the folder and read it aloud, "'average height, slender build, red dress' and a man, 'tall, full suit, no facial hair,' at the scene." He replaced the paper in the folder. "Now, I'm not stupid, Miss Walker. I know there are a lot of couples that fit that description. I don't want you to think I'm accusing you of anything. We're just running through our list of people who were in the area that night."

Kathy nodded nervously, afraid her voice would betray her if she spoke. After a moment, she cleared her throat and asked her next question: "What makes you think a skirmish is worth investigating?"

"The pier was covered in blood. Everywhere. Messy job. And," again he dug through the folder, "we found this at the scene." He showed her a photograph of her missing heel. The one she'd worn to dinner that night. The one who's matching pair was in the trash out by the curb, nearly ten feet away from them.

"That's horrible. I mean, I didn't see anything. We left right after dinner."

He nodded and put the photo away. "Okay. I'll be in touch if I have any other questions. Thank you, Miss Walker. Have a nice night."

* * *

Inside, Kathy found Samantha at the end of the dining room table.

Her papers were scattered around her, and her glasses were perched on the end of her nose.

"Do you have time to talk?"

"Not really." Samantha punched some numbers into her computer and made some notes on a piece of paper next to her.

"This will only take a second," Kathy said. She took a seat across from her sister.

Samantha realized that she wasn't getting any more work done until the conversation was over, so she closed her laptop and pulled off her glasses.

"I had a vision last night," Kathy started.

"In your dream? That's not unheard of."

"Vepar was in it."

"Do you think he's back?"

Kathy shook her head. She didn't want to think what would happen to Officer Warner's investigation if Vepar were back. "Impossible. This was the past. There was this woman who must've been his leader. It looked to me like she was ordering him to attack—I'm assuming that we were the targets, given that he came here when I was alone."

"You were the target. None of us actually saw him, thankfully," Samantha noted.

"Right. In the vision, after Vepar left, Will was there arguing with this woman."

"Why?"

Kathy shrugged. "I don't know. I went down to ask him today, and he said it's nothing suspicious—"

THE FULL MOON

"Of course he's going to say that! Kathy, don't be so naïve with this man. I don't trust him."

Kathy put up her hand. She did not want to be yelled at. "I know. He's going to explain everything tomorrow. If it doesn't add up, I'll break it off."

Samantha sighed. As much as she wanted to control her sister, she couldn't. "So who was this woman?"

Kathy shrugged again. "I don't know. I tried to ID her in the magic book, but there wasn't anything there. I'm hoping Will can give me a little more insight tomorrow."

"Maybe I should whip up a potion for you to take tomorrow when you meet with him? Just in case."

Kathy rolled her eyes. "If it'll make you feel better."

Chapter Six

I want you to be careful tonight," Samantha warned. She maneuvered pieces of Kathy's hair, putting it into a French braid so it wouldn't be in the way if things turned ugly. She had argued that Kathy wear jeans, too, but she lost that battle. Together they settled on pants instead of a skirt and shoes that wouldn't prevent Kathy from running if she needed to. "Call me if anything happens."

Kathy sat on the edge of her bed and watched in the mirror as Samantha braided her hair. "Yes, *Mom.*"

Samantha yanked a little harder on Kathy's hair and smiled when Kathy winced. "Just remember that the last time you went out with him, he pulled out a sword and started hacking someone up."

Kathy thought of the officer from the night before. She needed to tread carefully and definitely talk to Will about it. They'd messed up, and it could lead to major exposure—or, at the very least, some serious jail time.

"*Something* up. There's a difference," Kathy noted. "And besides, he promised me that he wouldn't ever hurt me. I believe him."

"What makes you think you can believe him? He hasn't been particularly truthful yet." Samantha used her teeth to pull the hair tie off her wrist and wrapped it around the end of the braid, holding it in place.

Kathy handed her sister some bobby pins. "That'll end tonight. And last time, for the record, he saved my life. So I think I owe him the benefit of the doubt at the very least."

Samantha sighed and stuck in a few bobby pins, pinning the loose strands of Kathy's hair in place. "You're right. I guess I'm just nervous because I don't know him."

"Well depending on how tonight goes, maybe I'll suggest our next date be here so he can meet the family," Kathy said. "I'm sure he's curious about you guys as well. I talk about you enough."

Samantha smiled. When her husband had first left, she'd thought her family had been fractured forever. But since then, Kathy had stepped up. While she could be a little freer with things than what Samantha would have liked, she was still a good aunt to the boys.

"There, I think you're set."

Kathy turned and faced her sister, wrapping her in a hug.

"Thanks! I promise I won't do anything stupid. Well, I'll try not to."

* * *

"Asian?"

Will placed the cloth napkin across his lap. "Yeah. Who doesn't love Asian?"

Kathy could name quite a few people who didn't like Asian, though her empty pockets usually prevented her from indulging in such delicacies. "I guess I didn't peg you as an Asian kind of guy," Kathy said. She flattened her napkin on her lap as well. Picking up the menu, she asked, "What's good here?"

Will pulled it away from her and said, "Don't worry about it. I've got it."

Kathy snatched the menu back. "You need to understand that I don't like being told what to do."

The waiter came over and asked if they were ready to order.

"Yeah, I'll take the, uh," she scanned the prices along the right side of the pages and picked out the two most expensive, "salt-and-pepper shrimp, and he'll have the abalone." She closed her menu and took Will's from him, delivering them to the waiter. "Oh, and could you bring us your soup special? Thank you." Will was going to learn through his wallet not to make decisions for her.

Will sat back and smiled. "Do you know what you just ordered?"

"I guess we'll find out when it comes." She took a sip of her water.

"So, did you find out anything else about that woman in your dream?"

"Nope. She isn't in our magic book and…" She cringed, wishing she hadn't mentioned her magic book. Sure, it was commonplace for witches to have magic books or spell books of some sort, but she didn't want to tell Will more than he had to know until she was positive she could trust him. She really hoped she could. "And, I've, uh, never seen anyone like her."

Will sat back in his seat and took a sip from his water. "Her name is Jubila. She's the leader of the banshees—was one herself, but she's trying to organize the chaotic underworld."

"What do you mean she *was* a banshee? I thought once you were a banshee, you were for life?"

He scrunched his face and rolled his head from side-to-side. "She is still technically a banshee, yes, but she's not going to be the one warning you when death is around the corner. Her scream will still make your ears bleed, though."

Kathy was intrigued but tried not to show it. She resisted leaning forward and hanging on each new bit of information Will shared. Instead, she folded her hands on her lap and asked, "So how did she become the leader of the banshees?"

Will chuckled. "I don't know. Maybe her scream was the loudest? Maybe she's the oldest? It doesn't matter, really. The leader is more of a figurehead. Whenever the banshees need to be spoken for, she's the one you turn to."

"All right, let me get this straight. She's in charge of the banshees, and they only exist to warn people when death is near, right?" She was trying to remember her banshee mythology. "But I thought they had white hair and wore gray?"

"And witches are supposed to be green with warts," he countered. "The details get lost in the retelling of the tales among humans."

"Okay, so then what was a creature that warns of death doing with a water creature and you?"

Will leaned on his elbows on the table. "It's complicated."

"Don't treat me like I'm stupid, Will. You said you'd give me answers, now start talking."

The waiter interrupted them to bring over their soups, but Kathy didn't even look down at hers. "I'm waiting. How do you know about Jubila and where she stands with the banshees?"

"I'm a Dark Knight."

"A what?" Kathy had never heard of such a thing, and she was trying to figure out if he was lying. His face was hard to read. Despite that, she had a feeling in her gut that she could trust him. She was putting on the demanding act to get answers for Samantha, not necessarily for herself.

"A Dark Knight. We're typically bodyguards or spies for the higher-ups of the demonic underworld. For a time, I served Jubila as her bodyguard."

"What happened that made you leave her?" She thought about the timeline. Will must've left his post within the last few weeks if he had been Jubila's bodyguard when Vepar was given his target.

He waved his hand at her. "You saw. She ordered Vepar to attack random people along the lake. It was a way to bring up her body count and prove to the rest of the demonic world that she was powerful enough to take over. I didn't agree."

Kathy felt a little light-headed with the flood of emotions she was feeling. She had asked for this information and here he was giving it to her. She couldn't pass up this opportunity.

Still, she couldn't help but feel a little foolish. Vepar wasn't being careful when he murdered people along the lake, yet he never left a trail or got caught. Of course, he wasn't assimilated into society like Kathy was, so he didn't have a permanent address where anyone could find him. Still, Kathy was doing good by killing Vepar, and she was under investigation because of it. She meant to tell Will about the investigation, but more important questions came out first.

"So when you were arguing with Jubila after Vepar left, it was to save people?"

"Not exactly that reasoning, but yeah."

"What do you mean?"

"I didn't think racking up her body count would matter much to the other demonic leaders," Will explained. "She needed to prove that she was smart as well as strong. Her strength would only increase with her control over others, but she needed to make intelligent choices in order to achieve that power."

"You were trying to help her take over the underworld." Realization was coming over Kathy. "You were helping one of our enemies!"

"Keep your voice down," Will grumbled through his teeth.

Kathy bit her bottom lip to silence herself. She had grown a bit too loud. "You're evil."

"Technically."

"There's nothing *technical* about it, Will. You have been helping the bad guys get badder." She wasn't sure if she could trust him anymore. Would she really benefit from telling him about the investigation or just crucify herself further?

"Not entirely sure if that's a word, but yeah."

Kathy's eyes fluttered as she thought of her next response. She stood and said, "I have to go."

Tossing her napkin on her chair, she raced out of the restaurant and onto the street. The streetlight prevented her from crossing, so she hooked around the building to the next intersection. Before she had a chance to cross, Will put a hand on her shoulder, pulling her back.

She whipped around and pushed him against the building, pinning him between the wall and her forearm.

"Leave me alone," she warned.

"I love you," he blurted.

She wanted to slap him. They had known each other for three weeks. He only said that so she would trust him and have a false sense of security. She knew better.

But as she looked in his eyes and her hold on him softened, she considered the idea that maybe he wasn't lying. Maybe he really was in love with her? Worse, maybe she loved him back? Here they were with their secrets in the open. He had the upper hand here. If he'd wanted to make his move and kill her, she would've been dead shortly after their first meeting.

"Kathy, I'm being honest. I told you I would never hurt you. I meant it and still do," he pleaded. "You're the reason I'm no longer working for Jubila. That client I was meeting with the other day? That was her. I terminated our contract, and now I'm not serving anyone."

She let her arm fall to her side and leaned into him. She didn't want to trust him so easily, but she did. She knew she was being stupid, but she was hoping her hesitations were all wrong. She leaned back and kissed him. When they parted, she held his face in her hands. She brought her right hand down hard and slapped him across the face. It felt good.

"What was that for?"

She pointed a finger at him and said, "Just a glimpse of what I'm going to do to you if I find out you're just using me."

"I'm not. I promise." He tried to scoop her up into his arms, but she pulled away. "What more do you need to know?"

"There isn't anything else you're leaving out? You didn't know about me and my family before you met me?" She might be putting herself in danger by loving him, but she wasn't about to drag her family into it with her.

"No, absolutely not. You captivated me all on your own."

She stood with her arms crossed over her chest and studied him. She believed him, but the nagging voice in her head—her sister's voice—still told her to be wary. That voice was getting fainter and fainter as the realization struck her that she loved him too, no matter how stupid and clichéd it sounded.

"Will, there's something you need to know."

He looked at the crowd forming next to them as the light

was about to change. "Let's go somewhere quiet to talk." He wrapped his arm around her and led her to a coffee shop. They sat at a table by the window.

"I didn't think the restaurant would let us back in," he said with a smile. Kathy didn't return it, and his face dropped. "Do you want anything?"

"No, just sit." She pointed to the seat across from her.

"What's going on?"

"A policeman came to see me the other day."

"About what?"

"Vepar. I guess some people saw us."

He lowered his voice. "And they suspect us? Why didn't you call me? I could've prevented you from saying anything stupid."

"I didn't say anything stupid, Will!" The fact that he thought she was so ignorant didn't sit well with her. He should've given her more credit than that. She had told her share of fibs with her lifestyle, though not to this extent. "I don't need you to come and save me."

"So what did he want?"

"Just to ask me some questions. I guess the hotel cameras put us there that night. But nobody saw our faces. Just descriptions of us."

"Did he say who he does suspect?"

Kathy bit her bottom lip momentarily. "No."

He snorted. "Then it's probably us."

"Why? It's not like we're known criminals."

"No, but sooner or later they're going to get more evidence

that puts us there. They'll find the body, find my car, our clothes, anything." His eyes widened. "What about your other shoe?"

She looked down at her hands. "They have that."

He tapped on the table and looked around. "Okay…what did you do with the other one?"

"Threw it in the trash."

"Kathy!"

"What was I supposed to do? I thought the other heel landed in the lake!" She noted the barista shooting them looks, and she lowered her voice. "I didn't think there'd be an investigation. What are we going to do?"

He held out his hand. "Do you trust me?"

She hesitated a moment. Finally, she placed her hand in his and they stood.

"Since we never actually ate, I figured we could have dinner at my place," he suggested.

She shook her head. "I'm not hungry."

"Do you just want me to take you home instead then?"

She shook her head again. "No. Let's go to your place."

Chapter Seven

Kathy was locked in another vision within her dream. Of that, she was absolutely certain, and it terrified her. It wasn't a complete vision like she usually experienced. This was just a glimpse, as if something or someone were blocking her power.

Typically during her visions she had the sensation that she was a fly on the wall, or sometimes she even felt as if she were right there living it, but was still not able to register any of the senses in the room. As if her body were numb and everything was surreal—almost like a dream.

But this vision spooked her right to the core. Samantha lay on the floor at their house, covered in blood—whether it was her own or not, Kathy couldn't tell. She was clutching her side and calling to someone. Kathy saw that her sister's eyes were shifty as they darted about the room, likely looking for her attacker.

THE FULL MOON

The idea she might be seeing the present unnerved Kathy. It wouldn't have been the first time, even though it was rare. By the way Samantha was dressed, Kathy could tell it was probably sometime during the day, maybe even late afternoon. Either way, she needed to see her sister with her own two eyes to confirm that she was okay.

The problem was that she was still locked in the vision, unable to break herself out of it. Kathy couldn't look away from the sight of her defeated sister crumpled on the ground and screaming for help, as if she were meant to see more. But whatever or whoever was blocking her prevented the complete vision from coming through.

Finally, the vision ended and she sat bolt-upright. Sweat had matted some of her hair to her head. It was a mess from taking out her braid the night before. The sheet clung to her bare body.

She remained a bit disoriented before she remembered where she was. Will was sound asleep next to her, and she remembered the night they'd had.

Pulling on some of her clothes, she walked into the bathroom and splashed water on her face. The clock on the wall said it was just after five in the morning. She needed to get going. Samantha would be up this early for a run. She liked to stay active because her mind specialty didn't allow her to be out of shape.

Kathy ventured out into the bedroom and gathered the rest of her clothes. Taking the bus this early would be a "joy" for her, with all the late-night weirdos and early risers judging her on her walk of shame.

In the kitchen, she tried to find a scrap of paper to leave a note for Will. She didn't want him to think that she took off without saying good-bye—which was exactly what she was doing.

"What are you doing?" His tired morning voice startled her and she jumped.

"I...uh, I have to go," Kathy said. She self-consciously combed her fingers through her messy hair knowing full well it was useless.

"Oh." He seemed disappointed, and she felt like she owed him an explanation.

She walked up to him and wrapped her arms around him. "No! Not because of you. I...it's my sister. She asked where I was since I never came home. No matter how old you get you never stop having a big sister, right?"

He kissed her and then asked, "Wouldn't a text work?"

Kathy looked at the clock on the wall. It had already been fifteen minutes since she'd woken up from the dream. It would take another fifteen to get home. She needed to get going. "Uh, no. I have to drop the boys off at school. She doesn't want them to see me coming in, and she doesn't want them asking where I was last night." She was hoping he'd momentarily forget the fact that she didn't have a car.

Will nodded. "Right. Forgot about them."

Kathy felt a little disheartened that the boys had so easily escaped Will's mind. Maybe he didn't want to meet her family as much as she thought?

He ran his fingers through her messy hair and said, "Let me drive you home. I wouldn't want you scaring anyone on the way."

THE FULL MOON

She laughed and swatted at his chest. "Fine. But hurry up! The boys usually wake up at six!"

They pulled into the driveway at ten to six. Kathy pecked Will on the cheek and turned to leave, but he grabbed her arm and pulled her into a deeper kiss that took her breath away.

"I'll see you tonight?"

She pressed her forehead against his and smiled. "Yes." She lingered for a minute before her mind drifted back to the vision that had woken her up.

When she burst through the door, she let it swing and slam into the wall. Samantha came running from the kitchen. Sweat had stained the back of her tank top.

"What the hell is going on?" She was holding her bottle of water.

Kathy hugged her sister tightly.

"You're alive!" Kathy exclaimed with her cheek pressed against Samantha's.

"What did you see?" She had lived with Kathy long enough to know when she'd had a vision.

The sound of the boys' alarm clock prevented Kathy from answering.

Samantha fixed her eyes on her sister's hair. "Go fix yourself before they see you," she said.

Kathy headed up the stairs and managed to escape into her bedroom moments before the boys emerged from theirs.

At breakfast, Samantha was dishing out eggs to Josh and Chris when Kathy finally came downstairs.

"Did you oversleep?" Samantha asked for the boys' benefit.

"Yeah, I must've." She pulled over a plate that had been made for her and started nibbling on some toast. "Are you going to be free for lunch?"

Samantha poured herself some milk. "I can be, yeah. You want to come down to the office? I'm not sure I'd have enough time to get home and back."

Kathy nodded. "Yeah, I'll do that."

"Where were you last night, Aunt Kathy?" Chris asked.

The sisters both stopped and looked at each other, waiting for the other one to step in with an explanation. Finally, Kathy decided to tell the truth.

"Well, you know how I've been dating this guy?"

"Will?" Josh asked. He scooped up the last of his eggs into his mouth.

Kathy smiled and started to continue, but Chris held up his hand. "Nope, don't want to hear it!"

Samantha laughed, relieved that she didn't have to have that conversation so early in the morning.

Kathy's face heated with embarrassment. "Okay! Get your stuff together, I think it's time for school!"

* * *

Kathy was just walking out the door to the bus stop when she saw Officer Warner pull up. He stepped out of the car and she waved.

"I'm sorry, but this is a bad time! I'm meeting my sister for lunch and I need to catch the bus," she pointed toward the direction of the bus stop. "Could we reschedule?" She wasn't in the mood to dodge his questions again. Besides, Will wasn't exactly clear what his plan was to get rid of this mess, and she didn't want to screw it up for him.

"Actually, I would prefer to talk now. I could drive you to your sister's."

She hesitated, but she was out of options. Finally, she nodded. "Okay."

After she gave him directions, he jumped right into the case, wasting no time for small talk.

"I'm not sure you ever told me about the guy you were with the night of the twenty-fifth."

"No, I don't think I did."

He smiled and pressed on. "Was it Will Brown, by any chance?"

She opened her mouth to answer, but paused. "What makes you say that?"

"The reservations at the Sheraton that night were in his name. Plus, I saw you two yesterday at the coffee shop on Fifth."

"Yeah, we were there."

"You two looked pretty serious. What were you talking about?"

"How is this relevant?" She looked at him, but he kept his eyes on the road.

"A farmer out in McKean found what looked to be some

remains in one of his empty fields. The body seemed to be wrapped in seaweed or something else from the lake—my guess is that's where they were murdered. Very likely related to the blood that was found on the pier. We're still waiting for the test results."

"How do you know it was murder?" Kathy's palms were sweating and her anxiety showed in her voice, but she needed to try to defend herself. Saying nothing would only crucify her further.

"I don't mean to ruin your lunch, but the body was chopped to pieces. This wasn't an accidental death."

Kathy's head was swimming. "What does this have to do with me and Will?"

"I'm just trying to understand the relationship you two have."

"Are we suspects?"

"We have a lot of suspects right now. We know it's a duo and you both fit the profile that the eyewitnesses gave—"

"Eyewitnesses can be wrong," she cut in.

He smiled. "Absolutely. But in this instance several gave the same report. Odds are, they're not wrong."

Kathy was drowning, racking her brain for anything that would pacify him and get him off her trail. Luckily, he pulled up to the building Samantha worked at and Kathy moved to get out. Cutting the conversation short would work just as well. She had fewer opportunities to damn herself.

"Miss Walker," the officer started. She turned and looked at him. "Be careful. If you know something about that night, you'd be better off telling us. Just because he's a lawyer doesn't mean he's got the best intentions for you."

* * *

"So what was this vision that caused you to rush home early?" Samantha asked. She and Kathy were perched on the windowsill in the lobby of the floor Samantha's office was on. She worked for an accounting firm in the city. Her office had a beautiful view of the lake.

Kathy had brought them food from home since they were tight on money. She was hoping that she'd hear from the day care soon so that she could start bringing in a paycheck of her own to help Samantha out.

"Maybe lunch isn't the best time to have this conversation," Kathy said, popping a grape in her mouth.

Samantha waved her hand. "I think we both have pretty tough stomachs."

"I saw you bloody on the floor, gasping for air," Kathy blurted. She did it quickly, like ripping off a Band-Aid. She didn't want to think too much about the actual vision, more about what it meant.

Samantha paused and then shrugged. "You've seen us in bad situations before, right?"

Kathy shook her head. "Not like this. Sammy, this was different."

Sensing the change in her sister's tone, Samantha continued carefully. "Okay. So did you see who was attacking me?"

"No. That's the thing. I feel like it should've been a full vision, but something was blocking my magic."

"How so?"

"Usually when I get visions, it's as if I'm right there. I get the full spectrum of the room with the exception of the actual feeling, you know? This was focused solely on you."

Samantha wiped the corners of her mouth with a napkin and brushed the crumbs off her skirt. "Maybe nobody else was around?"

"You were talking—yelling—to someone. And it was as if a spotlight was on you and everything else was black…it's hard to explain."

"I wouldn't worry about it too much. Maybe it was just a dream?"

"No, this was definitely a vision," Kathy confirmed. She reached over and picked a piece of lint off Samantha's shoulder. "We have time. You weren't wearing this in my vision."

"So relax! We'll do a protection spell tonight at dinner just to be sure."

Kathy nodded. "Good."

"So how was your date? I'm guessing it went well."

Kathy smiled. "Very well! I'm seeing him again tonight."

"Did you ever find out what he is?"

"What do you mean?"

"Is he a witch? Wizard? What?"

Kathy bit her bottom lip. "Oh. Yeah, he told me."

"And…?"

"He's actually a Dark Knight." She sipped from her water bottle and looked out at the lake. She wanted to pass this off quickly, but she knew Samantha wouldn't let it go. "You gonna eat that?"

"A what?"

"Your apple?" Kathy played dumb, but Samantha cocked her head to the side and glared at her until she explained further. "Like a supernatural guardian–slash–bounty-hunter mix."

"From the 'Dark' in 'Dark Knight' I'm guessing he's demonic." Samantha's eyes were locked on Kathy. She was not about to let her off the hook.

"Technically."

"Absolutely not. Kathy, are you out of your mind?"

"Sammy, chill! I've been seeing him a couple of weeks now and nothing's happened."

Samantha was standing now, forcing herself to keep her voice down. "He's sizing you up. Gaining your trust, learning your weaknesses. I want you to break up with him."

"No!" Kathy also stood.

"He could very well be a danger to our family."

"You just don't know him like I do."

"Obviously not! I'm not jumping into bed with the first guy who bats his eyes at me!"

They were starting to gather attention. They could see the heads poking through the windows of the offices and people stopping on their trip to the elevator. Kathy grabbed Samantha's wrist and pulled her close.

"Keep your voice down, damn it. Just because you're bitter Steven left doesn't mean the rest of us have to be just as miserable." Kathy could hardly believe the words she was spewing, but at that moment she was so enraged with her sister that she didn't care.

"I don't want you to be miserable, but I don't want you dead, either," Samantha murmured. She tried to pry her sister's hand off her wrist.

"I love him. He's not going to hurt me."

Samantha studied her sister. "Has he hexed you? You seem to have fallen hard really fast."

"Screw you." It took all of Kathy's energy not to slap her sister across the face. She was fuming.

The sound of Samantha's phone interrupted their argument. Kathy finally freed Samantha's wrist so she could answer it.

"It's the school. Hello?"

Kathy gathered their garbage and walked away so she could calm down. When she got home she was going to go for a run or something. She needed to relieve some stress. This quick temper was new to her.

Before she returned to the windowsill, Samantha ran up to her in a panic.

"Josh is gone!"

CHAPTER EIGHT

Gone? What do you mean gone?" Kathy asked.

Josh was not one to run away, but he was always so busy doing one thing or another at school that he wasn't very often home. He was usually gone.

"That was Chris. He said no one has seen Josh at school since this morning." Samantha was pacing now, one hand on her hip, chewing the thumbnail of the other hand.

"There isn't any chance that he went home sick?" Kathy was trying to look at all the options before they overreacted.

"Is Josh one to go home sick? Especially without a phone call? We have to find him." Samantha said. Sure, the boys had been in danger before, but they had never been targeted without her present. Josh's powers had just developed. He didn't have full control yet. "I'm going to tell my boss I'm going home, then we'll have to pick up Chris and search the book."

Kathy put her hands on Samantha's shoulders and said, "We need to get home now!" In a flash they were standing in their living room.

"What did you do?" Samantha asked.

Kathy looked around. "I don't know."

"How are we home?"

"Maybe it's an extension of my power?"

"Your specialty is time. How did you manage to transport us here?"

"Well, the few times I've time traveled, I was able to transport us to another time and *place.*" Kathy shrugged. "Maybe I can transport to another place in the same time?"

"Like teleporting?"

"I guess."

Samantha rolled her eyes. Her sister was always getting the cool powers. Samantha's specialty was the mind, which allowed her to do some cool things, but none of it was as flashy as Kathy's specialty. "Okay, why don't you head up to Josh's room and try to get a vision from his stuff. I'll grab the book and start the basics of a potion."

Kathy nodded and in an instant she was in Josh and Chris's bedroom. At first, her sudden appearance in another room disoriented her a little. This new power would take some getting used to.

She sat on Josh's bed and closed her eyes, trying to take in his presence. Sometimes, if she focused enough, she could connect to the person she was trying to see and could trigger a vision on her own. Other times it was spontaneous, although she had better luck the more she knew the person she was trying to find.

Slowly, as if she were looking through dense fog that was clearing, she saw her nephew. He was tied to a post in the center of what looked like a pyre.

A man stood nearby, looking at Josh with his arms folded. He was dressed in black and Kathy had a hard time seeing his face in the haze of her vision. He had a black scarf draped over his mouth and a black tattoo of a flame above his left eye. His clothes hung loose but allowed him the ability to move freely.

Kathy was trying to focus harder in order to hear if they were saying anything, but the vision grew hazier the harder she tried to see more. Eventually, she lost her concentration, and she was looking at the boys' bedroom.

In the kitchen, Samantha was working on a lethal potion. She prided herself in making the best potions out of all the witches in her family and had reluctantly begun to teach Josh some of her tricks. Her hesitation to teach the boys magic stemmed from the pain she still felt from her ex-husband leaving her for the boys developing witchcraft. When he walked out the door, they had never heard from him again. As much as it broke her, his words still rang in her ears: *You're turning them into killers.*

"Sammy!" Kathy shouted.

"Huh?"

"Are you going to answer this?" Kathy was holding up Samantha's phone.

"Oh, yeah. Thanks." She wiped her hands on the dish towel and answered her phone. It was her boss. "I'm sorry, my son called and…well, my other son is sort of missing so I'm looking for him." She didn't like to lie any more than she had to, and most of the time she really had to. "I'm sure it's nothing to worry about too much, but I'll feel better once I see him. I finished some of the accounts on the Jackson file, and I'll bring the rest home tonight or tomorrow to finish."

Kathy was seated at the kitchen table, flipping through the book. By the time Samantha was off the phone, the magic book sat open to the page on Josh's kidnapper.

"This guy! Yon King," Kathy read.

"Yon King?" Samantha repeated. Some of the names of their enemies were so strange.

Kathy skimmed the article, reading the important parts. "Hybrid: half-demon, half-human…well-trained swordsman… he does have some powers, but mostly focuses on his sword-fighting…oh, and no known spell to kill him. Fantastic."

"Then we'll have to make one," Samantha said. She added a few more herbs to the potion but had no idea if they would be effective. With him being a hybrid, she didn't know if the toxins that killed some of the magical would hurt him the way they did the others.

"Maybe we should ask Will for help?"

"Your demonic boyfriend? No thank you. I want you to stay as far away from him as possible."

Kathy rolled her eyes. "Okay…we'll discuss that one later. But

I really do think he'd be able to help. He has more connections with the demonic world than we do. Maybe he could get us some insight on where Josh even is?"

Samantha wanted so badly to say no. She didn't want help from Will because that would be opening up a whole can of worms that she didn't want to let loose. But Kathy had a point. If Will was as involved with the demonic leaders as he said he was, he would be able to ask around and find out where Josh was—maybe even without drawing attention to himself.

"How can I count on Will's loyalty to me and the boys? We haven't even met him yet. He doesn't care about us," Samantha argued.

Kathy sighed. "Maybe so. But he cares about me. Who cares why he helps us, as long as he does?"

"Fine."

Kathy closed her eyes and debated whether or not she should say anything. She knew it was huge for Samantha to agree to asking Will for help. Ultimately, she decided against it and left the room to call him.

Suspecting that he had his phone off during business hours, Kathy called Will's office line.

"William Brown Attorneys," a woman's voice answered.

"Wi—who's this?" Kathy was taken aback. She wondered if Will had signed on another attorney to his firm and hadn't told her.

"This is Mr. Brown's secretary. How may I help you?"

"His secretary?" Will had told Kathy he didn't have the payroll to take on a secretary. Here he was hiring someone else while Kathy still waited to hear back from the day care—something she wasn't originally looking for. Something he had steered her toward.

"Yes, ma'am. Did you want to make an appointment with Mr. Brown or Mr. Claymore?"

"Uh, no." Kathy sighed, pushing her jealousy aside and focusing on the reason she called. "Could I talk to Wi—Mr. Brown?"

"I'm sorry, ma'am, he's in a meeting right now. I can have him call you back. He should be finished within the hour."

"Yeah, why don't you have him call me." Kathy left her name and number and hung up.

When Kathy returned to the kitchen, Samantha was bottling the potions.

"He's in a meeting right now, but his secretary said he'd call me back," Kathy announced. She didn't want to show her agitation with Will in front of Samantha. "Another hour, max."

"And in that hour Josh could be dead," Samantha said. She slammed the empty pot back on the stove for emphasis.

"Well, it's all we have to work with."

"Whatever, I'm going to pick up Chris from school. We may need him," Samantha said.

"Okay, but you're going to need me to take you back, remember?"

Samantha's march to the back door came to a halt when Kathy spoke. "Well then take me back to the office and then come back home and wait for Will. I don't want him riffling through the house alone."

The Full Moon

✳ ✳ ✳

"What's wrong? Debbie said you called," Will said when he called back ten minutes later.

"Josh is missing," Kathy said.

"What do you mean 'missing'? Isn't he in school?"

"No, Chris said no one's seen him all day. We're freaking out, Will." She wanted to stress how important this was for her, not just her sister. Will would be less likely to help if he thought Samantha was the only one concerned. "Who could've taken him?"

Will sighed. "Did Chris give any other clues about his disappearance?"

"No, just that he was gone. That's not like Josh. He's always at school."

"Yeah, yeah, brainiac."

Kathy didn't appreciate Will's dismissal of Josh, but she didn't say anything. She was still too hung up on him being missing. And Debbie.

"I'll look into a few sources and let you know what I find," he said.

"Hurry, Will. Whoever took him might not take mercy on the fact that he's a kid."

"I will. I'll meet you back at your place when I'm done."

He sounded like he was about to hang up, so Kathy shouted, "Will!"

"Yeah?"

"You know how Samantha's specialty is the mind?"

"Yeah." He seemed to be losing his patience a bit, but Kathy ignored it.

"With this whole investigation about Vepar, maybe Samantha could—"

"No, absolutely not!" Will said. "You haven't told her about this, have you?"

"No," Kathy said quickly. She was holding back that information from her sister because she knew she'd never hear the end of it and she just plain didn't want to worry her. But Samantha's specialty might be the solution to their problem. "I just thought it'd be the perfect way to make this all go away."

"Kathy, that cop that talked to you isn't the only one who is working on the case. It's a murder they're looking at. And even if he was, the rest of the police department knows about the case. If he suddenly gets amnesia, it's going to look suspicious. He could lose his job, his reputation, all because you were protecting yourself against a demon. Don't ruin his life to save yours."

She sighed. "Yeah, you're probably right." Will had a point. For all she knew, Officer Warner had a family that was relying on him to provide for them. If he suddenly lost his job and was unable to do that, what would that mean for him? Why was it fair for him to suffer the consequences of her sloppiness?

Besides, she wasn't even sure if Samantha would agree to something like that. She could be getting her hands messy, and it wasn't even her mess to clean up. Whatever the solution was, it was up to Kathy and Will to solve it.

"Give me some time to think of a solution. We'll fix this. We don't need to involve your sister."

"Will?"

Another sigh. She really was getting on his nerves now. "Yeah?"

"You got a secretary?"

Silence. Either he didn't want to admit that he had duped her, or he didn't know how to back out of this cleanly.

"You told me that you didn't have enough money to hire me as your secretary."

"Kathy…"

"No, it sucks that you lied to me. If you didn't think I was qualified for the job, you should've just told me." She knew that part of her anger was fueled by her fear for Josh, but she needed to say this when she had the courage to. "I'm a big girl. I don't need things sugarcoated."

"That's not what I was doing." His voice was growing more and more agitated.

"Then what was it?"

"You would be a distraction. I couldn't be professional if I hired my girlfriend as my secretary."

Kathy bit her tongue. She wasn't sure if she believed him, but she didn't want to waste any more time. They had other problems to worry about.

"Hurry back with information on Josh."

* * *

"We're home!" Samantha announced when she and Chris walked through the front door.

Kathy was sitting on the couch in the living room, writing in the pages of the magic book.

"What are you doing?" Chris asked. He pulled off his backpack and plopped it on one of the oversized chairs.

"I'm adding an entry on Will." She was still angry with him, and he was likely not too happy with her, but he was still out scouting information on Josh—whom he hadn't even met yet.

"Are we hunting him now?" Samantha asked. She wrapped an arm around Chris. With Josh gone, she wanted to keep a close eye on him to make sure that both of her boys didn't slip away from her.

Kathy shot her sister a look. "No. I just thought it'd be a nice inclusion. I added a page on Dark Knights, too." Her eyes darted to Chris and then back to her sister.

"I told him in the car," Samantha said. "I figured it was better that he knew."

"So is Will going to find Josh?" Chris asked.

Kathy nodded. "Yeah, he's checking into a few sources now. He says he'll report back as soon as he hears something."

"Do we have a game plan once he shows up?" Samantha asked. She crossed her arms and screwed up her face, unhappy that the search for Josh was taking so long.

"It all depends on what he finds," Kathy said. "But I was reading more on Yon King. Turns out he's driven by his pride. He has powers but chooses not to use them because he believes he doesn't need them. My theory is that if we can stab him with his own sword, that might hurt his pride enough to kill him."

"Outsmart him in his own swordfighting," Samantha added. "Could work. I don't have time to brush up on my swordfighting skills, but if you guys distract—"

"Actually," Kathy interjected, "I was thinking Will would be better to attack him."

"Oh."

"It's just that swordfighting comes naturally for Dark Knights. Plus, he can conjure up shields and body armor and stuff just in case…"

Samantha turned away. "I get it. I have no active powers, so I need to take a backseat to saving my son. Do you want me to be the weeping mom who sits on the sidelines while everyone else does the work?"

"Don't be stupid, Sam!" Kathy snapped. "Everyone is going to play a part in this."

The doorbell broke their argument. Chris jumped to answer it, feeling lucky to be away from the tension.

"You must be Chris, right?" Will asked.

Chris nodded and stepped aside to allow Will to enter.

"Samantha?" He approached her with his hand extended, but Samantha folded her arms. She stared at him and asked, "What did you find?"

"Sammy, be nice," Kathy warned. She stood and greeted Will with a kiss. His secretary was still on her mind, but kissing Will was more for Samantha's sake than her own.

"I found Josh. Yon King has him outside the city," Will said, attempting to wrap his arms around Kathy, but she shrugged out of his embrace.

"So he's alive?" Samantha asked.

"Yes. I kept my eye on them for a while, and the entire time Yon King just stared at Josh, as if he was guarding him."

"For who?" Chris asked.

"I heard that Jubila hired Yon King, but I didn't see her so I'm not sure," Will responded.

"So it's the same woman you used to work for?" Kathy asked.

Samantha rolled her eyes. "What a coincidence."

"I think she's trying to make a power move by killing a witch," Will explained. "The more witches she kills, the more powerful she seems."

"What does killing witches have to do with power? Why wouldn't she just kill the nonmagical like she was doing?" Kathy asked. "Or some other supernatural entity?"

"Witches, for the most part, are the only ones actively fighting against the dark side," Will explained. "Sure you get a few sorcerers or oracles who use their powers the same way, but witches are all so unique that they each bring a different power to the table. If you get them in a coven, they're unstoppable. You get one alone, and you can sometimes break the connection in the coven and weaken them."

"Sounds like you know a lot about how to kill a witch," Samantha said.

"Samantha!" Kathy snapped.

THE FULL MOON

"So what are we going to do?" Chris asked before his mom and aunt could continue their fight.

Will shrugged. "Go after them, I guess. The problem is that Yon King can't be killed with a spell."

Samantha waved her hand at him dismissively. "Yeah, yeah. We think we found a way. Kathy should use her new power to take us. It'll be faster."

"You have a new power?" Will asked.

Kathy smiled. He wasn't the only one who could keep secrets. "I'll explain later. We need to get to Josh."

Chapter Nine

Who's that?" Kathy whispered to Will.

They huddled together with Samantha and Chris behind a line of trees. Kathy recognized the place as Presque Isle. She and Samantha used to go there all the time as kids. It seemed like it had been forever since they'd enjoyed some carefree fun.

Josh was down the beach, sitting in the middle of a pyre near the water, just like in Kathy's vision. Yon King perched a few feet away, keeping his eyes locked on her nephew. Jubila stood with a dark-skinned man dressed in all black. He had a strap tied around his right leg that held a short dagger.

"That's Kaiser. Looks like he's my replacement," Will responded. "He was one of my soldiers before I was…dismissed."

"What's the plan?" Samantha asked. She made sure to keep an arm around Chris, just in case they were approached from behind. She scanned the area for anyone else's thoughts and couldn't hear any. They were safe where they were. For now, at least.

"I think Will should be the one to take on Yon King," Kathy suggested. "Remember to make sure to kill him with his own sword. Chris can untie Josh when he has an opening. Samantha, you and I can take Jubila and Kaiser."

"We don't know what kind of powers Kaiser has," Samantha said.

"He's pretty powerful," Will said.

"So maybe Samantha should take him? Read his mind, feel out his weaknesses," Kathy suggested.

"That's probably a good idea," Will added. Samantha shot him a look.

"I'll go first, with my new power," Kathy said. "Will, you go next so that Yon King doesn't try to attack Josh while we're fighting off the others. Then Samantha, you run out after us, just in case Kaiser shows his powers beforehand."

"What about me?" Chris asked.

"You wait here until you can get a clean run to Josh. Once he's free, meet back here. Got it?"

He nodded.

"All right, here it goes!" Kathy closed her eyes and focused on controlling her new power. When she had first developed her time specialty, it took her weeks to learn the trigger. She constantly froze people by accident. But with this new power, the idea was simple enough that she had relative control already.

In a bright red flash she was suddenly standing next to Jubila. She dropped down to the sand and swung her feet under the banshee's legs, knocking her to the ground. Kaiser and Yon King looked up and moved to attack, but Will came charging out, wielding a large sword.

As he ran past Kathy and targeted Yon King, she held up her hand and froze Kaiser in place. That would hopefully give Samantha a chance to read his mind—unless his thoughts were frozen with him. She wasn't sure what Samantha's power allowed her to do. Either way, keeping one opponent at bay would only help them.

As she squared off with Jubila, Kathy saw Samantha run out of the trees and hurl a potion at Kaiser, breaking the magical freeze.

Jubila swung at Kathy a few times, but Kathy was easily able to dodge the attacks. Obviously Jubila was more used to giving orders to attack than executing them.

Another drop to the sand, and Kathy swung her leg under Jubila's and knocked her to the ground. She stood over the banshee and pressed her foot on Jubila's chest, holding her down. She tried to freeze her, but couldn't. Jubila must've been more powerful than she looked.

Samantha parried with Kaiser as he fired energy beams from his palms. She allowed him closer, only to make him underestimate her skills. Now far enough away from the pyre, Kaiser extended his hand to fire another attack at Samantha, but she grabbed his wrist and flipped him onto his back.

The Full Moon

Kaiser was stunned for a moment. Samantha glanced behind her to see how the others were doing with freeing Josh when she felt something slice open her arm. Snapping her head back to Kaiser, she grabbed her arm and her hand came back bloody. A warm trickle ran down her arm.

She jumped out of the way just in time to dodge another energy beam and landed in the sand. Her fingers started to go numb, and she wondered what had been along the blade he cut her with.

As she lay on the ground, Kaiser moved closer, preparing his attack. He loomed over Samantha. "No more potions?"

"Go to hell."

"We're trying," Kaiser sneered. He held out his hands to attack, but Kathy came up from behind and kicked him to the sand.

Holding up her hands, she froze him and then turned to her sister to help her up.

"Where's Jubila?" Samantha asked, still clutching her arm. She had gotten sand inside the wound and winced at the pain. She looked at her sister, who was soaked to the bone. "Why are you all wet?"

Kathy smiled. "Took a swim." Her teeth started chattering. "The water's freezing, though. Are you hurt?" She tried to look at her sister's arm, but Samantha had her hand clamped over the gash.

"I'm fine. Where are the boys?" Samantha scanned the beach.

Kathy pointed to the pyre. "Josh is gone! Chris must've untied him. Go back to the trees. I'm going to help Will." Before Samantha could protest, Kathy was gone.

Will was locked in a fierce battle with Yon King. Whenever Will had an opportunity to attack, he didn't take it. He needed to wait until he had possession of Yon King's sword, which the warrior held on to very well.

Swinging his blade around, Will had managed to slice up Yon King's right arm, giving him the disadvantage of fighting with his left arm. Still, the warrior was a great swordsman—even left-handed.

The two battled on, moving across the beach. The waves splashed up against their legs as they moved closer to the water. Finally, Yon King's foot sank in the sand enough to prevent him from moving as swiftly as he needed. Will was able to get the better of him, sending the warrior's sword flying across the beach.

Standing over Yon King, Will pressed his sword into his throat, wondering whether he would still die if he was killed with someone else's blade. He debated for a minute. Just as he made up his mind, Kathy shouted his name.

"Will! Use his sword!" She snatched up Yon King's sword from the sand and ran to her boyfriend, tossing the sword to him when she was close enough.

Will's sword dematerialized as he raised his hand to catch Yon King's. Without a second thought, Will swung the sword sideways, decapitating Yon King.

Kathy shrieked and brought her hands to her mouth. "A little gruesome, don't you think?"

The Full Moon

Will stared down at Yon King, breathing heavily as he tried to catch his breath. Finally, he dropped Yon King's sword and walked over to Kathy.

"Let's get back to your sister before—"

Kathy's magic on Kaiser had worn off, and he charged at them. Conjuring his sword again, Will pushed Kathy behind him with his free hand and moved to attack Kaiser.

"Where's your master?" Will asked.

Kaiser stopped in his tracks. "What have you done with her?"

Will clenched his jaw, wondering how long he could hold off Kaiser's attack.

"I threw her in the lake!" Kathy shouted, peeking her head out from behind Will's bulk.

Kaiser stared at the two of them a moment longer before speaking. "This is not over." He ran to the edge of the beach and dove into the water.

"What was that? Why did he run away?"

Keeping his eyes on the water, Will said, "Probably didn't want to take both of us on at the same time." He took Kathy by the arm and ushered her up the beach to where Samantha and the boys were hiding.

Once Kathy laid eyes on Josh, she pulled him into a tight embrace.

"I'm so glad you're safe," Kathy said. She grabbed Josh's face between her hands and looked at him.

"Mom, are you okay?" Chris asked.

Samantha's fingers on her right hand were now fully swollen. She wobbled in the sand, and Chris tried to reach for her, but she fell to the ground.

"Sammy!" Kathy shouted, falling to her sister's side. She felt her forehead, which was red hot. She remembered the gash she had and looked at her arm. It had turned an unhealthy shade of blue from the site of the wound all the way down to her fingertips.

"That's not good," Will said, confirming everyone's thoughts.

"Okay, let's get her home. Everyone, get in a circle," Kathy ordered. She pointed to her sister. "Will, do you mind?"

He scooped her off the ground and joined the circle. In a flash, everyone was gone.

* * *

"How's that potion coming, Josh?" Kathy asked, rushing into the kitchen. She was running around the house like a madwoman searching for antiseptics and gauzes to stop the bleeding, which was continuous. It was as if Samantha's body had forgotten how to heal itself.

"Good, I think," Josh said. He followed the recipe, but it was the first time he was making a potion that complicated. "Hopefully not much longer."

Kathy nodded. "Good...good job, yeah. That should help." The potion was called Venenum and was supposed to draw out any supernatural infections. Though it was one of the older potions in the book, the sisters hadn't used it, at least not that Kathy could remember.

In the living room, Chris changed the bandages on his mother's arm again. Will was standing behind him with his arms crossed. "Make sure it's tight," he reminded.

"How's it coming?" Kathy asked.

"The bleeding still hasn't stopped," Chris said. "She's losing a lot of blood." His hands shook as he wrapped the gauze around his mother's arm.

"Just keep it wrapped. That's all we can do for now," Kathy said.

Will pulled her into the dining room and lowered his voice. "I'm not sure there's anything that we can do for her. All these remedies are just hypothetical."

"It's the best we can do. We have to do something," Kathy urged. "I can't let her die!" She realized after the words left her mouth that she was being too loud. She glanced over at Chris, who had a sad look on his face. She smoothed the hair back on the top of her head. She had thrown it into a loose bun after her trip into the lake, but her hair was slowly slipping out. She lowered her voice and continued, "The boys have never seen her like this. Hell, it's been years since I've seen her like this."

Will sighed. "Did you find anything in the magic book?"

Kathy shook her head. "Just the potion Josh is working on. He should have it done soon. We just have to hope that after she takes the potion her body will start to take over."

"That potion will only remove the infection—if it does that.

We don't know how long it'll take to set in, and we don't know how much more her body can take once the infection's gone."

"It's all we have now." Kathy shrugged. "I'm doing the best I can." She hated that she was suddenly supposed to have all the answers.

Will pulled her into an embrace and kissed the top of her head. "Let's just hope it works, then."

She buried her face in his chest. "I'm glad you're here."

"Of course."

"And I'm sorry about yelling at you earlier." She pulled out of his embrace to look him in the eyes. "It's just that I was blindsided. Why didn't you tell me you hired a secretary?"

"Because I wanted to avoid this. The only reason I didn't hire you was so that I could keep my personal life separate from my professional life. You, of all people, should understand that with this lifestyle we live."

She didn't meet his eyes and looked down at their feet. Over-reacting would be an understatement. Even after she had yelled at him, he had not only saved her nephew, but was working on saving her sister as well, who hadn't shown him the most warm welcome. She didn't need any more proof that he was dedicated.

"Aunt Kathy! The potion's done!" Josh called from the kitchen.

Kathy ran to the next room.

"How's it look?"

Josh had his finger on the open magic book, marking the spot he was reading. "It says we're supposed to lather it on the cut to draw it out. But…" he lifted the wooden ladle and dumped some of the potion back in, "it's very watery. I don't know if it'll hold."

"Then we'll soak it in some gauze. Bring it over," Kathy said. She turned and raced back to her sister.

Chris was taking off another set of bloody bandages. "Look at all this." He deposited another soiled bandage into the trash can next to him, already half-full of the bloody bandages from Samantha. "That's too much."

"We have the potion, so hopefully this'll work." Kathy sat on the coffee table in front of her unconscious sister and soaked a few pieces of gauze with the potion before placing them on the open wound. It had started oozing with pus.

The group stared, waiting for Samantha to miraculously jump up and be completely refreshed, but she still lay there unchanged.

"It's too watered down. I should've let it boil a while longer," Josh mused. He stirred the potion in the pot that Kathy had set next to her.

"Give it time," Will said.

"She's really white," Chris noted.

Kathy ignored her nephews and squeezed her sister's hand. "C'mon, Sammy," she muttered. After another minute of silence, she turned to Will. "Should we put more on?"

"I would think that should be enough," he said with a shrug. "I don't really know."

"Chris, go get the book. We need to find out what poison was used," Kathy said.

"We've already—"

"Go get the book!" Kathy shouted. She was scared. The last time this had happened to one of them had been years before the boys were born. And still, even then it hadn't been this bad.

Chris turned to leave, but Will snagged his arm. "Wait!"

Samantha let out a breath of air.

The group leaned closer, watching and waiting for something else to happen. The color began to return to her face, and slowly the blue tinge from her arm softened and eventually subsided.

"It's working." Josh smiled.

"Wrap it up," Kathy instructed. "I'm going to get her some water."

By the time Kathy returned to the living room, Samantha was starting to rise.

"Relax, Mom," Chris said, pushing her back down on the couch.

"What happened?" She gave in to Chris's urging and rested her head back on the arm of the couch.

"Kaiser's dagger must've had poison on it," Kathy explained, wiping the errant hairs off her sister's face. "But it's all okay now. Josh used one of the potion recipes. He saved you."

Samantha smiled up at her oldest son. She reached for his hand and squeezed it.

"I'm guessing the poison on the dagger was Nihil Curaret," Will explained. "It disrupts your body's immune system and prevents it from fighting a disease. In the past, some people in the demonic world have distributed it into some food suppliers and infected a lot of people."

"Well that's nice," Kathy commented. She blinked the tears out of her eyes and laughed.

"You're lucky you survived." Will looked Samantha in the eyes.

"I'm lucky you were here," Samantha said. "All of you." And although it killed her to say it, she added, "Thank you, Will."

* * *

"Once again, I owe you a massive thank you," Kathy said, walking Will to his car. Samantha had been tolerant of him since they came home from Presque Isle—mostly because she had been sleeping for a good portion of the evening—but Kathy didn't want to press her luck and invite Will to spend the night.

He leaned against the hood of his car and pulled her closer. "You don't owe me anything. But listen, I've been thinking. This whole mess with the investigation, why don't we figure out a way to pin it on Jubila and Kaiser?"

Kathy was thrown off guard. After using the potion on Samantha, they had spent the remaining part of the day being normal. Watching movies, making dinner. To suddenly be pulled back into the magical chaos that they were slipping into was a shock to her.

"What?"

"Yeah, it'd take the heat off us and could even get the two of them out of the way."

"How are we going to do that?"

Will waved his hands around, thinking. "I don't know. We could use magic on the evidence to put them at the scene and not us. They're looking for a man and a woman."

Kathy took a step back and crossed her arms. "Are they even technically citizens? Does the government recognize banshees and demons? Besides, say we do succeed in framing them, what would happen when the police suddenly have to deal with two very magical, very powerful creatures? They're not equipped or prepared to handle that. It's not fair to them."

"It's not fair to us, Kathy! We were just protecting ourselves—and any future victims—from a different supernatural threat. One Jubila sent after you! Shouldn't she pay for what she's putting you through?"

"Yes, I want her to pay. But pawning her off on someone else is not the way to do it." She closed her eyes and took a deep breath, taking his hands. "I love it that you're trying to protect me, but even you know this plan has a lot of holes."

He nodded and kissed her. "You're right. Stupid idea. But it's the best one I've come up with since you told me they were investigating. I just don't want to see you being punished for doing your job."

She smiled and leaned into him. "We'll figure it out."

CHAPTER TEN

Kathy and Chris were laying out a tablecloth on the dining room table. They rarely used the room for dining, but they were expecting a dinner guest: Will.

In the week since Josh had been kidnapped, Samantha had lessened her grudge against Will and agreed, for Kathy's sake, to try to give him a chance. He had been instrumental in not only rescuing Josh, but saving her life as well. The excuses for hating him had run out. She didn't know him, and she knew she was prejudiced against him for being a Dark Knight. She knew that wasn't the best way to start a relationship with her sister's boyfriend. Especially since Kathy was so infatuated with Will.

Samantha really did want to see her sister happy, and Will brought out a side of Kathy that hadn't been present before. But the demonic side of Will still scared Samantha. She hoped that by giving him a chance to prove himself, she could put aside some of her judgments. Offering him dinner was the least she could do.

"Josh, honey, can you and your brother set the table?" Samantha called up the stairs. Her oldest son had barricaded himself in his room and consumed himself with homework. Perfection wasn't good enough for him.

She jumped when she felt arms wrap around her stomach. She could recognize her sister's thoughts and smiled. After their spat at the office and Samantha's close encounter with death, the two had made up.

"Thank you! Thank you! Thank you!" Kathy tightened her grip. The fact that Samantha was finally coming around with Will elated her. She hated being at odds with her sister. "Have I told you how much this means to me?"

"You've mentioned it a few times," Samantha said. She patted Kathy's arms locked across her stomach. "Let me go. Dinner's almost done. And besides, you need to get yourself ready."

Kathy gave Samantha one last squeeze and let go. "I know I've told you already, but I'm so glad you're doing this. I really do think that once you and Will sit down and have a conversation about something other than magic, you'll realize you're actually exactly the same."

Samantha turned to Kathy and cocked an eyebrow. "Really?"

Kathy bit her bottom lip. "Maybe that wasn't the phrasing I was looking for. But you're both strong and independent people. Very similar."

The Full Moon

Samantha nodded, trying to keep an open mind. Kathy was certainly the peacemaker in the family, always wanting everyone to just get along. It was only fair that Samantha try to accept Will.

The doorbell rang before Samantha could respond. Kathy jumped. "Is that Will? I have to get ready!" She darted up the stairs.

"Boys! Can one of you get that?" Samantha called over her shoulder. She turned off the oven and pulled out the lasagna.

The doorbell rang again. Samantha shook her head at her kids' selective hearing and tossed her oven mitts on the kitchen table. As she walked to the door, she pulled the clip out of her hair, letting her brown locks fall to her shoulders.

She took a deep breath before opening the door. This night was going to test her patience.

When she opened the door, Will was standing with a bouquet of wildflowers in his hands. He wore a black sweater with the white collar of his dress shirt poking up from underneath. Even Samantha had to admit that he looked sharp.

"Hello." She forced a smile and stepped aside to let him in. She took the flowers from him and immediately escaped to the kitchen to find a vase. "Kathy will be down in a minute," she called over her shoulder.

When she returned with the hydrated wildflowers, Will was peering at the family photos that filled the house. Back before her husband had left, Samantha was quite the photographer. Her favorite subject: her family. Now she worried that she worked too much and didn't spend enough time with them.

"That must've been…gosh, five years ago?" Samantha commented on the picture Will focused on. It was a photo of the boys in the backyard in the fall. You could just make out their faces in the large piles of leaves.

He turned and offered her a faint smile. "They look so young."

Samantha nodded. "Yeah."

"Aunt Kathy! Will's here!" Chris shouted up the stairs, snapping both Samantha and Will away from the photo.

"I should go check on dinner," Samantha lied. She was desperate for a reason to escape. She hoped the whole night wouldn't be like that.

By the time Samantha had made the salad, Kathy and Josh had joined Chris and Will in the dining room.

"I actually work with insurance companies more than I do doctors," Will said. "It's not the same thing you see on TV. Not usually."

"What are you guys talking about?" Samantha placed a large bowl of salad in the center of the table.

"Josh was telling us that he thinks he wants to be a doctor," Kathy answered. She had plastered on a giant smile, hoping it would help the evening go well.

"Yeah? That's great," Samantha said. She waited as the salad made its rounds at the table, picking up an errant lettuce leaf that spilled onto the green tablecloth when Chris scooped out his salad. "That's a lot of work, though."

"I think Josh could do it." Kathy wrapped an arm around Josh and patted his arm before letting go. "Well, I have some good news. I wanted to wait for dinner to tell everyone, but this is close enough. I got a call from the day care and they asked me to start Monday!"

"Kathy, that's great!" Samantha cheered.

Will leaned over and kissed her. "Congratulations, babe."

Samantha couldn't help but feel her stomach turn at the sight of them kissing. Suddenly she wasn't hungry anymore.

"I mean it's mostly just a glorified babysitting job, but it'll be fun," Kathy explained. "I have so many ideas for activities with the kids. The hours are a little earlier than what I'm used to. The center opens at six—"

"Ha!" Samantha blurted. "More than a little earlier, I'd say."

Kathy shot her sister a look and continued, "And I'll be done by two, but I'm hoping to eventually move to a ten to six shift. We'll see how it goes."

"Well, it's a start," Will said. He sprinkled dressing on his salad. "Newbies usually work the bad shifts."

Kathy curled her lip. "Yeah, I know."

"Mom, aren't you hungry?" Josh asked, noting Samantha's plate pushed to the side.

"Wrong dressing. I'm not really a fan of ranch," she lied.

Kathy reached across the table. "Well here, let's switch. I don't mind."

"No," Samantha said, a little more forcefully than she intended. "It's fine. Does anyone want anything to drink? Will? Coffee, water, anything?"

Will looked up at her hesitantly. "No. I'm fine, thanks."

When Samantha left the room, Will looked at Kathy and shot his eyes to the kitchen, trying to communicate with her without speaking. Kathy shrugged and turned her attention back to the table, trying to salvage the dinner. She didn't know what Samantha's problem was. After all, this dinner had been her idea.

"Chris, why don't you tell Will about that project you just finished in school? The one about our family tree?" Kathy suggested. She stood and said, "I'll be right back."

"What's going on?" Kathy asked when she got to the kitchen.

"I thought wine might be a nice gesture," Samantha said. She was looking at a few of their bottles. "All we have is white. Doesn't really go with lasagna."

"Sammy, I need you to really try here," Kathy said.

Samantha gripped the edge of the counter tightly, trying her hardest not to yell at her sister and draw attention. "I am trying, Kathy. I can't help it that I get a bad feeling from the guy." She had been trying all night to break into his mind but wasn't able to read a single thought. That troubled her.

"Well, stop it, because I love him."

Samantha's shoulders slumped. Her sister was already in too deep. She turned and faced Kathy. "Please, be careful."

"I feel like we've had this conversation a million times." Kathy's voice was rising, but she couldn't bring herself to lower it. Her face was hot with anger. "I get it, you don't like him. But that's not going to stop me from following my gut. I don't see the danger you see." She pointed a finger in the direction of the dining room. "When I look at him, I see a man who wants to take care of me. A man who is thoughtful and makes me smile every time I see him. Don't think that I'm some naïve little girl who ignores everyone else's threats. I know what he is. I know your hesitations. I also know deep down that he would never hurt me!"

Her voice had grown louder than she intended. No doubt the boys heard her in the dining room. She smoothed out her dress and said, "Now, can we please go back in there and finish this dinner?"

The sisters studied each other before either of them said anything. Samantha wanted more than anything to stop arguing with Kathy. She wanted to be able to trust her and the man she loved, but she couldn't shake the feeling that Will was not the right fit for her.

"You should bring bread," Samantha finally said. She slid over a tray with Italian bread that she had just cut into slices. There was a small dish of butter in the corner of the tray.

Kathy took the tray from her sister, and they stared at each other a moment longer before she finally returned to the dining room.

The rest of dinner went by rather smoothly. The boys didn't seem to have the same hesitations about Will as Samantha had, which made Kathy happy. Samantha eventually gave in and held a brief conversation with Will about a client they shared. It was short and very polite, but it was something.

"Mom, is there dessert?" Chris asked anxiously.

Samantha smiled and put an arm around her youngest son. They had just finished eating. "You can wait. I do have ice cream in the freezer, though. When everybody's ready."

"Well, before we move on to dessert, I would like to say something," Will said. "I also had something to share at dinner, but I guess Kathy beat me to it earlier with her wonderful news. Congrats again, baby." He kissed her and took her hand in his.

"I know we've only known each other a couple of months, but they've been the best of my life," Will started.

"Oh no," Samantha muttered, panicked.

"In the short time we've been dating, we've gotten to know each other very well. It didn't take me long to realize that you're the woman I want to spend the rest of my life with," Will continued.

Kathy gasped, beaming from ear to ear.

"Kathy Walker," he produced a small box from his pocket and opened it, brandishing a ring with a sparkling diamond in the center and black diamonds surrounding it, "will you marry me?"

CHAPTER ELEVEN

Kathy shrieked with excitement. Despite having only known Will for two months, she knew he was the one for her. No one else had made her feel this giddy and happy. She felt like a love-struck teenager again, and she didn't care how foolish it made her look.

Her smile slowly faded, though, when she saw Samantha's face. Her sister's jaw had dropped with surprise. When she tried to compose herself, she couldn't keep the look of disgust off her face.

What was it about Will that bothered Samantha so much? Yes, Will was evil, or at least, he had been. He hadn't shown any sign of being a threat since Kathy had met him—but he had been instrumental in saving them a few times already. Surely Samantha should be grateful.

All Kathy knew was that she hated this back-and-forth arguing about Will that ultimately solved nothing. She didn't want to argue anymore. She wanted Samantha to jump up and be excited about her engagement as much as she was excited about it herself. And when it came time for her wedding day, she wanted the biggest worry on her mind to be whether her dress would fit or if everyone had enough to eat.

She wanted this part of her life to be normal. But she would never be normal. It was the one thing she could count on, without a doubt. It was more likely that by the time her wedding day did come, she would have to worry about some sort of attack. Or, at the very least, a magical backfire that was supposed to make things easier.

No, normal was completely out of her realm of reality. She was marrying a demonic bounty hunter after all.

The thought of Will snapped her awake. How long had he been waiting for an answer? She flashed him a smile and said, "Yes, of course I'll marry you!"

He wrapped her up in his arms and kissed her. She knew by the way he clung to her tightly—like he didn't want her to slip away—that this was something he really wanted, too. No matter what any ulterior motive Samantha might think he had, at his core, Will truly did love Kathy. That much she was certain of.

When he finally let her out of his grasp, he slid the ring on her finger. It fit perfectly and she loved the way it looked on her. She placed her hands on his face and pulled him in for another kiss.

The Full Moon

"Okay, okay! Get a room!" Chris complained. "I'm trying to keep my dinner down over here."

Everyone laughed, except Samantha. Her gaze was fixed on Will and Kathy, their combined hands, and the ring Kathy now sported. She faked a smile for the time, but Kathy knew they would have another round of arguing later.

* * *

"You sure about this?" Samantha asked the next morning. They were the only two up. Kathy was busy trying to make a hot breakfast for Will, who had spent the night—much to Samantha's dismay. She was moments away from pouring the pancake batter on the skillet. Her breakfasts weren't usually a delicacy, and they hardly encouraged firsts let alone seconds, but it was the least she could do for her new fiancé.

"You're right," Kathy said, setting the batter down. She was wearing Will's dress shirt from the night before and a pair of shorts. "What if he'd rather have waffles? Maybe I should wait."

"I'm not talking about the food." Samantha was warming her hands around her mug of coffee. "I'm talking about marriage."

"What's not to be sure about? We love each other, why shouldn't we get married?" Kathy tried to keep herself busy by fussing with the dishes and rinsing them thoroughly in the sink before checking the sizzling eggs on the stove.

"Okay…" Samantha looked down at her coffee cup, trying to think of another way to approach the topic. She didn't want to

113

argue anymore either. "Look at it this way: you're a good witch, he's a Dark Knight. What sort of magic will your children have?"

Kathy shrugged. "So we adopt? Cut magic out of the equation. It'll be easier raising them, knowing they won't be targeted like Josh and Chris will be soon."

Samantha let that slide. She already kicked herself for bringing them into an unsafe world with a giant bulls-eye on their backs—something that caused a schism in her marriage and left the boys without a father. "Okay, well, you're good and he's evil. One of you will have to pick a side. You can't walk the line of both."

Finally, Kathy turned around to face her sister. She leaned against the counter and crossed her arms. "What are you doing?"

"I'm just trying to warn you of the challenges you're going to have to face going into this," Samantha said. "Forget about my suspicions for now. Say Will really is trying to be good and he has nothing up his sleeve. How are you going to manage fighting off his enemies and yours?"

"That's too much to think about right now!" Kathy exclaimed, frustrated. She wanted to celebrate her recent engagement, not dwell on the pitfalls they'd inevitably face. "I've been engaged for less than twelve hours. Let me be happy for a little bit. Please."

Samantha opened her mouth to press further, but the sad look on her sister's face stopped her.

"Something smells good," Will's voice chirped as he bounded down the stairs. He greeted Kathy with a kiss, wearing the same clothes as before, minus the dress shirt he wore under his sweater. "Hey, I was looking for this." He tugged at his shirt on Kathy.

THE FULL MOON

"I wanted to surprise you with breakfast," Kathy said, leaning into his embrace. She smelled the eggs burning and rushed to the stove. "Oh no!"

Will laughed. "Baby, it's okay."

"I guess I have to work on my domestic skills." She laughed as she scooped the blackened eggs into the garbage.

"I love you for trying," Will said. He wrapped her in his arms again and kissed her. "I actually have court later. I have to get going so I can shower and change."

"Mmm, can I join you?"

Samantha couldn't stifle her groan. She tried to pass it off as a cough.

Will shot her a glance and returned back to Kathy. "Something tells me that if you come, I'll never make it to court on time. I'll be back tonight. Promise."

* * *

Kathy's new boss at the day care, Amy, was very impressed with how fast she was able to adapt in just a week. It helped tremendously that Kathy loved working with the kids. She couldn't help but think she was refreshing her maternal instincts for when she and Will had kids. The last time she'd taken care of a baby had been when Josh and Chris were little.

Amy had decided that Kathy was equipped enough to handle a classroom on her own. It was her first day with her own room. The week previous, she had been shadowing another teacher.

Now that the school year was over and the summer program was starting, enrollment had shot sky-high and Amy was desperate to get Kathy started on her own.

Kathy had just arrived and was tidying up the room before parents began dropping off kids when she heard a familiar voice behind her. She turned and saw Jubila, with her long, silky black hair framing her whitewashed face.

"What are you doing here, Jubila?" Kathy demanded. She wasn't sure if the banshee would attack with children present or not. She didn't want to take the chance.

"Actually, I would like to be called the Queen now. Since I will be the ruler of the demonic world soon." Jubila took a step forward.

"I asked you a question." Kathy wasn't dressed for a fight. She wanted to make a good first impression on the parents, especially since she had no previous background working with kids. Blood would definitely stand out on her khakis and white blouse.

"I wanted to warn you." Jubila circled the room, running her hands over the various toys and tiny chairs that filled the room. "It's not usually customary to warn my targets, but I like a good chase—something I know you and your sister are certainly good for."

Panic ran through Kathy's mind. She had only seen Samantha for a brief second this morning, but maybe that had been a shape-shifter? If it was, were Josh and Chris in trouble too? Her mind filled with images of her vision. "What did you do to her?"

Jubila rolled her eyes. "Oh, nothing. Stop looking so worried.

You really are a beautiful girl. I'd hate to see you adding stress wrinkles so close to your funeral and all."

"Cut the crap and get to the point." Kathy glanced at the clock. The kids would be arriving any minute. She hoped that Amy or any of the other teachers didn't pop in to check on her before the day started. She could hear small voices from down the hall and knew they were likely preoccupied with their own kids.

"Okay." Jubila stopped and looked at Kathy. "You took something of mine. I have no interest in getting him back since you tainted him, but know that you are certainly my next victim," she warned. "And no one's escaped me yet."

She had to be talking about Will. Unless she meant Josh? She had kidnapped him, but he wasn't exactly *hers* to begin with. It must be Will.

"Will has," Kathy said.

Jubila smiled. "And I will make sure he pays for that through you and your sister."

Something didn't add up. If Jubila—or the Queen, as she wanted to be called—were about to become the latest demonic leader, why would she worry about two witches from Erie? She must have bigger fish to fry in the demonic world. "Why are you warning me?"

"I told you. I like a fight."

Kathy thought back to their fight at the beach when they'd rescued Josh. Jubila wasn't much of a fighter. One drop in the water and she had been out of commission. Of course, given that she was a banshee, Kathy knew her deadliest attack had yet to show itself.

"You don't seem like much of a threat to me," Kathy said.

Jubila smiled again. "Sweetheart, you have no idea." She stepped toward the door. "Don't say I didn't warn you."

Kathy wasn't sure if she should let her go. What if Jubila did something to someone in the center? No, that wouldn't be to her benefit. She would expose herself, and the respect she demanded from her followers would be lost with the sloppy use of her powers.

Before the Queen walked out of the room, she turned on her heels and said, "Oh, I do believe I owe you a congratulations. Let's hope you can hold on to the Dark Knight longer than I could."

Chapter Twelve

When Kathy got home, she raced upstairs and grabbed the magic book from under her sister's bed. She wanted to find a way to take out Jubila. Kathy couldn't help but think that Jubila only wanted to be called the Queen as a way to bolster her following.

From her bedroom, she kept an ear out for the sound of someone coming home. Since she was home much earlier than anyone else, she knew she had time. School was over but neither of the boys were home. Josh was at the Maritime Museum out on the bay, and Chris was at the mall with his friends.

The visit in the classroom scared her. Jubila was now targeting Kathy and her family, and it was all thanks to her. She wondered: If she wasn't with Will, maybe the Queen wouldn't be after them?

No.

Kathy couldn't let herself think that. Will was her fiancé. They were going to be a team—they were a team. The Queen was only using Will as an excuse to target her family. She had already shown that she had a thirst for witch blood. Kathy just needed to get the upper hand.

Flipping to the section of the magic book on banshees, Kathy studied the creatures and tried to devise a way to kill Jubila. The potion or spell would have to be stronger than it would be for a regular banshee, but it might still work. Even though the Queen was the leader of the banshees, she was still a banshee after all. The poisons that ailed the rest of them would at least have some effect on her.

After flipping through a couple of pages, Kathy found a spell that would work. She just needed to figure out a way to reword it to strengthen it. Either that or couple it with a potion that would weaken Jubila before they recited the spell.

The sound of the front door slamming shut stopped Kathy in her tracks. She stuck a scrap piece of paper in the book to mark her place and shut it. Tucking it under her bed, she went to greet whoever walked in the door. If it was Josh or Chris, she could probably still get away with working on the spell and taking out the Queen before Samantha got word of it.

"Hey, what've you been up to?" Samantha asked when Kathy joined her in the dining room. She was setting up her laptop, ready to work on stuff she brought home.

"Oh, just wedding stuff," Kathy said.

Samantha slipped on her glasses as her computer lit up.

"Already?" She didn't look up when she spoke, consumed with whatever was projecting on her computer screen.

Kathy shrugged, trying to act natural. "I'm excited, what can I say?"

Samantha forced a brief smile. "That's great. I'm glad you're happy."

"Yeah."

Finally, Samantha looked up at her sister. "You mind putting something together for dinner tonight? Henry dumped a whole new client on me, and his records are a mess."

"Oh, I'm sorry." Kathy really hated it when Samantha worked so hard. She knew she would rather be spending the evening with her kids or doing anything else.

"It's okay. But this will probably take me a couple of hours just to sort through the chaos that is his filing system. So I'm not even sure I'm going to have dinner." Samantha spread out crumpled receipts across the table.

Kathy contemplated her available options. She had been hoping to dump the dinner cleanup on Samantha and head out to ask Will for help with the Queen. She figured that after working with her, he probably knew her best. But it sounded like she was stuck for the night.

"Um, I think I might head over to Will's tonight after dinner." She knew Samantha still wasn't his biggest fan, but she was thankful for her trying to be civil.

"That's fine. I'll see you tomorrow at dinner then?"

"Yeah. Wouldn't miss it."

* * *

Kathy debated whether she wanted to drive or use her power to go to Will's. Driving would allow her more time to think of how exactly she was going to tell him that Jubila threatened her, but she didn't want to have to worry about returning the car to her sister. Samantha would probably suggest the bus, which Kathy was tired of taking. Plus, she was running short on cash until payday.

"Aunt Kathy!" Chris shouted from downstairs. "There's someone here to see you!"

Kathy looked out her bedroom window and saw a police car in the driveway. She cringed because every other time Officer Warner had paid her a visit, nobody had seen him. Her luck had run out this time.

She raced down the stairs and greeted him in the foyer. Her heart beat faster when she saw Samantha deep in conversation with him.

"Yeah, the house was built in the nineteenth century and has been in the family since. I guess we're the fourth or fifth generation to have it." Samantha was great at hiding her emotions under the veil of small talk. Through the years, she had discovered that talking about the history of their home was a great way to distract from any questions regarding their supernatural lifestyle.

Kathy gave Officer Warner a tight smile, and he politely ended the conversation with Samantha. He ushered Kathy outside to talk. She didn't want to think of the twenty questions Samantha would have once he was gone. She also didn't want to know what else he had to show her in the manila envelope that he had in his hand. It was thicker than the last time she had seen him.

"I haven't heard from you in a couple of weeks, so I just figured you found your guy," Kathy said, forcing a smile. Her heart raced in her chest, and she wondered if Officer Warner could tell. Weren't police officers trained to pick up on anxiety like that?

"Oh, we have, Miss Walker." He produced a photograph from the envelope and she took it. "Recognize that?"

It was a blurred photo of the back end of a car. He handed her another photograph that had been zoomed in on the license plate. The number was blurry but still very visible.

"I don't own a car, so that's not mine," she blurted.

He smiled. "Of course not. Those plates belong to William Brown. The same man you went on a date with that evening of the twenty-fifth. The same night there was a skirmish on the pier."

"That still doesn't mean Will's the one that did it." She knew she came across as defensive for Will, but she didn't worry about it. The point needed to be made.

"That's what we're stuck on. We have no hard evidence to convict or even arrest Mr. Brown, except for placing him at the scene of the crime."

"What did the blood tests show? Maybe that farmer used fish as fertilizer and whatever happened at the pier has nothing to do with Will?" She wondered why she'd never asked these questions earlier. If she was supposed to be truly innocent, she knew she should've asked them before. Hopefully, her nerves would make her seem like she had no idea what had happened. Still, she wasn't optimistic Officer Warner was buying her act.

"We tested the blood. It was certainly human—"

"It was?"

He paused and gave her a crooked smile. "Yeah, definitely not a fish. Besides, that pier hasn't been used as a fishing dock in a long time."

"Okay, so there was a crime and you suspect Will, but you can't arrest him—why are you telling me this? Didn't you say you suspected a couple?"

He smiled again, which was getting on her nerves. It was as if he thought of her as a naïve little girl. "You two were together that night. Eyewitnesses place the couple at the scene shortly after hotel security cameras caught you two exiting the restaurant. Unless he brought you back here and went back to the pier in a matter of minutes, you were likely his accomplice."

Kathy was suddenly out of breath. In all the excitement of the wedding and her new job and Jubila, she had forgotten to figure out a reasonable alibi for her and Will. Her knees went weak, and she sank down onto the first step of the porch.

Officer Warner, who remained standing, said, "Obviously, if we don't have enough evidence to arrest Mr. Brown, we don't have enough to arrest you, Miss Walker. However, this investigation is ongoing. We could find something that could change everything, and you both could be facing some serious jail time."

She looked up at him then. "So why are you telling me this?"

THE FULL MOON

"We believe that Mr. Brown is the one who planned every-thing, although we are stumped on his motive. You just happened to be in the wrong place at the wrong time. Now, we might be able to work something out if you're able to provide us with any information about that night that you haven't already disclosed. Anything that we could use to convict Will."

Her head was spinning. She either needed to throw Will—her new fiancé—under the bus, or she would go down with him.

She kept her gaze on the sidewalk when she answered him. "I have nothing to say." Her voice was hollow, emotionless. She just wanted this all to go away.

* * *

Kathy leaned against the front door once she was back inside. She tried to think of the best way to bring this up to Samantha. She knew there would be questions, and she needed to address those. Besides, Samantha was her only hope at this point to get them out of this mess.

She slowly walked into the dining room where Samantha sat among a clutter of papers on the table. Her glasses were perched on her nose as she read them over, her head bouncing between the paper in her hand and the computer.

"What was with the cop?" she asked without looking up.

Kathy pulled out the chair across from her sister and sat down. "I need to talk to you."

Samantha jerked her head up. "Is this about the cop?"

"Yes."

Taking a deep breath, Samantha removed her glasses and closed her computer. "What did he want?"

"To warn me about an investigation they're working on. Involving Will…and me."

Samantha's eyes widened. "What did you two do?"

"Remember our first date?"

Samantha's eyes narrowed for a second as she recalled the memory of her sister's first date with Will. "Someone saw you? Kathy, this is exactly why I told you to be careful around him. Not only is he demonic, but he's nearly exposing us as well!" She ran her hands through her hair. "What are we going to do? How many people know?"

"This is not Will's fault, Sammy. He was saving me!"

"Keep your voice down," Samantha nearly spat. "We don't need to be telling the boys that you're about to get arrested for a supernatural murder."

Kathy sighed before continuing in a quieter tone. "I don't know how many people know. I think just the precinct. Maybe. I don't really know how much cops talk to each other about their cases."

"How much evidence does he have?"

"Not enough to arrest us, obviously. But he's identified Will's car. He has his license plates."

"And what did you do with the body? You buried it, didn't you?"

Kathy nodded. "In a farm field out near McKean. Which the

farmer found."

"Now that the body is in the hands of the police, he'll forget about it. I'm more worried about traffic cameras tracking Will's car from the pier to the field."

"They can do that?"

"They might," Samantha said. "I don't know. We need to make this thing go away before they find anything else."

"So you're going to help?" Kathy couldn't help but smile.

"I'm keeping you out of jail. Will just happens to be wrapped into this with you."

* * *

Samantha walked into the precinct the next day on her lunch break and asked to speak with Officer Warner. As she sat waiting for him, she closed her eyes and head-hopped between everyone in the room, trying to decipher who knew what about the case. Some had overheard it discussed over lunch but hadn't paid much attention to it. She was able to clear the subconsciousness of each pretty easily. Officer Warner, and whomever else he'd discussed the case with at length, would be a harder fix.

"Ms. Harper?"

Samantha jumped at the sound of her name. "Yes." She smiled and tried to recover from being caught with her eyes closed. "Sorry, I didn't sleep well last night."

He smiled. "I've had those nights. Why don't you come over to my desk and we can chat?"

Samantha hesitated. With Warner knowing the most about this case, she would need to place her hands on his head in order to clear his mind. She couldn't do that without drawing attention in the busy police department.

"Actually, do you mind if we go and grab coffee instead?"

He groaned. "I'm sorry, Ms. Harper, but I don't have that much time today. I could get you some coffee from here, though. It's instant, but it's the best I can offer."

She smiled and nodded. "That'd be great, thanks." When he turned to fetch her the coffee, she pulled out her phone and texted Kathy: *Get over here now. Need your power.*

He returned faster than she expected and led her to his desk. "So what can I do for you?"

Samantha glanced around the room, searching for her sister. With her power, she could be there in an instant. She gripped her phone tightly but hadn't felt it vibrate with a response. Kathy had the day off, so she should've been at home.

"I…uh, was just wondering if you…" she looked over her shoulder again, "I mean…" She smiled and tried to think of anything to say. The room suddenly fell silent as everyone froze in place. She turned around and saw Kathy behind her.

"Do what you need to do. I'll clear the security footage. The cameras are still rolling," Kathy said just before she disappeared to a different room.

Standing, Samantha placed her hands on either side of Officer Warner's head and closed her eyes, losing herself in his mind. She focused on Kathy and everything he knew about her, erasing his memories one by one. Samantha was surprised to see memories of herself. He spent a lot of time thinking of her. They had only chatted once back at the house, but she was popping up in various corners of his mind. She decided to leave those. No sense in erasing his entire memory of the sisters.

Finally, she was finished sorting through and erasing his memories. When she pulled out of his mind, Kathy was standing by her side, sorting through the papers on his desk.

"We need to hurry! He had to have filled out paperwork for this case."

Samantha snatched up the manila folder that contained the images of Will's car. "Put it all in here. We'll burn it later."

Kathy had found a stack of papers related to the case and stuffed them inside the folder.

"What about the chief? He has to know about the case, right?" Kathy asked.

"I'll have to clear his mind, too. How much time do we have left?"

Kathy looked up at the clock. "Not much."

Samantha shoved the envelope in Kathy's hands and said, "Get out of here! I'll call you if I need you with the chief."

Kathy nodded and disappeared in a flash of light.

When the room started up again, Samantha smiled at Officer Warner and said, "Would you like to get coffee sometime? I'd love to finish that conversation we had the other day."

* * *

"You got the files from the chief's office, too?" Kathy asked, tossing another stack of papers into their fireplace. The flames curled around the edges of the files that were so powerful and now forgotten.

"Yep. Cornered him at the gym and cleared his mind there. Did you get all the files from their computers?"

"Went back after you left, so we're all set there. I was also able to properly dump the body far away from here."

"How far? You still need to be careful not to pin it back to you."

"Africa?" Kathy smiled. "I really like my teleportation power."

"So this whole thing should finally be over," Samantha said. "I just hope we're not forgetting anything."

"I don't even want to think about that. I'm just glad you agreed to help."

Samantha's head snapped to her sister. "Why wouldn't I?"

Kathy shrugged, tossing more paper onto the fire. The light from the flame flicked across her face. "Will."

"I'm not particularly thrilled that he was involved, but it's over now. Let's just move on."

Kathy smiled. "Are you warming up to the idea of Will being my husband?"

Samantha fought back the urge to cringe. "No. I'm just glad that you came to me for help even though you know how I feel about him."

"Well, I needed your power." Kathy smiled and Samantha smacked her arm with a stack of papers. "But seriously, you helped me figure out what to do. Will would've freaked out, and I was already freaking out enough for both of us."

"Not that he would say thank you, but if Will does, tell him he's welcome."

Kathy stayed silent. Will had been adamant about not telling Samantha about the investigation. She didn't know how he'd react to her cleaning it up for them.

* * *

In a flash, Kathy was at Will's front door. As soon as he opened it, he scooped her up in a kiss, pulling her into his apartment.

"I'm glad you're here," he said. "I wanted to talk to you about the wedding."

She smiled at him. He was sweet. She almost hated to bring the problems of reality into his world, but that was the reason she'd come. Not that she didn't enjoy the kiss.

"What's wrong?" he asked, noticing the concern on her face.

"I need your help." She hated waiting an extra day to tell him about the visit Jubila had paid her, but she needed to take care of the investigation first. Especially while Samantha was still willing. Now that that was taken care of, she could address her next concern.

"With what?" He was running his hands up the sides of her arms.

She took a step back, needing to separate herself from him. His touch was too distracting.

"The Queen—" She stopped, catching herself. Maybe Will

wouldn't know who the Queen was? "Jubila threatened me. And Sam and the boys."

Will's face lit up in a rage. "She did what?"

Kathy knew she should stop before Will got angrier, but she couldn't help the flow of words that escaped her. "She said that I stole you from her and that we were going to pay for it."

He clenched his jaw. "I'll take care of it." He turned and stepped through the room to open a wooden cabinet at the opposite end. It contained five shelves, two of which were filled with small vials of potions lined up; two others had various weapons, knives, machetes, even a small handgun; and the last shelf held ritual instruments.

"Will, honey, it's okay. I think I found a way to defeat her," Kathy pleaded. She didn't like it when he was like this. The last time she'd seen him in this state was when they killed Vepar—*he* killed Vepar. And that had resulted in a bigger mess than she expected. He had been reckless then. If the investigation Samantha cleaned up taught her anything, it was that they needed to tread carefully with their enemies.

"No, it's not. I'm going to take care of this." His fingers hovered over a few bottles, scanning the labels on the potions before selecting just the right one. "You should go back home. If anything happens, at least you won't be alone."

She tugged on his arm as he moved toward the door. "Will, stop!"

He looked at her hands gripping his wrist and then up into her eyes. "I told you I'd protect you."

She ran her hand against his cheek. "Then let me help."

He stared at her, considering her proposal. "No. It's too dangerous." He pulled away from her grasp and turned toward the door. "If Jubila personally threatened you, that means she'll use her own powers to kill you. You won't survive that."

"What am I supposed to do if you're the one who's dead?" Kathy shouted when he was halfway out the door.

He stopped, struck by her words. He dropped his head and closed the door.

"Please, Will. I don't want to lose you." She could feel tears welling up in her eyes and tried to blink them away without success. She hadn't expected to be so scared.

Will shut the door and wrapped his arms around her. "Okay. I'll stay." He paused for a moment, resting his chin on her head. "It's probably better, anyway. Jubila will be expecting a retaliation now. We should take her by surprise."

"Thank you." She pulled away from him and wiped the tears from her eyes. She laughed at how ridiculous she looked.

He smiled. "You're never going to lose me."

She pulled him into an embrace and pressed her cheek against his chest. "Good."

"You know, I've been thinking." He resumed his position with his chin on the top of her head, and they swayed a little throughout the small apartment as if they were dancing.

"Yeah?" She lifted her head to look into his eyes.

"I know we haven't even been dating for two months, and we've only really been engaged for about a week," he lifted her hand and twisted her engagement ring around on her finger, "but I think we should move up the date of the wedding to the end of the month."

Kathy was immediately ripped away from the sweet moment they were enjoying. She let go of him and stepped back to get a better look at his face.

He had to be joking. They didn't have anything planned out yet. The past week she had been so consumed with her new job that she hadn't really even seen much of Will.

She crossed her arms. "What?"

He shrugged. "Yeah. No sense in waiting, really."

"Will, there is a lot of sense in waiting. I haven't found a dress, we haven't picked a hall, set a guest list, found a caterer—we're completely unprepared!"

"Wha—I thought you'd be happy!"

"People are going to think I'm pregnant! Sam—" She stopped herself. Samantha would have a fit if they got married after only two months of dating. She already had trust issues with Will; Kathy didn't want to add fuel to the fire.

"Samantha? Is that what this is really about?" He was angry, and Kathy didn't want to pit them against each other—especially with Samantha already having a problem with him. She needed to try her best to calm things down before they got any worse.

"No, Will. We've only known each other a short time. This is a big step. I just don't want to jump into it," she said. She tried to reach for his hands, but he pulled away from her. "Just give me some time to process this. Everything is happening so fast."

The Full Moon

"If you needed time to process, why did you agree to marry me?"

He had a point. Kathy knew it wasn't fair to be giving mixed signals like this.

"I do want to marry you. I just need some time to plan the wedding first. I want to celebrate this—us. I don't want a shotgun wedding," she said. "Besides, with the Queen targeting us, it's probably not the best idea to be giving her an opportunity to attack us. It'd be the perfect time for her. Our guards will be down and the whole family will be there."

She could see that Will was cooling off. This had not turned into the evening she had hoped it would be.

"Okay. So tomorrow I'll go after Jubila, and once she's dead we can decide on a wedding date."

Kathy gave a tight smile. "Yeah." She hated the idea of Will going after the Queen alone, but she needed to pacify him for now.

He pulled her into another hug. This had been a roller coaster of a night.

"I'm going to make that bitch pay for ever threatening you," he said.

Kathy didn't respond. She was worried that he would do something rash that would have a ripple effect and bring in more enemies than they cared to have—especially when planning a wedding.

* * *

"Absolutely not!" Samantha exclaimed that night when Kathy told her about Will wanting to move the wedding date up. "You two have only been dating two months! Two months! What sort of example is that setting for the boys?"

"Sammy, I told him no," Kathy said.

They were sitting in the living room on the couch. It was late, and she knew she should go to bed—the six o'clock start time was already exhausting—but she knew she wouldn't get a wink of sleep without first telling Samantha everything. She didn't want to hide anything from her anymore.

"You're damn right you told him no! How much of this wedding have you actually planned?"

Kathy bit her bottom lip. "Not much. But I think Will is more looking to elope or something." She saw Samantha's face flare up in anger and quickly added, "With you and the boys present, of course!"

Samantha tucked her hair behind her ears and tried to calm herself with a deep breath.

"I just think this whole thing is insane. I mean, what do you really know about the guy? How old is he? Does he have a family? Parents? Any kids? Siblings? What's his deal?"

Kathy felt guilty that Samantha was right. She didn't really know where Will came from. She almost felt like she shouldn't pry because she was afraid of what she might find. What if he had been married before? What if his body count was higher than she could fathom?

But she knew all she needed to know. Will was the one for

her, and she was tired of convincing herself and anyone else of the truth.

"Why did I think I could talk to you about this?" Kathy stood up from the couch.

"Well, Kathy, I've told you how I feel about him and yet you insist on marrying him," Samantha said. "I don't blame you for falling in love with him. He's a charming man. But he has secrets. That's what I don't like. If you're going to be his wife, you should be entitled to know those secrets. With our lifestyle and his background, they'll come back around if you aren't prepared."

Kathy didn't respond. It was nearing one in the morning and she needed to be up by five. She and Samantha had gone in circles on this topic over and over again. It was tiring, and Kathy decided at that moment that she wasn't going to run anything else by Samantha again. At least not when it came to Will. She didn't have the support she wanted or expected.

"I know you love him," Samantha said before Kathy could walk away, "and this is hard to hear. I get that. But open your eyes. He's too good to be true."

Kathy kept her gaze on the floor. "I'm going to stay at Will's for a few days." She couldn't stand to look at her sister and left without a response.

Chapter Thirteen

The sound of heavy fists on the front door woke Kathy immediately. She sat up and looked around the room. The morning sun was just starting to creep in through the windows. More pounding came; this time she heard her name.

"Who's that?" Will asked. They were at his apartment now that Kathy had basically moved in with him.

"I don't know," Kathy said groggily. "I'll get it. You get some more sleep." She pulled the hair tie out of her hair and let it fall to her shoulders. She ran her fingers through it, twisted it, and brought it to the side, then pulled on her jeans and tried to flatten out the wrinkles in the T-shirt she wore to bed.

The sound of the fists pounded harder.

"I'm coming!" Kathy barked.

THE FULL MOON

When she finally answered the door, she saw Samantha; her fist was raised, ready to pound on the door again.

"It's about time." She pushed past Kathy and walked in.

"What are you doing here? How did you know where I was?" Kathy demanded, slamming the door.

"Searching ritual." Samantha had her hands in her jacket pockets. Kathy knew her well enough to know that Samantha was concealing a potion.

"What are you going to do? Blow me up? Just because I'm not going to let you boss me around?" Samantha had always been a bit of a mother figure to Kathy, but they were both adults now. Samantha had to cut the cord eventually.

"I need you to come to your senses. Will has obviously put some sort of curse on you, and I—"

Kathy put up her hand to stop Samantha. "No. You're the one who is feeding me lies. Just because you're a lonely old broad doesn't give you the right to be such a bitch to me."

Samantha gritted her teeth. "This has nothing to do with that, Kathy. Will's manipulating you and you're so blinded by lust that you can't see it."

Kathy cocked an eyebrow. "Lust? This isn't just some booty call. Why can't you accept the fact that your screw-up little sister is finally grown up?"

"Grown up? You call running to me to clean up your mess *grown up?*"

"Shut up," Kathy hissed.

Samantha pursed her lips, trying to control her temper. She

could see Kathy had already lost hers. "Where's Will?"

"What do you care?" Kathy retorted, crossing her arms. She knew Will likely heard everything from the next room.

Samantha opened her mouth to speak, but the sound of Will's voice stopped her.

"I'm right here." He stood in the doorway, barefoot in a plain black T-shirt and jeans.

Samantha snapped around and hurled the potion in her jacket pocket at Will. Kathy shrieked and froze it.

"What do you think you're doing?" Kathy shouted, snatching the frozen potion out of the air. "What's in this?"

"It's just a truth potion, so he can finally explain what he's up to," Samantha explained.

"Subtle." Will folded his arms.

"Well, I can't imagine you'll be coming over for dinner again anytime soon," Samantha said. "What do you want with my sister?"

"You need to leave," Kathy said. She put her hand up to ward off her sister.

Samantha ignored her and locked eyes with Will. "I asked you a question."

"What makes you think I'm hiding something?"

Samantha rolled her eyes. "Please, Will. I'm not stupid. An alleged reformed Dark Knight is suddenly interested in a witch? How coincidental. I don't believe that Jubila fired you. I think you rebelled so you could start your own campaign to kill her. Doesn't sound like the typical actions of a Dark Knight to me."

She had studied up on Dark Knights. She knew they remained

loyal to their leaders until either of them were killed. That was their nature. If Will was rebelling, he had another agenda up his sleeve.

"What makes you think I rebelled?" Will asked.

"Jubila's still alive, Will! That's proof enough!" Samantha said.

"Get out!" Kathy shouted.

"Kathy! He's up to something and he's using you to get to it!" Samantha turned her stare back to Will. "I knew I couldn't trust you from the moment I met you. Something wasn't right. But then I figured it out. I could hear everyone's thoughts but yours. Why would someone who doesn't have anything to hide be protecting their thoughts when they know a telepath is around?"

"Maybe because I don't like the intrusion? You ever think that maybe you shouldn't be granted that much access to people's private thoughts?"

Samantha rolled her eyes. "Come on! You know I can't read everything. You've been around enough telepaths to know that."

"Where are you getting this information?" Kathy asked. A few days ago, Will had still been a mystery to Samantha, and now she seemed to know more about his past than Kathy did.

"I've done my research," Samantha said. She was fairly well-known in the magical community. She had connections with all sorts of people, people that Kathy didn't even know. Before she had kids, Samantha would often travel throughout the Northeast looking for ways to help people with magical problems. "I figured since you decided to choose him over your own family—"

"Oh, please. Stop being so melodramatic!" Kathy said.

"I'm not kidding, Kathy. If you marry him, consider us gone. I don't want to put myself or my boys in danger because you have a little crush! This is serious."

Kathy could feel her blood boiling. Her fists were clenched tightly and her fingernails dug into her palms so hard that she started to draw blood.

She didn't know how her own sister could turn on her. They had been inseparable before, and now their relationship was torn apart. She refused to believe that Will was the reason. Well, Will specifically. If it had been any other man, Samantha would still have an issue. She had been almost motherly throughout their lives, and the thought of letting her go was killing Samantha. That much Kathy was sure of. The whole deal of Will plotting against them was a ruse Samantha was using to hide her true feelings.

No, Samantha just didn't want to lose Kathy. After her husband left her, Samantha had become even more possessive of her family, always checking to see where they were, afraid to leave the house, and unwilling to trust anyone new. Kathy had put up with it at the time, but it had been long enough. This was getting old, and she wasn't going to let Samantha dictate her life anymore.

Before she knew what was happening, Kathy was pouncing on her sister, pushing her to the floor and pressing her knees against her shoulders, pinning her down.

Samantha squirmed to get up. She was used to being taken by surprise and hand-to-hand fighting. But so was Kathy. In fact,

The Full Moon

Samantha had been the one who taught her how to fight.

Kathy punched Samantha in the face, screaming, "It's! Not! A! Crush!" with each blow. It wasn't until Will wrapped his arms around her waist and pulled her off that Kathy stopped. Even then, she punched and kicked at the air until she realized how useless it was.

Samantha sat up, wiping the blood from her nose on the sleeve of her jacket. All three of them were breathing heavily from the ordeal. Will still held Kathy firmly against him.

"If you want me gone, then I'm gone!" Kathy shouted, her voice hoarse. "Stay away from me and my fiancé!"

Samantha stood and looked between Will and Kathy. She felt betrayed and confused. If Will really was after them, why would he stop Kathy from beating her to a pulp? Wouldn't that be the perfect scenario? No blood on his hands.

She wondered for a minute if Will really did love Kathy. The thought of Kathy being guilt-ridden for killing her sister would be crippling to her, and Will would lose the woman he fell in love with.

If he could love.

From her experience, evil wasn't capable of such an emotion. Not only were evil-doers unable to love, but they had a hard time comprehending the concept at all. No, Will was definitely up to something.

And then there was Kathy. Samantha looked at her little sister, restrained by Will. She had Samantha's blood on her hands and tears were spilling from her eyes. The girl was a mess.

"

For a long time now, Kathy had been extra sensitive. Quick to get angry. Quick to fall in love. She had fallen faster for Will than she had with any other man—and Kathy had had her share of boyfriends through the years. Something was up with her. Samantha couldn't shake the feeling that the cause of it was magical and that Will was the root of it.

She looked up at Will and concentrated all her energy into blocking out Kathy's thoughts—filled with obscenities directed at her—and homing in on Will's thoughts only.

It was useless. She couldn't hear anything, as usual. Especially now that she was staring at Will. He probably knew what she was trying to do. He was using his own magic to block out hers.

But she was still confused as to how he was doing it. The magic Dark Knights wielded was confined to that of their leaders. If they were teamed with a powerful leader, their own magic was enhanced, but only to protect or serve their leader. They weren't granted access to the powers of the universe simply because their leader was that powerful.

No, Will was doing something else. She believed that he wasn't under anyone's orders at the moment, but that didn't explain the strength in his powers. He must've figured out a way around the restrictions placed on him and his magic. She needed to figure what exactly he was up to and how to stop him before he corrupted Kathy any more than he already had.

That's when the thought hit her: What happens if she's completely wrong and Will has nothing planned out? What if he genuinely loves Kathy? Killing him would be a surefire way to completely sever the bond between her and her sister. Kathy would never forgive her for that. But her gut was telling her otherwise.

Samantha took one last look at her sister squirming in Will's arms.

"You stay away from us until you remove whatever hex Will has on you. Do you understand me?"

"Screw you!" Kathy croaked, her voice completely shot from screaming all morning.

Samantha looked up at Will momentarily. He seemed to be hiding a smile that made her skin crawl. She was disgusted with him.

After she left, she walked swiftly to her car. It wasn't until she was by herself that she finally broke down. She had just left Kathy with her worst enemy.

And he was going to destroy her.

Chapter Fourteen

It took Kathy a good hour after her sister left to calm down. She had sat curled up on the floor of the shower, letting the warm water rain over her. She knew she should apologize for attacking Samantha like that, but she just couldn't bring herself to do it. Samantha was wrong about her suspicions of Will.

What was worse was that Kathy kept having these waves of anger that would completely consume her. One minute she despised Samantha for what she'd said, and the next she was crying over their broken relationship.

What finally roused her were the words Samantha had said just before she left.

"You stay away from us..."

It was Samantha's decision to kick Kathy out of her life—and the lives of Josh and Chris. Naturally, they would side with their mother. Kathy guessed her sister was brainwashing them now about how horrible of a person Kathy was. If they listened to her, they were the enemy just as much as Samantha was. The three of them were likely plotting to kill Will—and possibly even Kathy—at this very moment. This gave Kathy enough strength to pick herself up and prove them all wrong.

When she emerged from the bathroom, Will was sitting at the breakfast bar reading the paper.

"How're you feeling?" he asked, wrapping his arms around her.

"Better, I guess," Kathy said. She rested her head against his shoulder and leaned into him. Everything with Will seemed easy, except their rocky start. But that had been from Samantha's suspicion that crept into Kathy's head. She needed to move past that now.

"How about we go somewhere? Get your mind off things for a bit?"

She patted his back and pulled away from him. "That's sweet, but I'm wiped." She was thankful that it was the weekend and she had two glorious days to recharge.

Will shrugged. "Okay, whatever you want to do. We can stay in and watch a movie or something."

He was trying so hard to make her feel better and not point the blame at Samantha. Kathy stared into his eyes for a moment before planting a kiss on his lips.

"I love you."

He smiled and kissed her back.

This moment, wrapped up in Will's arms, was perfect. She knew she wanted every weekend to be like this—minus the explosive morning. But she knew he had heard how Samantha had cleaned up the investigation. She needed to tell him herself if they were going to move forward.

"I take it you heard Samantha this morning," she started.

"I think the whole building heard you two this morning."

"About the investigation."

He sighed and dropped his eyes. "Your sister's the one who took care of it, isn't she? After I told you not to involve her." There was an edge to that last sentence, and he refused to look at her.

She closed her eyes and pulled away from him. She didn't want to have another argument this morning. Her voice was still hoarse from screaming at her sister.

"Will…"

"I don't understand, Kathy. I thought we were going to take care of this? This was *our* problem! Your sister didn't need to know about this at all. It just gives her more reason to hate me. You and I both know she's not short on that."

"They were about to arrest you, Will!" She couldn't hold it back any longer, and it all came slipping out in a hysterical cry. "All they needed was to find your motive. Sooner or later they were going to have enough evidence to arrest you."

"So they arrest me. That still doesn't give you the right to tell your sister!"

"Samantha cleaned it up! She wiped their memories and we burned the files. You couldn't kill your way out of this mess, Will.

You were too tangled in it all."

"How do you know they were about to arrest me?"

"The officer working the case wanted me to turn on you and give him details about the murder. He's been stopping by for a while now. So yes, I told my sister. I wanted her to clean it up because I couldn't stand looking over my shoulder every day. I didn't want to worry about you going to jail for protecting me!"

She was crying again, and he pulled her close.

"I didn't know he had been questioning you. You cleaned it up the best way you know how. At least that weight's been lifted now."

She let her tears dry as she thought about how much she loved him. Sure, they had their problems, but things were still easier with him than they were with Samantha. He made her feel better, and she wanted that feeling to last forever.

"Why don't we get married?"

He laughed and raised the hand that displayed her engage-ment ring. "I think I already beat you to that question."

She giggled. "No, I meant now. Today. This weekend, what-ever."

Will furrowed his brow. "Where's this coming from? I thought you didn't want to rush it?"

"Well, that was when I wanted a big ceremony, you know? Friends and family," she explained. "And since my family seems to be against this wedding, I'd say we can scratch them off the guest list."

"Are you sure? I don't want you to regret anything."

She kissed him again. Even now, when she was giving in to his request, he was thinking of her first. How could Samantha not think he could make a good husband? Then she realized: Samantha usually only saw things in black and white—good and evil.

"Trust me, I won't. I'll have you and that's all I need."

"Okay!" He smiled and Kathy jumped in excitement. "Let's do it! Let's get married!"

Suddenly the list of things to do before the wedding came rushing back to Kathy. She still wanted to find a dress, then there was the marriage license and finding someone to perform the ceremony. The list was still persistent even after simplifying it.

"What is it?" Will asked, sensing her sudden decline in excitement.

"I'm just thinking…maybe we should wait a week or two? You know, just to make sure everything cools down with… everything…"

Slowly, he nodded. "Yeah, okay. We can do that." He kissed her again and Kathy melted.

"Maybe you are bad."

"Never said I wasn't."

This stopped Kathy cold. Her stomach dropped and she asked, "What?"

He shrugged, trying to play it off. "I've been honest about who I am. I understand why your sister thinks—"

Kathy held up her hands. "Okay, let's just leave her out of this for now." She didn't want to cloud her thoughts with her anger toward her sister. "You're still evil? I mean, *actively* evil?" Her world was spinning. An hour earlier she had screamed herself hoarse defending him, and here he was admitting to it.

"*Dark* Knight, sweetie." He smiled, trying to smooth things over. "C'mon, it's not news. And besides, with your family against you, maybe this could be a new path for you, too."

She raised an eyebrow. "What are you saying?" She backed away from him.

"I'm saying that a union between a Dark Knight and a witch has never been done before. We could be unstoppable." Will stepped over and reached for her hands. She didn't stop him. He ran his thumb over her ring.

Kathy wanted to tell him no. She wanted to push him away and tell him that it was against everything in her nature to be a demonic witch and use black magic.

Actually, she wanted to run home and talk it over with Samantha, but that was out of the question. Kathy hated herself a little bit that the idea had even flashed through her mind. After everything she'd said this morning about Samantha treating her like a little kid, she was falling right back into the same routine that had dictated her entire life.

No, she needed to make this decision on her own. Will wasn't asking her to use black magic. He was just asking her to stand beside him, as his wife. Just as she had agreed to when she accepted his marriage proposal. For better or worse. He had seen her worse, now it was time for her to see his. She considered this to be her first test as his wife. She wanted to do right by him.

Still, the thought of becoming a demonic leader with Will scared her. But she couldn't hide the fact that it was enticing. No more taking the moral route. No more following the rules Samantha had set for their use of magic. With this new way of thinking, Kathy could do whatever she wanted, whenever she wanted. She didn't have to answer to anyone.

"So…what would I have to do?"

He tried to stifle his smile, but couldn't help flashing his brilliantly white teeth. "I'm not entirely sure. I've never been married before." That answered one question Samantha had about him. "But I do know where we can find out how to perform the ceremony. It'll be a little risky."

Kathy gulped. "How so?"

"In your magic book, is there a spell to summon a dark priest?"

She thought for a moment. It wasn't a spell they had ever used before. Why would someone practicing white magic need a spell like that? Then it hit her: a dark priest performed many forms of rituals and would likely be in possession of many foreign ingredients that were hard to come by in the nonmagical world. One of the previous owners of the book may have devised a spell to call upon a dark priest in order to acquire those ingredients.

"Maybe."

"You need to get it. That's the only way we can do this."

Kathy still looked uncertain. Will put a finger under her chin and brought her eyes up to meet his.

THE FULL MOON

"If you're having any doubts—"

"No. I want to do this. I'll get the spell."

* * *

In a flash, Kathy appeared in her bedroom at Samantha's house. She listened for any sign that the boys were home. She heard the sound of the TV downstairs and figured it was Chris. As long as she stayed out of the living room, she would be able to avoid him. If worse came to worst, she could freeze him. But she didn't want to have to do that.

She crept out of her room and tried to listen for any sign of Josh. He usually spent his summer vacations reading, so it was harder to listen for him. He had so many reading spots throughout the large house that she wasn't sure where exactly he would be. When she couldn't spot him in his room, she hoped he was outside.

With the boys both occupied, she needed to find the book as quickly as possible. First she searched upstairs, stepping carefully throughout the old house to avoid any squeaky floorboards. Having spent her whole life in this house, she knew exactly where they all were.

The magic book wasn't in any of their bedrooms. Samantha must have hidden it, which was irritating but totally predictable.

Kathy stood at the top of the stairs, listening for the sound of the boys moving and considering her options. The attic would have to be a last resort. If anyone thought the floorboards in their bedrooms were bad, they had obviously never gone up another level to the attic.

Samantha had used the same hiding spots for years; surely Kathy could find the one she was using for the magic book now. With the boys home, Samantha would likely keep it somewhere they would frequent. In case anyone would try to steal it, they would have the obstacle of the boys to get around. Which was exactly the issue facing Kathy. Still, she knew she would be able to get around them. She knew them and their habits.

Glancing at the clock, she saw it was just before noon. If she moved now, she could search the kitchen before Chris raided the fridge. If she needed to, she could search the living room while he was in the kitchen. She was suddenly very thankful for her new teleportation ability.

Kathy hesitated at the top of the stairs a little bit. She didn't know what she would say if the boys spotted her. She wasn't sure what they knew, but she couldn't afford to waste any more time. The sooner she found the book, the sooner she would be Will's wife.

In a flash she was in the kitchen. She opened all the cupboard doors and came up empty. Placing her hands on her hips, she looked around and thought about all the places they had hidden the book in the past. She glanced at the clock above the stove to check the time and got an idea. She opened the door and saw the magic book resting on the racks in the oven.

Just as she was pulling it out, she heard the TV click off, and she used her power to pop upstairs. She sat on her bed and flipped through the pages. She wasn't positive the spell they needed was even in there. But she needed to move quickly. She didn't want the boys to find her, and she needed to put the book back where she found it so Samantha wouldn't know she had been there.

Just as she flipped to the right page for the spell, she heard Josh come up the stairs. He was yelling down to his brother as he came up.

"Mom's going to kill you if you don't rinse out your dishes again!"

Locating a scrap piece of paper, Kathy frantically scribbled down the information from the page. She snatched the book up and held it to her chest as she pressed herself against the wall. When she heard Josh in his room, she popped downstairs into the dining room and hid behind the table, listening for Chris's location.

Dishes clattered in the sink and then the TV clicked on again. Before she stood, she took a look at herself in the reflection of the china cabinet. Here she was, a grown woman, hiding from her teenaged nephew. What had her life become?

Shaking the thought from her mind, she stood. She needed this wedding to happen without any interruptions. She slipped the scrap piece of paper in her pocket and replaced the book back in the oven. Before she disappeared, she looked in the sink. Chris's dishes were thrown in without water.

* * *

The day finally arrived. In the two weeks since Kathy had declared her independence from Samantha, she and Will had summoned a dark priest and had set the altar, preparing for their dark wedding.

Kathy decided against the traditional white dress, opting instead for a strapless black dress with a matching veil. She stood alone in an old barn, fussing with her hair in the reflection of the tiny mirror she brought from Will's apartment—her apartment. Home.

The setting was not what she had originally envisioned when she used to think of her wedding day as a little girl, but the dark priest said that in order to get the best use of the full moon—which would amplify both of their powers and more completely bind them together—they would have to be outside.

When Kathy was a little girl, she used to say that she wanted to get married in a greenhouse or botanical garden that would be filled with flowers and other decorations. For years, she had placed Samantha as her maid-of-honor. She tried not to think about her previous fantasies and how different they were from her reality as she fussed with her appearance.

The barn that Kathy was in was abandoned and didn't offer much light, besides what came from the full moon creeping in through the cracks in the walls. The wedding was scheduled for midnight. That, coupled with the full moon, was the only time the dark priest would perform the ceremony. Both Kathy's and Will's powers would be strongest at midnight under a full moon.

She had been so worked up over the wedding, worried that somehow Samantha would get word of it and would try to stop it. Kathy was actually a little disheartened that Samantha *hadn't* tried to stop her. It was like her sister had completely given up on her.

Kathy fought back the sadness. This was her wedding day. She would remember this day for the rest of her life, and she wanted to remember being happy. So she put on a smile. Just outside, Will waited for her.

The barn doors slid open with a creak, signaling that it was time for the wedding to start. Just before Kathy stepped into view, the sound of a gong rang slowly three times.

The beaten path from the barn down into the middle of the field was lined with black candles that flickered in the night breeze. Kathy could see Will and the dark priest at the end of the path, surrounded by more black candles and illuminated by the light of the moon. Will was dressed in a black dress shirt and pants. He smiled when he saw his bride.

At the end of the path, Kathy took his hand, and together they faced the dark priest.

The dark priest held a small, worn book in his hands. Once Kathy and Will were facing him, he opened it and read aloud.

"I call forth the power of nature and the darkness within. Consecrate this place with the power of love, darkness, and the strength of magic. In the joining of these forces, William and Kathleen shall be one."

The dark priest produced a tall red candle from within his robes. With a snap of his fingers, the candle lit. He held it above him, letting the wax dribble down the side.

"I call upon the element of fire to come serve us. Ignite the passion between Kathleen and William and fill them with all-consuming lust for each other." With a flick of his hand, he let the dripping wax fall on Will and Kathy's joined hands. Kathy winced at the pain, but didn't let go.

After blowing out the candle and returning it to the hidden pocket within his robes, the dark priest raised his hands above him and said, "I call upon the element of air." The wind began to stir, yet the candles remained lit. "Knowledge flows! Let this couple share a mutual wisdom and unified vision!" He let his arms fall to his side, and the wind stopped immediately.

The dark priest continued the ritual by calling on the elements of earth and water, sprinkling a fistful of soil over the couple's joined hands and causing a brief rain shower that fell only over Will and Kathy. She couldn't help but think that the time spent making herself look nice for her wedding had been a waste.

"Provide these lovers a place of solace and protection." Pulling out a thick golden cord, the dark priest wrapped it around the couple and said, "Up until this moment, you have been separate in thought and action. As the cord binds your hands, so do your lives become bound as one."

They were ordered to say their vows to one another.

"Will," Kathy started, "I have only known you for a short time, but that's all the time I needed to be sure of one thing: that I love you and want to stand by your side forever. You have brought out a side of me that hadn't been alive before. As your wife, I will do my best to return the love you've shown me."

The Full Moon

The dark priest motioned for Will to begin. Clearing his throat, Will said, "I pledge my soul ever to your service. My love for you will be strong and enduring so that our lives will be ever protected. Accept it, and what is mine will become yours." His voice was even and precise. Kathy had never seen him like this before. She wanted to believe that he was just nervous, but if she was being honest with herself, it scared her a little.

"Your vows have been made to each other and before the forces of darkness," the dark priest said, continuing the ceremony. He produced the wedding rings. "These rings, like your vows, are without beginning or end. These are the physical representations of your love."

He handed off one ring to Will, who slid it on Kathy's finger while speaking foreign words. Next, Kathy did the same, only she repeated after the dark priest.

"I now pronounce you husband and wife."

Kathy leaned in to kiss Will, but the look on his face stopped her.

"Upon the first kiss as husband and wife, you will be forever bound until death do you part," the dark priest said.

Will leaned down, lifted Kathy's veil, and gently kissed her. It felt different, almost impersonal. Not like the way he had kissed her before when they'd first agreed to move up the wedding.

As his lips met hers, she could feel the cord tighten over their joined hands, and the wax seemed to burn once again. Once their lips parted, both sensations stopped immediately.

"The ceremony is over. Go on and spread the magic of

darkness," the dark priest said.

With the ring of the gong, he concluded the ceremony. Kathy knew that she had just changed her life forever.

Chapter Fifteen

Any apprehension Kathy had about Will during the ceremony was gone when they got back to their apartment. Once they dismissed the dark priest and were alone, Will returned to his regular self, flashing Kathy a smile and sweeping her up in his arms. She figured he'd been probably just trying to show indifference in front of the dark priest.

They couldn't afford to take on any enemies. Kathy knew there were some people among the evil community that disliked the fact that Will had chosen a white witch to marry. Some were very likely questioning her loyalty. Convincing them would be a struggle.

Still, she tried to push these thoughts out of her mind. It was her wedding night and she was going to enjoy it. While she fussed with her hair in the bedroom, she heard voices coming from the kitchen. Will had been looking for the bottle of champagne he had been saving for a special occasion. Glancing at the clock, Kathy saw that it was nearing two in the morning. This wasn't one of Will's neighbors.

Pulling her robe tight and tying it off, Kathy placed her ear against the door and tried to recognize the voice. It was certainly a woman's. She spoke slow and throatily. Within seconds, Kathy had placed the voice and reached for the doorknob just as Will crashed through the door. Luckily, she stood just out of the way.

"Will!" Kathy shrieked. He clutched his shoulder as he lay on the smashed door, his hand trickling blood.

"Watch out!" Will pointed out of the bedroom. Kathy turned and saw the Queen charging after them.

"The honeymoon is over, sweetheart," Jubila said. She pushed Kathy to the floor.

Kathy swung her legs and dropped the Queen to the floor beside her. She moved to pin her in place but stopped when she saw Will standing over the Queen with his sword pressed against her throat. Blood slowly beaded from her neck under the blade's edge.

"If you scream, you're dead," Will promised. He waited until Kathy was by his side before continuing. "You know, I thought I would be able to celebrate my wedding night in peace, but it seems you had other plans. So tell me, what are you doing here?"

The Queen looked first at Will, and then at Kathy. She had her hand gently holding the flat parts of the sword, trying to prevent Will from pressing any harder.

The Full Moon

Losing her patience with the pause, Kathy delivered a swift kick to the Queen's side. "He asked you a question!"

Will placed a hand on Kathy's arm. "Easy."

A smile began to creep across the Queen's face, but Will warned her by pressing the sword a hair farther into her throat.

The Queen opened her mouth to speak, but no sound came out. Frustrated, Kathy froze her.

"Let me just unfreeze her head so she can speak," she suggested. "Can you do that?"

Kathy shrugged. "I've never tried, but I'd say it's worth it. I don't want her or anyone else thinking they can barge in on us like this. We need to find out what's bringing them here. Then maybe we can make an example out of her."

Will smiled, loving the way his wife was embracing her new destiny down the dark path. He kissed her and then said, "What if she screams? She's a banshee, it'll kill us and anyone else around."

Kathy shook her head. "She won't scream. I'll be ready to freeze her head."

He didn't look convinced. "I don't know…"

She rolled her eyes. "Then you have the sword ready in case you need to decapitate her. I'm not sure if that'll kill her, but it'll shut her up for a bit." She didn't know how resilient banshees were to death, or if the Queen, being the leader of the banshees and a hopeful leader of the demonic world, would even be able to be killed the same way as a banshee. Kathy knew she hadn't done enough research on her enemy.

The added protection of the sword seemed to give Will comfort. He stood over the Queen's head, placing his sword against her neck, ready to swing it like a golf club if he needed. "Okay. Unfreeze her."

"What are you doing here?" Kathy demanded after reversing the magic on her head.

"Are the rumors true?"

"What rumors?" Will asked.

"Now that you two are married, there is talk that you are after my crown," the Queen said.

Kathy raised her eyebrows. "And you came here personally to ask us? Don't you have lackeys to do that?" She thought of their battle at the beach when Josh had been kidnapped. The Queen's lackeys didn't seem to be strong enough for any of the witches. In hindsight, Kathy wondered if the Queen just didn't want to show her hand too soon.

"I wanted to respectfully inform you that I won't let you stand in my way of becoming queen of the underworld."

"Respectfully?" Kathy spat. She looked to Will. "Is this a thing? Does respect matter among the demonic world?"

Will shrugged and nodded. "For something this important, sometimes." He turned his attention back down to the Queen. "But it still doesn't explain why you needed to show up tonight, which happens to be our wedding night! We haven't even been married two hours yet!"

"I'm done," Kathy said. She froze the Queen's head before she could respond. Kathy looked up to her husband. "Get rid of her. I have a spell to cast." She walked off to the bedroom.

As she dressed, she couldn't seem to quell her anger. How dare the Queen show up like that and give some half-ass explanation about wanting to warn them that she's going to kill them. Since when do demonic leaders give people a heads-up they're being hunted?

"What are you doing?" Will asked, stepping over the broken door.

"If people think they're going to show up uninvited all the time, they have another thing coming." She pulled her hair back out of her face.

"The Queen is just upset that someone she used to order around is now outsmarting her," Will said. "She's small fry compared to anyone who really matters, and we're not on their radar."

"I don't care, Will. I don't like it!" Kathy pulled on a T-shirt and said, "I'm going to get a spell from the book. Be right back."

Before he had a chance to argue, she was gone.

* * *

When they woke up the next morning, it was late. Kathy had risked a trip back to Samantha's to find a protection spell. She wanted their presence to be completely unavailable to all other magical beings. This was their home and it needed to be sacred.

Back before Kathy had met Will, she had suggested Samantha use it on the house so that they could guarantee the protection of the boys, but Samantha said no. She thought that by having their house open, they would be the targets for any potential threat instead of the innocent people who didn't have powers to protect themselves.

By the time Kathy finished brewing the potion and chanting around the apartment, it was nearing four thirty in the morning. Will had zonked out, leaving Kathy to protect the space by herself.

Now that the sun was up, beckoning for Kathy to join the rest of the world, their places had reversed and Will was the one fussing around the apartment while she slept.

The smell of eggs sizzling on the stove woke her. She pulled on her robe and wandered into the kitchen.

"What are you doing up? I wanted to surprise you with breakfast in bed!" Will said. The toaster popped and he rushed to get a plate.

Kathy walked up and kissed him. "I love you. And I wanted to apologize for last night. The Queen got me so mad, I just had to do something. I felt like a sitting duck here, unprotected."

Will turned off the burner and scooped some eggs onto two plates. "Yeah, I wanted to talk to you about that spell you cast last night."

Kathy plopped down at the breakfast bar—the closest thing they had to a dining room set. "Sorry, did I wake you with the incense? I tried to be quiet in the bedroom, but that stuff was potent."

Will waved it off, placing her plate in front of her. "No, that's not it. It's just…where did you get that spell from?"

Pushing her eggs around on her plate, Kathy diverted her eyes from Will's. In a small voice she said, "Um…from the magic book."

"The one at your sister's?"

Kathy briefly turned her hands palms-up. "Yeah, it's the only one I have."

He reached out and took her hand. "Kathy, it's not your book anymore. When you married me, you chose to abdicate any allegiance to white magic."

"What? Will, you never told me that when I agreed to marry you. You just said that I would be your wife while you became a big, bad demonic leader!"

"Oh, don't be so naïve, Kathy. You knew what you were signing up for. Even if I didn't explicitly tell you, you knew deep down that once you were my wife, you could never practice white magic again."

Kathy dropped her fork on her plate and crossed her arms, staring at Will. He was right. She'd known exactly what she was walking into when she married him. She'd been the one who suggested they move up the wedding. She had even gotten the spell to summon the dark priest.

"The spell you cast won't be able to hide us against people like your sister," Will said in a careful, even tone.

"So what do you suppose we do if the spell I spent half the night making was a waste?"

"I think that's the best we can do for now. Against the Queen, that is," Will said. "There are a few things we could do with black magic that would protect us against your sister's magic. But you need to prepare yourself for the reality of it all. Once she realizes you've chosen the dark side, we'll be her targets. She will become our enemy."

Kathy dropped her eyes. She'd never thought of that. Samantha would not stand for spreading evil. She would try to convert Kathy back to the good side, but in the end she knew her own sister would strip her powers if she had to. Maybe even kill her.

Will was beside her now, wrapping his arms around her. "Promise me you won't go back there to do anything. Not even to look at the magic book or collect anything from your old room. If you need something, we'll figure out the best way to do it together. That house isn't your home anymore."

* * *

Kathy had just finished up another day at the day care. She used to find the children so fun and entertaining, but these days she found them exhausting. The only thing preventing her from quitting was the fact that she felt she needed to contribute something to her new marriage. That and her lack of qualifications for any other position.

Leaving the day care, she walked a couple of blocks toward the crook in between two buildings she always hid in to teleport back home. Today, she noticed a man following her. She took a few odd turns to try to throw him off her tracks, but still he persisted.

The Full Moon

She turned into a random building and acted like she had intended to enter the building from the start. It was a hotel—with less of a crowd than she was hoping for. Still, the presence of any witnesses would divert a street thug from doing anything.

She took a seat at one of the large leather chairs and busied herself by digging through her purse. The window she was perched next to overlooked the busy street.

Chancing a look up, she let out a shriek of surprise when she saw the man—he wore a heavy jacket with the hood pulled up, concealing his dirty face. He stood still for a moment and then began pounding on the glass with his fist.

He shouted through the glass, "The Queen will be the end of you! You're dead!" He continued pounding and shouting threats until finally a few policemen arrived—apparently the people inside the building had called 9-1-1—and pulled him away.

As the hotel clerk and the doorman circled Kathy, asking if she was okay, she could only hear the thought that screamed in her mind: the Queen was sending a message, this time with one of the lackeys Kathy had teased her about. She was coming for Kathy and Will.

* * *

"I think we should steal the Queen's crown," Kathy suggested that night when she climbed into bed.

Will put down the newspaper he was reading and asked,

"What makes you say that?"

She didn't want to mention the man and the Queen's threat. That would only enrage him—the same way it had when the Queen visited her at the day care.

"Well, the Queen is only the first in a long line of people who are more than likely going to be after us anyway," Kathy explained. "I mean, I haven't exactly shown proof that I'm on the dark side yet. I'm sure not many people are happy about that. I think in order to prevent these attacks, we need to be feared."

"Kathy, bringing ourselves into the spotlight like that will only be inviting more attacks," Will said. "Are you sure that's something you want?"

She could see in his eyes that it was something he wanted, but was afraid to push it. Right now, he was satisfied enough that she was his wife. She wondered what his attitude toward the Queen's undertaking would be like once the buzz from their marriage was over. Kathy wanted to be proactive in making him happy. Plus, she wanted to put the Queen in her place and take the very thing she wanted most: to be the leader of the underworld. She still resented her for ruining their wedding night.

"You said it yourself that a union between a Dark Knight and witch has never been done before. This is our chance to embrace our full potential."

Will sat up and faced her directly. "You're serious about this?"

Kathy rolled her eyes, tired of trying to convince him. "Yes!"

"Understand that this will require a big sacrifice, especially for you."

"I don't care." She had already sacrificed so much to be with him. There wasn't much left for her to sacrifice.

He got out of bed and went to the main part of the apartment.

"Will, honey, what are you doing?" She got up and followed.

He opened the cabinet that held his magical instruments and potions. "To start the process, we'll need to be bound as one," he said, testing the sharpness of a blade against his fingertips.

"We're not bound as one? What was all that mumbo jumbo at the wedding then?" After the dark priest continued to tell them that they would be united forever, she thought that she'd feel different. She didn't. Not really.

"This is different. The wedding was binding us as lovers. This ritual would bind us magically, the same way you were bound with your sister and nephews," Will explained. "Blood will have to spill." He turned toward her with the knife pointed in her direction.

She backed away. "What? Why?"

"You and your sister share the same blood. By extension you share the same blood with your nephews, too," he said. "In order for us to become stronger together, we'll need to mix our blood."

Kathy chewed on her thumb before asking, "So…what will that do?"

"It'll connect us. Amplify our powers when we're together. Make us unstoppable. No single force has the power to destroy us if we remain together." He added, "Especially since we're married. They would have to separate us and destroy us individually—if they could even do that."

Kathy took a deep breath. "Okay, so what do we need to do?"

He raised the knife. "Do you trust me?"

She hesitated, staring at the glint of the blade that was about to pierce her skin.

Offering her arm to him, she said, "Yes."

Chapter Sixteen

And that," Kathy swung Will's sword, slicing off the head of Demetria, the evil witch in charge of the latest faction they were after, "is how it's done." They were just outside the city, hidden beneath the shelter of trees that blocked the sound of traffic from the 90 thruway nearby.

The rest of the members of the faction were scattered around, bewildered. Some clutched bleeding limbs, others lay dead. Those lucky enough to evade an attack were awestruck by Will and Kathy's ruthlessness.

The witches who made up the faction were tricksters, focusing on random people on the streets and infecting them with paranoia. They were like Kathy in the sense that they lived normal lives for the most part, but they were sinister in their evening activities.

As Will and Kathy hunted them, they discovered that these

witches met and plotted out their next victims a few times a week. If left unattended for too long, they could become a powerful group capable of stopping the husband-and-wife duo.

Will thought the specialties of these witches could be useful to them. They had already gained a few followers, and now Kathy was hungry for blood and eager to kill, so it didn't take much convincing on Will's part.

Since Will and Kathy had fused their blood to enhance their magic, she could feel the extra power whenever she was near her husband. It was a power she craved if she spent any time away from him.

She was proud of the following they had gained, a small handful of factions, not much more. But they were powerful. For someone who had once been a white witch, with the dark community skeptical of her conversion, Kathy thought she had changed their minds.

"Anyone else want to try me?" Kathy bellowed to the remaining witches. She scanned each of the survivors, sizing them up. No one met her eyes. She let down her sword and smiled, knowing she had scared them. Will began the spell.

> *To those of you who have fallen,*
> *I call you now to follow me.*
> *From now on this is your calling,*
> *none of you will try to flee.*
> *In the night and in the morning,*
> *you will follow, so let it be.*

THE FULL MOON

He had devised it as a way to make the factions they had overpowered follow him without the thought of rebellion. He didn't figure it would work on the few stronger followers he and Kathy had gained but it was still better than not casting the spell at all.

Kathy stood by her husband, admiring the work they had accomplished. It had only been a month since they began this journey, and already they had four factions following them.

Once the spell was complete, Will crossed his arms and stared down at the new followers. He opened his mouth to speak but stopped dead when he saw movement amid the trees.

Kathy followed his looked. "Shit."

Samantha sauntered into view. She looked Kathy in the eyes before turning her attention to the faction. Pulling out two knives from her jacket, she moved quickly, launching potion after potion at the members of the faction.

Smoke filled the air as the magic took effect on as many members as she could reach before they could run away. One man tried to tackle her, but he got a blade in his belly before he could do any damage. However, when Samantha pushed him off her and moved to stand up, she felt a force pushing her down onto the ground.

Will had his hand extended, using new magic acquired from his newfound ranking in the demonic hierarchy to keep her in place.

"You think you can just show up and kill me with some little bitch blade?" Kathy asked, standing over her sister.

"I just want to talk," Samantha said. She fought against the magical barrier holding her down.

"Bullshit! You just killed half our fleet!" Will barked.

"Let her up," Kathy said. "She won't run."

Reluctantly, Will lowered his hand and released his magic. She sprang to her feet, taking a step back.

"Talk," Kathy said. Her eyes shot daggers into her sister. She wondered why she was here. She hadn't heard from Samantha in a month.

"You can't keep doing this," Samantha said. "If you want to go off and marry Will—"

Kathy held up her left hand, brandishing her wedding ring. "Already did that." She could see the hurt look briefly cross Samantha's face before she replaced it with her cold stare.

"Still, you don't have to do this. He's using you to get what he wants," Samantha pleaded. "Do you understand that what you're doing is going to have serious consequences? What happens if you slip up and expose yourself?"

"Do *you* understand that I'm doing this so I don't have to worry about the consequences?" Kathy said. "For once I can do magic without worrying about how I'm going to justify it to you. All my life, you have had me right under your thumb, suffocating me. I'm not dealing with it anymore."

"I was protecting us," Samantha started, but Kathy cut her off.

"You were controlling me!" She pointed the sword at Samantha. "And now that I've broken free, you don't like it." She locked her arm with Will's, who watched the argument carefully, ready to step in if either of them decided to strike.

"You don't have to listen to him, either. He has you on a path that will lead right to the demonic throne," Samantha said. "I just hope you're not one of his casualties."

Kathy smiled, knowing her sister didn't have the whole story the way she alluded to. "No. This path we're on? It was my idea. Moving up the wedding? Also my idea. You think he's corrupting me? I'm the one calling the shots here!"

Samantha's jaw dropped momentarily. She studied Kathy's face, hoping beyond hope that she was bluffing, but knowing deep down that she wasn't. She had lost her sister, and Will, who she was quick to blame, wasn't even the reason.

Still, Samantha couldn't help but think that Will was at the root of their sudden fallout. It wasn't until Kathy met Will that things started to change between her and Samantha.

A smile briefly flickered across Will's face, and Samantha was consumed by her hatred toward him. She charged after him, brandishing the blade in her hand. It wasn't the smartest attack she'd ever made, but at that point she didn't care.

Samantha was able to nick his cheek before Kathy plowed into her, pinning her down. Wrestling on the ground, Kathy was able to eventually find her footing and stand. Samantha hopped up not long after. She stood between Will and Kathy.

Tears had started to build up in Samantha's eyes, but she fought them. She didn't want to give Will—or even Kathy—the knowledge of how much it hurt her to know that she had failed to protect her sister. That she was the reason her family was so damaged.

"Kathy...why?" Samantha managed to croak, letting her

arms fall to her side, without care of whether Will would attack her from behind.

Catching the look in her sister's eyes, Kathy hesitated. She thought back to their younger days when they had been the two tag-team witches who were nearly unstoppable against any enemy. Back then, she'd had such faith in her sister, knowing that Samantha always had her back. She still had her back, even when Kathy had completely turned on her.

Behind Samantha, Kathy caught Will moving to strike. He had conjured a sword and had it raised over Samantha's head.

"Will, no!" Kathy shouted. Samantha cowered and moved out of the way, just in time to miss his swing.

The three of them stood still, sizing each other up. Both Samantha and Will looked to Kathy for an explanation.

"Samantha, just get out of here," Kathy said weakly. When she hesitated, Kathy shouted, "Go!"

* * *

Back at the apartment, Will was furious. He had left a trail in his wake: broken doors, smashed lights, tipped furniture. Anything that was in his way felt the wrath. Kathy had been a little scared that she would be the next thing in his way, but her anger compensated for her fear. She felt a sense of bravery as she challenged him.

"How could you let her go like that?" he demanded.

"She's my sister!"

"That didn't stop you from beating the shit out of her before!"

Kathy clenched her fists, thinking back to her brawl with

Samantha right in this very room.

"That's different. I wasn't actually trying to kill her."

"You had me fooled. I thought that's what we've been trying to do? Overpower your sister."

"I'm not going to kill my sister, Will," Kathy said.

"Back before we started all this, I told you she was the enemy. You said you were okay with that!" He stepped closer to her, lowering his voice. "If you're having second thoughts, you need to tell me before I go making fools out of us in front of everyone. They will kill us, Kathy. If they find a weakness, they'll take advantage."

Kathy thought of the faction that Samantha had attacked. The half that had lived ran away before they could hear anything.

"If we don't have a united front, nobody will respect us and we're dead in the water," Will continued in a soothing voice. "If you want to stop, we'll have to repair some of the bridges we've already burned. But if we go ahead, your sister and her boys will eventually become our priority."

Josh and Chris flashed into her mind. Right now Josh was likely doing homework. Chris was probably hanging out with one of his friends or watching TV. She wondered what they thought about her conversion to the dark side. It was probably contingent on what their mother told them. Kathy guessed they probably hated her now.

"I warned you of the sacrifices," Will said, interrupting her thoughts. "Here they are, staring you right in the face. It's your decision to make. Choose."

He started to back away toward the door, but Kathy stopped

him. "Will, wait." She twisted the wedding ring around her finger, staring at nothing in particular. Her eyes snapped up to him and she said, "You're right. I need to let them go."

He wrapped his arms around her, kissing the top of her head. "I know it's not easy for you, but they're no good for you. Not with what we're trying to accomplish."

"I think they need to die," Kathy said into Will's chest.

"They will. Depending on where we stand when the time comes, you may not even have to do it," Will said.

Kathy looked up him. "No. It's up to me. I'll kill them. That will convince anyone who has any doubts that I'm in this completely. No one will ever question my intentions again. This will be good for us."

Will met her eyes. "Honey, you don't have to do this right now. We can wait until some of this has passed. Let the wounds heal a bit."

Kathy shook her head. "No, we need to do it as soon as possible. I know my sister. She thinks she has a hook in me. She thinks I'll be easy to convert back. I need to show her that I'm staying." She also knew that Samantha was resilient and wouldn't stop trying to get her back until one of them was dead.

"What are you thinking?"

"I have a plan. We'll kill the boys first and let her watch," Kathy explained. "She'll be so blinded by emotion that she'll let her guard down. Between you and me, we should be able to finish the job."

After fighting with her sister for so many years, she knew Samantha's strengths and weaknesses. She had watched them change through the years as well. Before, her soft spot used to be Kathy. Now it was her boys. She always tried so hard to protect them—hovering, smothering—that she would lose her focus. Couple that with her sometimes overconfidence in her abilities and she was a sitting duck.

Kathy didn't allow herself to think about the morbidity of it all. Her nephews were almost like her kids, too. Killing them, especially with their mother watching, wouldn't be easy for her. She needed to look at it objectively. This was a means to an end. Josh and Chris were just casualties—sacrifices, as Will put it—along her road to the throne.

They had to die.

Chapter Seventeen

Kathy waited as she rode the elevator up to her sister's office. She leaned against the handrail with one hand and tapped the top of it with her fingernail. She was nervous. This whole thing could blow up in her face. She worried that Samantha would see through the ruse. For as well as Kathy knew Samantha, she knew her sister knew her just as well. It's why they always made such a good team.

The elevator dinged when she reached the correct floor. Kathy took a deep breath and prepared herself. Confidence would be key in luring Samantha into her plan.

She strolled through the glass doors marked Darius Wilcox, CPA and located Samantha's office.

"What are you doing here?" Samantha asked.

Kathy closed the door behind her and leaned forward on

Samantha's desk.

"I want to cut you a deal."

Samantha raised her eyebrows. "A deal? What do you have that I would want?"

Kathy smiled. "Your life."

"You wouldn't dare." Samantha turned serious.

Rolling her eyes, Kathy said, "Not me. The Queen—Jubila, if you haven't gotten the memo. She's hunting us. Not just me and Will, but you and the boys, too. She told me so last month."

"She threatened us and you forgot to mention it?" Samantha shouted. She realized where she was and immediately lowered her voice. "You should have told me. When was this?"

"Back when I first started at the day care." She waved her hand dismissively. "But listen, I have a way to defeat her."

"I thought we could just use the spell to kill a banshee and couple it with a potion?" Samantha asked, tossing her glasses onto her desk and leaning back in her chair.

"Will doesn't think that'll work." She saw her sister roll her eyes and added, "You know, if we're going to do this, you're going to have to work with us."

"You're not the problem. He is."

Kathy stood and moved to the door. "Fine, let the Queen kill you. I just hope she's quick when she kills the boys."

"Wait!"

Kathy wiped the smile from her face before she turned her attention back to her sister.

"What do we have to do?" Samantha sounded defeated, and

Kathy loved being the one who held the cards.

"Will and I can lure her to us, but we're going to need more manpower once she's there," Kathy explained. "Will used to work for the Queen, so she'll know all his tricks. I haven't exactly been discreet with my powers lately, so there goes me. That leaves you and the boys."

"I don't want to bring the boys into this if I don't have to," Samantha countered.

"You do have to. Your mind specialty won't be enough. I'm sure your mind games won't work on someone of Jubila's level, anyway," Kathy said. "We need Josh's power."

"He doesn't even know how to use it yet," Samantha said. Josh's specialty was the wind. He had just developed it six months ago, and because she had tried her best to keep them out of any magical situations, he had limited control. The memory of Steven walking out after Josh developed his first power still stung her like an open wound.

"Well, teach him!" Kathy snapped. "You're not helping those boys by hiding this world of ours." She paused. If her plan was successful, Josh and Chris wouldn't have a future to learn their powers in—Chris hadn't even developed his specialty yet. Her heart sank at the thought. She wondered if she would be able to pull it off when the time came—not that she had a lot of time to decide.

"Where are we meeting?"

Kathy knew her sister was not going to offer the house, so she offered her spots. "The apartment is too small, so maybe out in the woods? Where you found us before."

Samantha considered a moment and then said, "No, I don't know if you guys hid any traps or anything like that. We need some neutral ground where neither of us has the upper hand."

Kathy crossed her arms and let out a deep breath. "Okay. How about Presque Isle? We fought her there before. We already know she doesn't like water."

Samantha nodded. "Okay. When?"

"Tonight." She didn't want to give her sister—or herself—too much time to reconsider. Or worse, come up with an effective backup plan in case it turned ugly—and Kathy was planning on it turning ugly.

"Okay," Samantha said, picking up her glasses from the desk.

"Okay." Kathy turned to leave, but the sound of her name stopped her. "Yeah?"

"What if Jubila—the Queen—brings her new right-hand man? The one who took Will's place? What was his name?"

"Kaiser," Kathy said, recalling the entry she found on him in her magic book—Samantha's magic book; it wasn't hers anymore. She had completely forgotten about him, but surely they would be able to take him on while finishing the job. He might even help by offering a distraction.

"That's it!"

Kathy cocked her head toward her sister. "Don't worry about Kaiser. We've got him taken care of."

* * *

"Are you ready for this?" Will asked. "It's a big job. Not like the others."

Kathy zipped up her hoodie. "As ready as I'll ever be."

Will nodded. "Let's run through this one more time: We summon the Queen. When she attacks us, you send your sister and your nephews after her, distracting them so that we can…" He trailed off, not wanting to finish for his wife's sake. "With any luck, the Queen will be the one to seal the deal, and we won't have any blood on our hands if one of them gets away."

"They're not going to get away," Kathy said. She slipped a knife into her belt and tried to cover it with her hoodie. "And I've been thinking…maybe we don't summon the Queen." It didn't cover the blade, and she pulled the weapon out, tossing it onto the kitchen counter.

"What? That's the crux of the whole plan."

Kathy unzipped her hoodie and walked to the bedroom. "I think it'll still work without her there." She flipped through her few things in the closet—most of her clothes were still at Samantha's house—and tried to find something that would allow her room to move and conceal her blade.

"How do you figure?"

She pulled off her hoodie and snatched a brown leather coat from the hanger. "Well, it doesn't really matter if they know we're the ones who killed them. They'll be dead, who are they going to tell?"

"What if one of them gets away? There's three of them and two of us," Will said. "It's quite possible we'll have our hands tied."

Kathy pulled on the leather jacket and flipped her hair out from under it. "Will we? Samantha's mind manipulation won't work on us, Josh doesn't know how to use his specialty, and Chris doesn't have any powers." She counted off each on her fingers. "Seems pretty easy to me."

Noticing the time, Will decided to let it slide. "Okay, okay. Your family, your call."

"Not my family. Not anymore," Kathy muttered, walking to the kitchen and collecting her knife from the counter. This jacket hid it much better. "You're my family. We're stronger together, right?"

She wondered how it all worked. Since she and Will had fused their blood, she felt stronger when she was with him. But prior to that, she always seemed stronger when she was with family. Her blood had been naturally fused with her family's, and there was no way to break that bind unless one of them died. How would she feel when she was in close proximity with both her sister and Will?

* * *

Walking up to the beach, Kathy could see Samantha, Josh, and Chris all standing near the water. Again, her heart sank seeing her nephews. She hadn't seen them in over a month and didn't realize how much she missed them.

Samantha's early arrival didn't surprise Kathy at all. She knew her sister would want to be the first one there so she could scope out the area for any tricks.

"Before we get started, I want to know how we're going to kill the Queen," Samantha said. She looked to Kathy. "You slipped out of the office before you told me that bit."

Kathy put up her hands and tried to freeze her nephews. She knew that with Will standing next to her, her magic would be strong enough to do it. As soon as her magic touched them, they seemed to evaporate into thin air.

"Where'd they go?" Will demanded, extending a finger to the spot where they had stood.

Samantha cocked a thumb next to her. "You believed that? Guess my mind manipulation is good for something."

"Damn it," Kathy muttered, running toward her sister. She was kicking herself for thinking that Samantha would bring the boys into a fight unnecessarily. She didn't want to think of having to make a second trip to kill the boys. She wondered if she could convince Will to convert them and raise them with black magic. They hadn't really started using white magic yet anyway.

After chasing Samantha down the hill, with Will close behind, Kathy decided to fight smart and use her teleportation to appear right in front of her sister.

Samantha stopped in her tracks and sized Kathy up, waiting for her to strike so she could evade it and hopefully find a way to counterattack.

Looking into her sister's eyes, Kathy felt conflicted. She could feel her sister's pull—they're blood bond stronger than she remembered—but as Will drew nearer, she could hear her dark thoughts creep back into her mind.

Samantha must have been reading Kathy's confusion, because Will was able to sneak up right behind Samantha and lock her in a bear hug.

"Kill her!" Will shouted to his wife. He fought to keep Samantha restrained. She was squirming and trying to break free from his hold.

Kathy was even more confused as Will wrestled for control of Samantha. She could feel the pull from both of them. She froze. Both sides pulling her toward them. Both sides amplified by the heightened emotions of the fight.

"Kathy!" Will shouted.

Finally, his pull proved to be stronger and she placed the knife back in her belt. "I have a better idea. Do you have any rope?"

"Can you freeze her?"

Samantha's eyes pleaded with Kathy, but she shook them off.

"I'll try." Putting up her hands, she concentrated on the energy radiating from Will and froze her sister in place.

"What happened to you?" Will asked, breathing heavily.

Kathy debated whether she should tell him. She thought Samantha's pull was something he should know, but she knew he'd be angry about it and try harder to kill Samantha. Whatever was happening with her, she needed to figure it out for herself without the influence of her sister or her husband.

She needed to figure out a way to keep her sister alive and her husband pacified until she was able to make a decision about whom to side with.

"Where's the rope?" she asked, holding out her hand.

Will conjured a long stretch of rope and handed it to his wife.

She tied up Samantha's hands, trying not to look at the pleading expression still frozen on her face.

"What happened to killing her?" Will asked, watching Kathy tie the rope.

She focused on pulling the rope tight. She didn't look him in the eyes. "New plan."

CHAPTER EIGHTEEN

Before Samantha had opened her eyes, she could hear Will and Kathy talking—arguing—in a hushed tone. She tried not to stir too much. She didn't want Will and Kathy knowing she was awake. She needed to get as much information out of them as she could. Will's control over Kathy was obviously stronger than Samantha had originally anticipated. That was, if Kathy's actions were the result of Will's influence.

"I thought we had a plan," Will said. "You said you'd be able to kill her. Are you having second thoughts?"

There was a pause, then Kathy responded, "No, I'm not. I…I just thought we could better use her alive than dead." Samantha noted the hesitation in Kathy's voice, and she was sure Will did too, but he didn't seem to let that be known.

"How so?"

"You and I made a blood bond. She and I already had one, and it still exists," Kathy explained. "We should be able to extract her magic and use it to our benefit."

"I've never heard of that. How would we extract her magic? With a spell? Potion?"

"Blood."

Samantha nearly jumped out of her skin. Will and Kathy took notice.

"Well, well, well. Looks like sissy is up now," Kathy said, strolling closer. Her tone had changed from hesitation to arrogance. She grabbed a fistful of Samantha's hair and yanked her head back. With her eyes now open, Samantha saw that she was inside—likely Will's apartment.

"Why don't you guys just kill me?" Samantha muttered between gritted teeth.

Will stepped into Samantha's field of view, which was limited to the ceiling and Kathy's face. "A quick kill doesn't really do it justice, does it? After all the trouble you put Kathy and I through?"

Samantha tried her hardest to maintain her composure, but the strength at which Kathy was pulling on her hair made her wince in pain.

"Whatever you're going to do, just go ahead and do it," Samantha said. She had a feeling—and she was hoping she was right—that Kathy wouldn't do anything too harmful to her. She hadn't been able to kill her on the beach, so Samantha figured she was probably safe. Still, she didn't trust Will for a minute. Her suspicions had now been verified.

Finally, Kathy let go of Samantha's hair. She stepped over to Will, who hooked one arm around her. Samantha hated the sight of him being so possessive of her.

"I'll get the syringe," Will offered, walking off into the bedroom.

"Kathy, think about what you're doing," Samantha pleaded. The few moments she had in Will's absence were essential. "You don't have to do this. It's your choice."

"This is my choice!" Kathy shouted. She saw Will emerging from the bedroom and pulled up each of Samantha's sleeves.

Will passed Kathy the syringe, but when she grabbed it, he kept his grip and leaned in, dropping his voice to an almost inaudible volume. "Are you sure you know what you're doing? A witch's blood in the wrong body could do serious damage."

"She's my sister. I'll be fine," Kathy said. She tried to pull away, but Will held on. "Fine, if you're still nervous, I'll only inject it into me. I'm a witch too, so my body will be less likely to reject it." She was just guessing about her body being able to hold it. She had no idea.

"Kathy, don't!" Samantha pleaded.

Ignoring her, Kathy carefully drove the needle into her sister's arm, filling the syringe. She pulled it out and stuck it in her own arm, depositing it into her body.

Samantha watched Kathy's reaction. Her eyes were shut tight and she pinched the bridge of her nose like she had a bad headache or brain freeze.

"Babe, are you all right?" Will placed his hand on his wife's shoulder.

Kathy swatted him away. After a minute, she opened her eyes. "Yeah, I'm fine. Just a head rush getting all that power."

The look on Kathy's face didn't seem to emit power. In a matter of a few minutes her skin was paler. Samantha thought the addition of her blood looked more like deterioration. Mixing blood was something alchemists dabbled in, not something witches got involved with.

"Are you sure you're all right?" Will asked. Samantha knew that he was genuinely concerned.

Kathy's knees started to give way, and Will gripped her arms, guiding her to the closest chair.

"I'm fine. I just need to sit down for a minute. Let the swell of power pass by a bit." Kathy looked at Will and smiled weakly. "By the time we've drained her completely, I'll have both of our powers, and you and I will be unstoppable."

Will returned the smile and nodded. "Yeah, okay. But maybe we should wait a bit before we take the next dose, okay?"

Kathy nodded. Half an hour later, she had returned to her normal self—the head rush having passed—and she was once again at Samantha's side, draining more blood and injecting it into herself.

All night long they took syringes of blood from Samantha and injected them into Kathy. By morning, neither Kathy nor Samantha were feeling great.

Although she seemed to become more and more hungry for the head rush that never seemed as strong as the first, Kathy was looking ragged. Sunken eyes, yellowing skin, shaky hands.

Samantha, on the other hand, was exhausted. Not only from the significant loss of blood, but also from the lack of food or water. With each dose of blood they took from her, she got even weaker.

A few times Kathy began to doze off, but Will woke her to continue the process.

"I have to run down to the office," Will announced the next morning, looking at his phone.

"Why?" Kathy croaked. She was in desperate need of sleep.

"My assistant booked a client for this morning," he said. "I'll be back by noon." He pointed at Samantha. "Keep going. We've almost got her." He leaned down and kissed Kathy on the cheek. "You're right, so much better than killing her."

Kathy smiled weakly at his praise as he walked to the bedroom to change. She had almost drifted off to sleep again when he came back out and announced he was leaving.

Once he left for work, Samantha was finally able to rest. She let herself fall asleep, knowing that Kathy was worse off than she was.

She snapped awake a few hours later. She was still groggy, but she felt much better. She craned her neck back to catch the time on the stove and saw that it was just after eleven. Will would be home in an hour. She needed to get to work.

Kathy's name was on the tip of her tongue, but she stopped herself before she spoke it. She needed to figure out what was going on inside Kathy's mind before she figured out a way to talk her down and bring her back to reality.

The short nap she had was enough to let her regain a bit of her energy. She certainly wasn't back to full strength, especially not after all the blood Kathy had drawn, but she knew she had enough power to do what she needed to do.

Probing into Kathy's mind, she first saw the dream her sister was having. Samantha herself was lying on the floor in her house, bloody and screaming off into the distance. She saw Kathy sitting off to the side, clutching at her leg, and Will lying on the floor a few feet away, one eye open, with a sly grin on his face.

Samantha pushed past that before she could see any more. She had witnessed a few of Kathy's visions this way, through her mind specialty, and she didn't want to experience it again. The gift of sight wasn't always a gift. Besides, Samantha was hoping beyond hope that what Kathy was dreaming of wasn't a vision. If the three of them were together, defenseless and facing an unidentified threat, then who was the target? Who was Samantha screaming to?

Digging further into Kathy's mind, Samantha looked in places she had never dared go before. She launched into the good memories Kathy had and ignored any of them that involved Will—which weren't as prominent as she would have thought. In fact, most of Kathy's happy memories of Will were before they were married, nothing recent—at least not that Samantha could tell.

Finally, she ventured to the place in Kathy's mind from before she even knew Will. The good memories she shared with Samantha and the boys—her family.

Usually, if Samantha was at full strength, she would be able to bring these memories to the surface and make them Kathy's conscious memory. Make her see what was buried in the depths of her memory. But with the blood loss and the significant weakness in her powers, she wasn't able to do that.

In fact, she knew she was losing strength by being so deep in

Kathy's memory. She decided to float further to the surface, sorting through the memories—good and bad—of Will. She needed to know how Kathy perceived him. Obviously, Samantha didn't see him the same way, so she tried to understand why Kathy had fallen in love with him in the first place.

She replayed the memories of their short romance—the first time they met, when Will first asked her out, their first date, the proposal, their wedding—all leading up to the present.

"Kathy! Kathy, wake up!" Samantha called.

Her sister began to stir, and Samantha called her name again.

Kathy was disoriented for a minute. She looked around, confused. When her eyes turned to Samantha, it took a moment before she really saw her sister, still tied to the chair and weak from the loss of blood. "I need to take more blood." She was in no position to stand, and she knew it. She didn't get up from her seat.

"Do you remember when we had just moved into the house by ourselves, and we spent all night cloaking it in the protection incense, chanting like idiots?" Samantha laughed, hoping Kathy would catch on.

Kathy raised an eyebrow. "Yeah, I actually used that same spell here last month. Stole the recipe from the book while you guys were sleeping."

Samantha tried not to look too surprised. She had missed that memory on her trip through Kathy's mind.

Sidestepping her sister's attempt at dodging conversation, Samantha pressed on. "That same year we almost blew up the house with that potion to kill the shapeshifter."

This brought a smile to Kathy's lips. "That was before we knew the house could fix itself." She quickly resumed her taut expression.

"You used to go on dates and tell me to call you with a family emergency if they were going bad," Samantha continued. "Of course, the dates that went well were usually interrupted by *real* family emergencies. You used to come home every night and tell me all about them—good or bad. That seemed to all stop with Will. Which is a shame because he's permanent now."

"Yeah, he is."

"What confuses me, though, is that you used to be someone to talk things out and rationalize and discuss how you felt before really admitting to how you felt," Samantha said. "Remember Jeremy? You dated him for almost four months before you even allowed him to call you his girlfriend. But with Will…it all went so fast. You've barely even *known* him four months, and you're already his wife."

It had actually been about five months since she first met Will, but Kathy didn't say that. "I guess it's just different with Will."

"Good different?" This was the test. Kathy's reaction would determine just how far she was gone.

"He just…charmed me. From the moment I met him," Kathy said.

"From the moment you met him?" Samantha pressed. "If you met any guy you could possibly have any sort of future with, you told me about it. You knew Will for a week before he asked you out. Obviously, he wasn't on your mind much before then, so what made you fall so hard so fast?"

Kathy chewed on her lip, thinking. She never thought about the way she was before Will versus after Will. Even she had to admit that she was different. With Will she was completely swept away. Yet she knew that she felt almost the same way with other guys, only not as fast. Is that what made Will "the one"? Did she believe in "the one"? Did she believe that Will fit her vision of "the one"?

She thought back to her and Will's tumultuous relationship. Her memories seemed to be fresh in her mind—she suspected Samantha had been lurking around. But she wasn't upset with her sister for the invasion. This was something she'd never thought of before, which was so against her nature. Something was preventing her from perceiving Will in any negative light. Suddenly it hit her.

"The earring."

Chapter Nineteen

The earring she'd supposedly lost on the day she met Will had been the turning point. She could see that clearly now. He must have done something to the earring because as soon as she'd taken it back, her feelings for him changed. Instead of just being a kind stranger who treated her to lunch, he was a potential suitor—and one she was very adamant on securing.

A thousand thoughts floated through her mind: Did she really love him? Was their whole relationship a fabrication? What else had he done to her to trick her into doing his bidding? How would she get herself out of the mess she was tangled in?

They were in so deep now. They had followers, plans set in motion to dominate the demonic world. She had pushed for it herself. Had it really been her idea? Or had it been fueled by the spell Will had placed on her?

THE FULL MOON

She looked up at her sister, still bound to the chair. Samantha had a quizzical look on her face, waiting until Kathy reacted.

More thoughts hit her: Was the earring hexed? Did that mean Samantha had been right about Will's intentions all along? She had suspected Will had placed a spell on her from the beginning. Would Samantha ever forgive her?

"Kathy," Samantha said, breaking into her thoughts.

"Sammy, I'm so sorry!" Tears poured from Kathy's eyes. She reached for her sister but immediately felt light-headed. She dropped the syringe to the floor and crushed it under her foot.

She wanted to take it all back—everything. The arguments, the harsh words, the demonic followers she had gained, the blood transfusion—all of it.

"It's okay," Samantha cooed. She let Kathy cry for a moment before continuing. "Kathy, he'll be back any minute. We need to get out of here."

Kathy leaned forward on her knees, letting her tears hit the floor. She wasn't sure she had the strength to even stand, let alone use her powers to take them back to Samantha's house— her house. Home.

"I can't." Her voice was nearly a whisper. She wanted everything to go away. Even though she was aware of the spell now, she still couldn't imagine disappointing Will. She didn't want to let down her sister anymore, either.

"You have to, Kathy. Please."

"I don't know what to do…I've made such a mess!" She began crying into her hands again, slumping over into Samantha's lap.

"Look at me," Samantha said, keeping her eyes locked on her sister, willing her to turn her head. Finally, Kathy met her gaze. "We'll deal with all of that later. First, we need to get somewhere safe. If he finds out that you didn't kill me, he'll do it himself." And, she feared, he might kill Kathy for breaking his spell.

Suddenly, Kathy's head perked up. "He's on his way home. I can feel his pull getting stronger."

"Then we have to move. Untie me and let's get out of here," Samantha said.

When Kathy stood, she wobbled a bit on her feet and grabbed the edge of the kitchen counter for support. Once the room stopped spinning, she stepped slowly to her sister, trying to loosen the knot. She could feel Will's power over her getting stronger and stronger as he got closer.

With one of her hands free, Samantha pointed to the bedroom. "Is there anything you want to take? You might not get the chance to come back. I can get the rest of these knots." If Kathy had snuck into the house to steal a spell from the magic book, Samantha didn't know if she had brought anything else from home that she would regret leaving in Will's possession.

Kathy nodded and crossed the apartment to her bedroom.

A few minutes later, once Samantha had freed herself and could stand without the room spinning, she crept slowly in Kathy's direction. She gripped various pieces of furniture along the way to steady herself. She was so weak. Her vision blurred and all she wanted to do was collapse on the floor and sleep.

"Kathy, are you ready?" Her mouth was dry when she spoke.

The Full Moon

Kathy was sitting on her bed, her head resting on her fist that was propped up on her knee.

"I can't do it, Sammy. I'm sorry!"

Samantha hesitated. She figured the sudden change in Kathy's attitude must have been because Will was getting closer. With the amount of blood she'd lost, Samantha wasn't up to strength enough to look into Kathy's mind to see what the real influence was. Even if she could, she didn't have that kind of time. Her only option was to talk her down.

"Kathy, listen to me. I know it's hard, but having him here and magically connected to you won't help you figure this out," Samantha said. Her mind flickered to her own divorce and the moment Steven had left. Her thoughts had been so clouded by him that she couldn't think straight. Samantha assumed being the one to leave would be even more difficult—unfortunately that wasn't the case for her own ex-husband. "He's already shown that he has no problem hexing you. You need to get away where you can think clearly. Away from him."

Wiping at her eyes, Kathy nodded. "You're right. We should go. Will's on his way up."

Samantha grasped her sister's hand. "Come on!"

Kathy closed her eyes and concentrated. Just as the door was opening, the sisters disappeared in a bright red flash.

* * *

The sound of shouting from outside roused Kathy from her nap.

She had passed out almost immediately on their arrival home. Fists pounding on the front door accompanied the shouting.

Kathy began to rise, but Samantha was by her side. "No! Sleep. I'll get rid of him."

"No." Kathy's voice was weak. She collapsed on her bed but kept her grip on her sister's hand. She didn't want to start a fight between Will and Samantha. Not again. She needed her space, but she didn't want him angry about it. "Be nice," was all she managed before she slipped back into her slumber.

When she woke again, the sun had set. She looked at the clock and saw that it was going on six in the evening. She felt rejuvenated. The effects of the injections had subsided. The sleep had certainly helped.

She rose and slowly made her way down the stairs to the kitchen. Samantha was there fixing dinner.

"How are you feeling?" she asked, wrapping an arm around Kathy. Even after this whole ordeal with Will, Samantha still welcomed her back with open arms as if no words had been exchanged. Still, Kathy could hear the nervousness in Samantha's voice when she spoke.

"A lot better. What about you? You really should be resting," Kathy said. Samantha had lost a lot of blood, and yet she seemed just fine. It made Kathy feel a little guilty for sleeping all day.

Samantha held up her hand and shook it. "Eh. A little woozy. I have to sit down a lot." She started toward the other end of the kitchen to sit. "I get these waves of light-headedness, but after I sit for a few minutes, they usually pass. I've been drinking plenty of water, too. Get yourself a glass."

Kathy carried over two glasses filled with water and handed one to her. "I'm so sorry." She tried to fight off the tears, but it was useless. Now that she was seeing things more clearly, she could see the extent to which her betrayal had gone. She had been horrible to her sister. She was in so deep with Will she wasn't sure if she could reverse it. Samantha was being too nice to her. She had no reason to. Just a few hours ago, Kathy was draining her blood to steal her powers.

"I wish I could take it all back."

Samantha, who was sipping her water, held up her hand as if to stop Kathy from continuing. "Don't. This isn't completely your fault. You were under a spell. You didn't know, I didn't know." She shrugged.

"But I'm still to blame." Kathy's eyes flashed to the red marks on Samantha's arm where she had stuck the needle in again and again in her vindictive drive for power. "All those horrible things I did to you—"

"You were trying to keep me alive," Samantha interrupted. "I know. I could see it in your eyes. Even though you were still trying to become Will's evil queen, you didn't want to kill me— no matter how much you threatened. Or tried." She smiled, reaching for Kathy's hands.

"I sacrificed you and the boys—"

Samantha put a finger to her lips and dropped her voice. "Shh! I didn't tell them anything about that."

Kathy was stunned. Even after the complete betrayal, which

involved the boys as well, Samantha didn't want to tarnish the image of Kathy in the minds of Josh and Chris.

"Why not?"

"I don't want them to hate you." Samantha was focused on her water glass, circling her finger around the rim. "And they don't need the added stress."

"Like I put on you." She paused. "I'll tell them tomorrow. Make them understand just how powerful the dark side can be."

"No! Kathy, I don't want them to ever know," Samantha said. "I don't want them watching their backs wondering if people are going to turn on them. That isn't the life I want for them. They should be able to trust the people they love."

Samantha's words stung. Kathy knew she'd forever be in debt to her sister—whether her sister punished her or not.

"What about you?" Kathy asked.

"What *about* me?"

"Are you ever going to trust me the same way you did before?"

Neither of the sisters looked at each other. Finally, Samantha let out a deep breath and looked up. "I don't know. We'll have to take it one day at a time. Figure some stuff out. I hope I'll be able to." She shrugged. "I just don't know."

Kathy nodded. They certainly needed to figure a lot of stuff out. She had no idea how far Will's spell on her went. She didn't know what would happen to the followers they had gained. Would there be an uprising?

She also didn't know what her future with Will looked like. She couldn't trust him; that much he had shown. But she knew she needed to talk to him and give him a chance to explain himself. Even if he did explain himself, she wasn't sure that they would still have a future together. Deep down inside she still loved him, but she wasn't sure if that was her true feeling or Will's spell talking.

"Who was at the door earlier?" Kathy had almost forgotten about the interruption of her nap.

Samantha hesitated. "Um…Will."

Kathy's eyes grew. "What did he want?"

"You." A simple answer, yet a loaded one. "He's still here."

Kathy was confused. If he was sitting outside, why didn't she sense his presence? Since their blood fusion, she was very conscious of where he was. She wondered if the spell on her had been broken. That didn't add up. She hadn't actually done anything to break the spell, and given that Samantha was a third party and not up to full strength, she was an unlikely candidate to have broken the spell while Kathy slept.

Samantha saw Kathy's confusion and added, "I put a protection spell on the house that prevents him from entering. It's only twenty-four hours, so it'll wear off tomorrow." That explained the disconnect.

"What does he want?" Kathy realized Samantha had already answered her, but she knew her sister would understand what she was asking.

"He was pissed at first. Pounding on the door, screaming your name," Samantha said, elaborating just the way Kathy knew she would. "It's a good thing the boys weren't home."

"So…why did he stop?"

"We actually had a nice conversation—after a few threats,

of course. I told him you snapped when you tried to take more blood and that you needed some space. That didn't sit well with him, of course, so he's been sitting out there waiting for you ever since."

Kathy sighed. It was things like this and the way he always gave Kathy an out during their journey down the dark side that confused her even more. If she was just a pawn in his mission to take over the underworld, then he would have found a new witch to sit by his side by now. He wouldn't have put up with all of Kathy's baggage.

"I'm going to go talk to him." She moved to stand.

"Do you think you're ready for that?"

Another sigh. Kathy turned to her sister and gave a sad smile. "No, but I'm going to have to do a lot of things I'm not ready for in order to clean up the mess I've made."

Outside, Will sat perched on the stone steps of the front porch. He leaned against the side of the house, his jacket pulled tight.

"Samantha says you've been out here all day," Kathy started, zipping up her own hoodie and taking a seat next to Will. She could feel his pull stronger than ever before, but she was determined to not let it sway her.

"What happened? Or is this part of some new plan?"

Kathy bit her bottom lip. Will still thought that she was going along with their original plan. So much had changed in just twelve hours.

"That's what I want to talk to you about. Look, Will, I know you hexed me when we first started dating," she started. Will opened his mouth to protest, but she put up a hand. "I don't want to argue about it. I can't say I'll ever forgive you for that, but what's done is done. All I know is that I need space to think about things."

"Are you saying you want a divorce? That's going to be complicated with our arrangement. We'd never really be completely separate," Will said.

Kathy didn't want to think about that. It was one thing to marry the wrong person and get divorced. It was another to eliminate the supernatural bonds they had formed as a demonic married couple.

"When it comes to you—us—I don't know what I want. But I do know that we need to stop doing what we're doing. I'm much happier as a white witch than a dark witch," Kathy confessed.

"That's impossible. We're leaders. We have followers. We can't just say, 'Nope, never mind! Sorry for killing half your faction!' Especially if you're no longer evil," he said. "That's putting a giant target on our backs. It's putting a target on your family's backs if they know they can get to you through them."

The turn the conversation took was suddenly too much for her. She could feel the supernatural anger building inside her.

"Make it disappear, Will!" She didn't want to have to dump it all on him, but she knew he would be able to take care of everything better than she could.

He stood and waved his finger at her. "This was all *your* idea! *You're* the one who wanted to steal the Queen's throne. *You're* the one who agreed to the demonic wedding." He shoved his finger in her direction with each accusation. "You can't blame this all on me. I was born evil, but you did a much better job at it."

Kathy could feel Will's dark power rising up inside her. She did her best to control it, shove it back down, but she still ended up slapping him in the face before slamming the front door.

Once she was inside, she could feel his power evaporate, clearing her mind of any heightened thoughts. She was in deeper than she wanted to be. At this moment she hated Will, but she wanted to make things work between them at the same time.

She didn't know what was real, and she just wanted to disappear.

Chapter Twenty

anticore. That's what the witches were up against.

Kathy flipped through the pages of the magic book while Josh wrapped Chris's wounded arm. He had a deep gash above his elbow from where the beast had managed to strike.

"Here it is." Kathy read aloud from the book: "'Manticores are mythical beasts with the body of a lion, bat-like wings, and the tail of a scorpion. They have three sets of razor-sharp teeth and are able to shoot venom from their tails that is capable of paralyzing their victims.'"

"Yeah, yeah, we already know that part!" Chris cut in. "They have really sharp claws, too!" He tried to lift his arm but groaned in pain at the movement.

Josh pulled Chris's arm back down and continued wrapping the bandage on. "Don't be stupid, Chris. Take it easy. Mom will be home soon, and she can give you something to speed the healing process." Samantha had been testing out new mixes of herbal remedies. Whenever she was stressed, she found herself in the kitchen crafting new potions to keep her hands busy. She had spent a lot of time at the stove lately.

"How are we going to kill him?" Josh asked, tightening the wrap on his brother's arm.

Kathy held up a finger and continued reading: "'Manticores' fur is impenetrable, leaving the weakest spots to be their orifices, such as the mouth or eyes.' Well, that's wonderful."

"Is there a spell or potion or anything that we could use?" Josh asked.

"No, that's all that's written."

"Great," Chris grumbled, "so we need to be able to get close enough to his face so that we can stab him in his eye—which might not even be enough to kill him. But we can't get too close, because then he'll bite our heads off."

"I still don't know why he even attacked. They're usually not city dwellers," Josh said.

Kathy was considering the same question herself. She feared that she was the reason her nephews were targeted. Had the factions already figured out that she was no longer interested in being their leader? Was this attack even related to the factions? It had only been a couple of days since she returned home. They had been randomly attacked before. She wondered if she would always be second-guessing every attack that was made on them from now on. How could she be sure that she wasn't the reason her family was being targeted?

"Hello! Aunt Kathy," Chris said, breaking into her thoughts.

"Hmm?"

"I asked if you think we could use a powder potion or something to sedate him before we attack."

Kathy drummed her fingers along the pages of the magic book. "Um…that's a question for your mother. I'm going to step out for a bit. Call me if anything else happens."

She moved toward the door, but Josh stopped her. "Don't go to Will."

Kathy wasn't sure exactly how much they knew about her marriage to Will. She needed to tread carefully. Spinning on her heels, she turned and faced her nephews. Luckily, Josh continued before she needed to come up with an appropriate response.

"Mom said he knows about us. Being witches, that is. Don't ask him for help yet. I know you just broke up with him, but I don't think we're that desperate yet. You don't need to put yourself through that."

Kathy's heart raced. She felt a little relieved that the boys knew, but she didn't know how to tell them that things with Will were more complicated than just their relationship.

She wished that she could tell the boys the truth so they could understand, but she knew Samantha wouldn't allow it. Plus, she was afraid of what they might say or think of her if they knew she had gone to the dark side, no matter how briefly.

"I have no other choice. I need to protect this family," she said. She bit her tongue so the words, "I have to fix my mistake" didn't slip out.

"Mom will know what to do," Chris said.

Kathy shook her head. "Your mom's knowledge of beasts is limited to what's in the book. Will specializes in this sort of magic. I'll be fine." She gave a faint smile. "I promise."

* * *

Kathy knew that Will wouldn't be happy with her asking for help. Especially since she hadn't changed her mind about being with him. She still wasn't sure how she felt and asking him for help was only muddying her mind and confusing her more. But she had to ask. She needed to save her family.

She opted to knock on his door like a visitor instead of popping in like she used to when she lived there. It had only been a few days ago that she'd called this place home.

When he answered, his head tipped back slightly and he scrunched his eyebrows together.

"I take it you're not here to see me," he said, stepping aside and allowing Kathy to walk through the door. "I haven't touched your things, so help yourself."

The first thing she noticed were the bloodstains on the floor in the kitchen. Despite the chair having been returned to its resting place and the rest of the apartment back in normal order, the stains still remained.

Samantha's bloodstains.

Kathy suddenly felt sick to her stomach. She tried to push

away the feeling of nausea. She couldn't help but think that she was a complete monster, but she was here to discuss a different monster.

"Yeah, I scrubbed the floor for hours, but nothing I had worked," Will said, coming up behind Kathy. Too close for her comfort, but she didn't move away. Her eyes remained locked on the stain.

She couldn't help but feel like Will was lying about trying to scrub out the stain. Surely he had more important things to worry about. His world was crumbling, too.

"Are you sure this isn't just a reminder that your wife betrayed you?"

Kathy could sense the anger building in him. The magical connection they shared was as strong as ever, maybe even stronger now that she'd spent a few days away from him. The surge of energy was like a drug, and it took all her self-control not to slip into the temptation of power once again and feed off Will's anger.

He stepped back and leaned with one hand on the counter. "What did you come here for? I assume it's not to rub it in my face that you chose your sister over me."

Kathy spun around to face him. "I should've never been put into the situation to choose between my family and you, Will. I told you, I haven't made a decision about us yet. But I know I'm certainly done being evil."

"I'm not!" Will shouted, jabbing a finger into his chest. "I didn't push the decision on you. If we weren't magical, you wouldn't have to choose, but that's not how it is. You needed to make the choice between good and evil. Your sister or me. You can't have it both ways!"

Kathy gritted her teeth, trying to calm herself before she spoke. His anger and surge of power was infectious, but she needed to remember the reason she had come.

"I'm not here to discuss the state of our marriage," Kathy started, meeting his eyes. "Josh and Chris were attacked by a manticore today."

A smile crept across his face. "Ah, so the factions have already rebelled. Can't say I'm surprised. We didn't really instill loyalty in them. Just simply killed their leaders. They're probably pissed at us."

"I'm sure they are, but it's not my nephews' battle to fight. It's ours."

"No, it's yours."

"I'm not asking you to kill the manticore. I'm asking you how I can kill him." She had her hands on her hips. Home was at the forefront of her mind in case she needed to flash out at any moment.

Will shrugged. "For whatever reason, I'm having trouble recalling the Achilles heel of manticores."

"Will, please. If you valued any of our time together, you'll tell me what you know."

"Why's that?" he asked. "Because we had such a happy marriage? I spent most of it keeping you from killing everything in your path! The dark side taunts you more than it does me."

The Full Moon

"Screw you!"

He smiled and shrugged. "That was never our problem."

Kathy rolled her eyes. "Just tell me what you know about the manticore. I know you've dealt with them before."

"I try not to live in the past. I'm too busy planning for the future," Will said. "Now, I think my memory might work better if you promise to return to my side as queen of the underworld. You know you'd be perfect."

"Don't push me, Will! I told you I needed time to think. This is not helping."

"You only have yourself to blame for that," Will fired back. "If you had stuck by my side, your nephews would be safe. They're still young, we could've turned them."

"At the expense of my sister! I don't think so," Kathy said. "I guess you're more bitter about being dumped than I thought you were."

Will grabbed her arm before she had a chance to disappear. He squeezed her wrist tightly.

"Be careful who you piss off, sweetheart." They held each other's gaze for a moment longer before he finally let go, and she disappeared in a flash of red light.

* * *

"That was really stupid of you to go to Will's," Samantha berated as they stood on the street where the boys had been attacked by the manticore.

The sun had set and the moon shone bright in the sky. The sisters each had a flashlight and were scoping out the area.

"I didn't think he'd still be so pissed," Kathy retorted.

"It's been three days, Kathy. Three days! You know how long it took me to stop being angry at Steven when he left," Samantha said.

Kathy had never thought of it that way. There were moments she was unsure if Samantha would ever stop hating her ex-husband.

"Well, he was no help anyway. So no harm done."

Samantha sighed and muttered, "Physically, at least."

Kathy stopped looking around in the nooks and crannies of the street that were out of reach of the streetlights and looked right at her sister. "What's that supposed to mean?"

"All I'm saying is that everything is still new. You haven't had a chance to really live without Will to see if you even can live without him," Samantha said. "It takes time. You can't just run to him whenever we have a magical emergency and expect to be able to sort out your feelings. It doesn't work like that. Besides, we've handled plenty of magical emergencies ourselves before he came along."

Kathy took a deep breath but kept quiet. Samantha was right, but she didn't want to admit it. Nor did she want to admit to herself that a part of her ran to Will because she missed him. She wasn't sure if that was pure longing or if that was the side effect of the hex he had placed on her. Or worse, the pull of their blood bond. That was a connection that she might not ever be able to sever.

The Full Moon

Both sisters snapped to attention when they heard the sound of a snarl coming from the parking lot nearby.

"I think we found our manticore," Samantha said before taking off in a run. Kathy wasn't far behind.

They followed the sound to a courtyard nestled between two buildings on the campus of Gannon University. Samantha pulled out a pouch from her pocket. She had found a sedative she could make into a powder in the book. She just wasn't sure if it was strong enough for the size of the manticore.

Kathy produced the same pouch from her pocket. They each had one in case they got separated. The sisters each pulled out a small blade that could be concealed in their jackets. The blades would be useless if he decided to charge them, but if the sedative worked, it'd be perfect for stabbing through his eye to his brain.

The manticore hadn't yet noticed the witches. He was currently devouring a squirrel that had been too slow to get away from the beast's attack.

Go to the other side and we'll get him from both sides with the powder, Samantha projected into Kathy's mind telepathically.

Kathy nodded and in a flash she was on the other side of the courtyard. The beast noticed the two flashes of light and became aware that he was the target. He let out a loud roar and moved in on Kathy.

Samantha shouted from the other side, but he paid her no mind. He had his sight set on Kathy and wasn't letting up.

Kathy tried to freeze him, but it seemed that not only was his skin impenetrable, but he was also immune to her powers, too.

She warily backed up until she nearly tripped over a bush lining the walkway. Still, the manticore continued to creep closer.

"The pouch!" Samantha shouted. She was moving to join her sister but trying not to make any swift movements to tip off the beast. She didn't know how quickly he could move, but she was sure it was faster than she was.

Kathy opened the pouch and threw it at the manticore, but the wind blew in the opposite direction and it floated away from him. She glanced over her shoulder and saw that beyond the bush lay a small strip of grass beside the brick wall of the neighboring building.

Mentally preparing to jump over the bush and make a run for it, she saw the manticore lift up his back end, and the scorpion tail curled around, ready to strike.

In an instant, Will was in front of her, blocking the attack with a shield.

"Use your power!" he shouted at her. He peeked over the shield to measure the manticore's next move.

Kathy was about to protest that he wouldn't freeze, but she understood what Will meant.

In a flash, she was beside Samantha, who grabbed her hand tightly. Together, they watched Will fend off the beast.

"We have to do something!" Kathy shouted.

"There's nothing we can do! If anyone can kill this thing, it's Will," Samantha said. She knew his skill as a Dark Knight was perfect for this situation.

The manticore lunged at Will, but he fended off the attack

with the shield. He managed to flip the manticore onto his back, but the beast recovered and got back on his feet.

The manticore let out another roar, and Will plunged the sword forward, pushing into the beast's mouth and slicing up, tearing his way through from the inside.

Staggering, the manticore eventually collapsed on the ground dead.

Chapter Twenty-One

Will stood, catching his breath. He looked at Kathy. Silently, they exchanged a thousand words.

Kathy stepped closer and Samantha called her name in warning.

"It's okay, Sam," Kathy said, motioning for her to stay where she was. Kathy kept her eyes locked with Will's as she approached him. "I thought you said you weren't going to help us."

"I'm helping you, not them." His weapons disappeared, and he took Kathy's hands in his. "I still love you. I know we can make this work. But I need you alive for that." He looked down, closed his eyes, and breathed deeply. When he met her eyes again, he said, "I'll help you eliminate the factions that are rebelling."

Samantha, who was still in earshot, was skeptical. "Why? Do you honestly think she's going back to you after you hexed her?"

"Sam!" Kathy warned, but Will was already snarling at her. "Stay out of this!"

"I don't want you anywhere near me or my kids." Samantha stepped closer and pulled her sister away from Will. "Do you hear me? My house is off-limits for you. If I see you so much as step foot on the sidewalk, I will kill you!"

* * *

"I'm sorry about what Samantha said yesterday," Kathy said the next day after work. Will had stopped by the day care after the kids had gone home.

"She doesn't trust me, I get it. As long as you trust me." His eyes focused on Kathy. "Do you?"

She hesitated. She didn't know the answer to that question. It was part of the reason she needed space from Will. Instead, she changed the subject. "So you said you had something for me?"

His face softened and his attention turned to the paper in his hand. "I've made a list of all the factions that are most likely to turn against us. It's not a complete list—we were busy in that short time—but it's a good start."

Kathy took the paper and skimmed it over. She remembered most of them and their weaknesses, but some sounded completely new. She wondered how strong the spell on her had been to wipe some moments from her memory completely.

"Okay…should we go on the offensive and attack them before they attack us?"

"Sweetie, I don't think that's a very good idea," Will said. Kathy felt her heart flutter a bit when he called her "sweetie." She hated herself a little for the sudden rush of emotion. "Not all of them are attacking. Besides, you're their target, not necessarily me."

She raised an eyebrow. "What are you saying?"

"They want you dead, not me," Will said. "It's not uncommon for evil beings to kill other evil beings with little reason, especially the ones we targeted. But for a good witch to turn to the dark side only to eliminate more evil beings…seems fishy. Especially now that you're back with your sister."

"So once again you're pinning this on me."

He reached for her hands, but she pulled away. "I'm saying I think it's foolish for me to get involved when I don't have to. When you need help, call me."

Kathy rolled her eyes. He wanted her to think that he was there for her and that she was safe, but in the end he was still putting her in the crosshairs and trying to cover his tracks as well as he could. "Save it. I can handle myself." She disappeared in a flash before Will could respond.

* * *

"A snake man?" Kathy asked, skeptical. She was sitting next to her sister at the kitchen table, flipping through the magic book.

Samantha shrugged. "I guess. I mean, he had arms, but everything else was like a snake. He could stand upright, but he had the creepy forked tongue and…" She shivered.

She had been attacked in the parking garage earlier on her way to her car. She had managed to evade attacks from the beast between the cars, but she was otherwise defenseless. Her hand-to-hand combat skills were almost useless against the swift moves of the creature. She was lucky the beast had slithered off when more people had entered the garage.

"Is this him?" Kathy asked. She turned the book over to her sister.

Samantha nodded. "Similar, yeah."

"He's an Anguis…'a species of half-human, half-serpent creatures that are brilliant and cunning. They disguise themselves as humans to spy on their prey before attacking,'" Kathy read from the book.

"But this doesn't make sense," Samantha added, skipping down further in the entry. "It says their natural habitat is warm, forested areas. We were in the city. It's not their usual hangout. Not to mention that it's almost October, so it's been getting colder."

"One of the factions must be sending these creatures," Kathy said. "I mean, we've dealt with mythical beasts before, but not this close together and in such foreign environments for them. Usually they're hunting someone else when we step in. These guys are targeting us…me."

Samantha shook her head. "No, you weren't even there. It was after me. This can't be related to the factions."

"Unless they wanted to use you as bait to get to me."

"Let's just look for a way to kill these things," Samantha said, returning to the book. "Okay…well, it says here that they hunt alone, but they nest with a tribe, so we don't want to uncover their tribe. We'll be too outnumbered. We need to lure him out."

Kathy knew what her sister was thinking. "No, Sam, you can't voluntarily use yourself as bait! What if he decides he does need a friend to help him hunt?"

Samantha rolled her eyes. "I'll be fine. Think about snakes, they never bring a friend to help finish the job."

"Snakes aren't sent to kill someone by someone else!"

"Keep your voice down," Samantha warned. "The boys are upstairs. I don't want them to know about the attack."

"Well what am I supposed to tell them if I bring you home dead? If there's even a body to bring back!" Kathy reached for her sister's hand. "I don't want you to die because of me." She already felt guilty enough that her selfishness and recklessness got her family into these situations.

Samantha took a deep breath. "Kathy, I told you, I don't think this is related to the factions."

Kathy shook her head. "I think you're wrong."

"Whatever the reason for the attack is, we need to kill him regardless," Samantha said, changing the subject to prevent further bickering. "Before he hurts anyone else."

Kathy glanced at the book. "The best defense is beheading. Don't ask me how we're going to get close enough to chop his head off without him moving beforehand."

"What's wrong with freezing him?" Samantha asked.

"If you're the bait, I won't be there to freeze him."

"I have an idea." Samantha stood and went to the kitchen.

Kathy followed her. "What are you doing?"

"I think I have a potion that will slow people down." She riffled through the cupboards. "Remember, we used it on that evil witch with the time specialty?" She found her battered potions book that had accumulated scraps of papers with experimental potion recipes through the years.

Kathy remembered that incident well. It had been back when Samantha was in college. She had sensed that the kid in her psych class was a witch, but it wasn't until he seemed to be moving in the blink of an eye that she guessed he shared the time specialty with Kathy. However, instead of his specialty developing into the ability to stop time, he was able to speed through time.

After some people in her dorm building complained about things going missing, Samantha assumed it was the speed witch and crafted a potion to slow him down and tell him to knock it off. Kathy had shown up for backup. The next semester he'd transferred to another school.

"Got it!" Samantha raised the paper in the air triumphantly.

"How are you going to get him to ingest it?"

Samantha wiggled her nose, thinking. "I could make it into a powder."

"And hope the wind doesn't blow it away like it did with the manticore."

"What about the sprinkler system?"

"How are we going to get it in the sprinklers and clear it out before it slows anyone else down?" Kathy asked.

"I need ideas, Kathy!"

"Okay…well, don't snakes absorb water through their skin? Maybe if you just got some on his skin, it would work? Bring a squirt bottle!"

Samantha laughed. "That might actually work."

* * *

Kathy stood in the empty office directly across the street from the parking garage, watching her sister taunt the stealthy creature with her vulnerability. She looked for any sign of movement around the building but knew that the Anguis was a natural at concealing itself. The darkening night wasn't helping either.

Samantha walked through the empty parking space. More than a few times she wandered behind a pillar and out of view from across the street. Kathy didn't like that.

"C'mon, Sammy, get out from behind there," Kathy muttered to herself.

Briefly, she saw Samantha step out from behind the pillar. A green scaly tail gripped Samantha's throat tightly and in an instant she was pulled back out of sight.

Kathy was by her sister's side in a flash. The beast had his mouth open, jagged fangs bared, ready to consume Samantha whole.

"No!" Kathy shouted, throwing her hands up and freezing the Anguis in place. She pulled out her machete and in one swift move sliced off the beast's head. He unfroze and collapsed on the cement, dead, his death grip still tight around Samantha's neck.

Samantha's face began turning blue as she grasped for the blade at her belt.

Kathy fell to her knees and sliced up as much of the snake's tail as she dared. Finally, after she split the snake's tail into three pieces, Samantha was free.

She sat up, covered in blood and gasping for air. Once she had caught her breath, she said, "I didn't even see him! When he attacked earlier, he made himself be seen. This was different."

Kathy narrowed her eyes. "He must've known you wouldn't come back without backup. I'm telling you, Samantha, some-one's trying to get to me!"

Samantha sighed, still clutching at her chest. "You're probably right. We need to figure out which of the factions hate you more." Kathy shot her a look. "But first I need to take a shower."

* * *

Kathy's knuckles rapped on Will's apartment door. She needed to talk to him. If anyone was going to figure out who could be targeting her and her family, it would be him. Or at least he would have a better idea of where to look. He'd been the one with a clear head through the whole ordeal. As she waited for him to answer the door, the fear that he was still in on every-thing they had started as a couple crept into her mind.

He finally answered, and the faint smell of smoke wafted through the open door.

"Did you have candles going?" she asked.

He waved his hand in the air. "Yeah, a few. Sorry. Come in." He stepped aside.

Will wasn't one to burn candles unless he was performing a ritual. Kathy didn't like that. If she was no longer what he was after, what was? Was he still determined to take over as leader? It didn't add up given that he had agreed to help Kathy fight off the factions. But besides the manticore, he never really got his hands dirty. Maybe it was all for show? Was he still trying to trick her?

She pushed the doubt from her mind and pressed on with the reason she'd come.

"Samantha was attacked by an Anguis," Kathy said once the door was shut. "Only a week after the boys were attacked by a manticore."

"It's the factions. They're pissed." Will pulled a beer out of the refrigerator and popped the top off with a bottle opener. "I told you they'd be using any methods possible to get to you." He tossed the cap in the trash and took a sip.

Kathy shook her head. "But they never seemed very interested in me. They seem to only be targeting Samantha and the boys. And besides, we gained followers like witch covens and demons, not beasts. These attacks were ordered by someone."

Will took another sip. "You're acting like this is all news. Kathy, this is what I've been saying since you left."

"But I haven't been attacked by any of the factions yet! I think this might be the Queen or someone else entirely. Someone who wants to sweep in and pick up where we left off," Kathy said.

"That makes me and my family their biggest threat. You too."

"Again, this is not news. I'm not at all surprised that someone is trying to replace us."

"I don't like it that my family is targeted when I don't know the reason," Kathy said. "I need your help. These attacks are scaring me. I can't promise that I'll come back to you, but if you help me save them, I won't forget it."

He leaned against the counter and looked at the floor. "Kathy," he started, but she rested her hand on his and stopped him cold.

"Please," she prodded. She didn't know if the hex still had a hold on her or if this was her own free will, but she couldn't help wanting to fold into him like she used to, back when they were two pieces of the same puzzle.

Will squeezed Kathy's hand and looked her in the eyes. "I'll take care of it."

Chapter Twenty-Two

I'm just going out with a few friends," Kathy lied. She stood in front of the mirror in the bathroom and checked herself out before slipping on her heels and fixing the clasp on each.

"Trisha?" Samantha was just walking in, pulling her hair out of her bun.

"Uh…no, actually it's Linda from work," Kathy said. Samantha knew Trisha, and she didn't want to get caught up in her own lies.

"Going someplace fancy?"

"Dancing downtown," Kathy responded. This wasn't a lie. "I'm probably going to be late, so go ahead and lock the door. I have my key."

Samantha didn't look convinced, but she didn't protest anymore. "Okay. Well, have fun. You look great."

"Thanks." Kathy smoothed out her dress. "Have a nice night with the boys." In a bright red flash, she was gone.

* * *

It was cold outside. Kathy cursed herself for not bringing a jacket. She stood outside the club waiting.

Finally, he showed up. Dressed in a baby-blue shirt and black slacks, he looked handsome. Kathy's heart beat a little faster. There was no way this was the effect of a spell.

"You look beautiful," Will said, leaning down to give her a kiss. She turned her head at the last minute, and he planted it on her cheek. She didn't want to give him the wrong impression about what this night meant.

"You look great, too," she said, letting him take her hand.

"How long have you been out here waiting? You're shivering! We should get inside." He opened the door, and they slowly migrated through the sea of people writhing on the dance floor.

It was still early, so most people seemed to be just enjoying themselves after a stressful workweek. A couple of people were very clearly already drunk.

Kathy clung to Will's side as he led them through the crowd to the bar. "You want something to drink?"

She nodded and he ordered before she could tell him what she wanted. After he paid, he handed her the drink he'd ordered: tequila sunrise.

Will sipped his beer and took her hand, leading her to a

quiet corner.

"How'd you know this is what I wanted?" Kathy asked, sipping her drink happily. She needed to shout a bit over the pounding music and the various drunken outbursts. She missed the nights she would spend in the clubs. Feeling the music in her chest, having fun with friends, and completely letting go of the world for a few hours. But she knew it couldn't last forever.

Will leaned in close, and she could feel his breath on her ear. "Our first date. You said you have a minor addiction to these."

She smiled. She'd made the comment in passing. They hadn't been in a situation since where she could order a drink to remind him. She wondered if he knew her better than she thought.

He leaned down to her again. "I'm a little surprised you agreed to go out tonight. And shocked that you chose this place."

A few days after Will said he would help her with the factions, he had asked her out on a date to test the waters of their marriage. He knew that he had to regain her trust, but he said he was willing to work on it.

"Our whole..." Kathy paused, looking for the word, "relationship has been so serious. I thought we both deserved a night off to have some fun."

Will smiled and the DJ started another song.

"Oh, I love this song!" Kathy shouted. She grabbed Will's hand, pulling him away from the safety of the wall. "Dance with me!"

* * *

They left the club just as the college kids started rolling in. They walked down the street, turning the corner so no one would see Kathy using her magic to take them home.

Kathy leaned against the building and pulled Will against her, kissing him.

"You were right. Tonight was a lot of fun," he said.

"Really?" She ran her hands up and down his arms, wishing he'd lean in closer to block the wind. And to be closer to him. She finally let herself admit that. "You seemed a little spooked when I first mentioned it."

Will laughed. "I'll admit, it's not usually my thing. But it was a good night. Because of you."

Kathy rolled her eyes and leaned in to kiss him again, but she stopped when she saw a black woman approaching them. Dressed like any of the other girls at the club, the woman had her eyes locked on Will. She ran her tongue across her teeth just before lunging at him and tackling him to the ground. She hissed and brought her mouth to his neck.

Letting out a shriek of surprise, Kathy tried to pull the woman off but her tight skirt and heels prevented her from being able to maneuver. Even trying to deliver a kick resulted in only a gentle jab to the woman's side.

Will produced a sword and tossed it up to Kathy. She didn't want to attack because she didn't know if the woman was human or not.

He pushed on the woman's chest, trying to fend off the attack, and managed to shout, "Vampire!" and Kathy swung the sword, slicing the woman's head off and splattering her and Will with blood.

Kathy dropped the weapon and tried to catch her breath. The sword was gone before it hit the ground. Will clutched his neck and sat up slowly.

"Will! Are you okay?" Kathy knelt next to him and pulled his hand away to examine his wound. There were obvious teeth marks, but the skin wasn't broken.

"Yeah. We should probably get out of here," he suggested. She placed her hand on his shoulder and transported them to his apartment.

Will looked around. "I thought you'd take me to your place." He leaned on the wall to help himself up.

Kathy ran a paper towel under the faucet. "Can't. I didn't tell Samantha I was going out with you. I said it was a friend from work." She pulled Will's hand away and pressed the sopping paper towel to his neck. Beads of water dribbled down and under his shirt, soaking into the cotton.

"You were able to lie to a telepath?" He gave up fighting her and let her nurse his wounds. They didn't need much tending, but he wasn't going to stop her.

Kathy shrugged. "She seemed to buy it. Hold still."

He shivered as the cold water ran farther down his chest. "Babe, it's fine."

She pulled the paper towel away and looked at him. "So are we back on 'babe' level, then?"

Will's mouth hung open. "Uh, I…that's up to you."

The Full Moon

Kathy pinched the bridge of her nose. She didn't want to have this conversation right now. The whole night was supposed to be fun and not serious. She didn't want them to be one of those couples that always seemed to have something going on between them.

"So that girl was a vampire?"

"No. Technically a Dhampir." He seemed happy to change the subject, too.

"She sure seemed like a vampire to me," Kathy said. She rang the paper towel out over the sink and tossed it into the trash.

"Dhampirs are half-human and half-vampire. They have some similarities with vampires—razor-sharp teeth, a thirst for blood—but most of them have compassion, which vampires lack. They feel bad when they kill."

"So why was she adamant that she feed on you?"

Will shrugged. "I'm not a vampire, but I'm guessing it's like an addict. The blood is like a drug for them, and they don't think clearly when they're on a high."

"So I killed a human?"

"You killed a monster."

She didn't seem convinced. Since she had started killing leaders of factions, she questioned every kill she made—even if it was for the greater good.

Will took a hesitant step toward her and slowly pulled her into an embrace, watching for any sign that she wasn't interested. Instead, she leaned into him, resting her head against his damp chest.

"Was she a part of a faction?" Kathy asked, speaking into Will's shirt.

Will sighed. "Probably. Dhampirs are like vampires in that they're usually part of a nest. Or family. That really depends on the individual."

"So we have a whole nest to go after." She couldn't bring herself to say *family*. That word was still too fragile for her. At least in front of Will. After tonight, she wasn't sure who she considered family. Both Samantha and Will claimed she was a part of theirs, but they were pulling her in two different directions.

"No. I told you I'd take care of it," Will said. "I'd never let anything hurt you."

The night only confused her more. She'd only agreed to this date so she could say that she'd given him a second chance, but she had genuinely had a good time. She missed him. A few hours earlier she had been sure that she didn't want to be with him, but he was still taking care of her even after she called him out on his betrayal. It all made her sound like the one who was messed up. She needed to set the record straight and declare what she knew to be true.

She looked up at him. "I love you. I don't know what that means or where we stand, but I have to be honest. With myself and you."

He smiled and opened his mouth to respond, but she cut him off.

"That doesn't change anything, though." She watched his face drop. "I'm still not sure if I can trust you. Not like I should be able to, at least. All I know is that I'm willing to work on it. Take it slow. Like we should have from the beginning."

Will nodded. "I'm sorry, Kathy. I'm not sure if I ever told you that, but I am. I never should've manipulated you that way."

This was the first time he had ever completely apologized and taken responsibility for his actions. She couldn't help but feel like a coward. If Will could own up to his mistakes, why couldn't she? Since she'd left him, she had been trying to place the blame on him and make him out to be the bad guy.

Stretching on her toes, she leaned up and kissed him. Her hands snaked through his hair, and he worked at her dress.

For the first time in months, she knew exactly what she wanted.

* * *

Kathy jolted awake as the front door came crashing in. Will woke up too and flung his legs over the bed to investigate.

"Kathy!" It was Samantha.

"Will, don't," Kathy said before he could open the door. She pulled on his shirt from the night before and scurried to the door. "Let me talk to her." She swung open the door and was immediately face-to-face with her sister.

"Sammy, let me explain!"

Samantha grabbed Kathy's wrist and pulled her closer.

"Let her go!" Will demanded, stepping out of the bedroom. He tried to make it to the door before Samantha, but she spun around and got in his face.

"I don't know what manipulative bullshit you're trying to pull with her, but I think Kathy's been through enough."

"Samantha, stop! It's not Will's fault! *I* brought us back here. We were downtown, and then we were attacked by one of the factions. Will was hurt and we needed to get out of there before anyone saw us!"

"And the fastest way to heal him was to jump into bed with him?" Samantha asked. She still had a firm grip on Kathy's wrist.

"I—" Kathy stopped herself from declaring her love. She knew that wasn't the best way to change Samantha's opinion of Will. "You don't always have to save me!"

"How can I be sure that you're not under the influence of your demonic ex-husband?"

"He's not my—" Kathy stopped herself again. She didn't know what Will was to her anymore. She was still trying to keep it simple with him, but everything was so complicated.

Will grabbed Kathy's other hand. "You can't control her! Kathy, what do you want to do?"

"Both of you, stop!" Kathy shouted, but they ignored her. Will and Samantha sized each other up. She felt like an insignificant object in the midst of the Samantha and Will war. Sure, their dislike for each other started with her, but were either of them really fighting for her anymore? Neither of them actually listened to what she wanted. Not that Kathy even knew what she wanted.

"Let go of her. She's not your puppet," Samantha said. "I'm her big sister. It's my job to save her."

Will clenched his jaw, but his eyes snapped to Kathy when she spoke.

"Will, let me go. Arguing is not going to help your case at all," Kathy said.

He sighed and after one last squeeze released her arm.

* * *

"This is stupid," Kathy said as Samantha tightened the ropes that bound her to a dining room chair Samantha had lugged up to her bedroom. "I'm fine. Everything I did tonight was completely voluntary."

Samantha pointed her finger in Kathy's face. "That's the problem. You just need a chance to dry out, so to speak, from the magic he put on you."

"He didn't put any magic on me!" Kathy protested. She tested the strength of the knots. There was no way she was getting out on her own. Creating sufficient restraints was one of Samantha's unique talents. "This is crazy, Samantha. How do I know you're not the one who's lost it?"

Samantha ignored her and placed an amulet around Kathy's neck. "This will prevent you from using your powers. Can't have you teleporting out of here."

"Josh! Chris! Your mother's gone crazy!" Kathy shouted. Her sister was scaring her. Hadn't Kathy done the same thing to her when she was at rock bottom? Was this payback? Knowing it was no use, she pulled at the restraints anyway, trying to free herself.

The ropes dug into her arms.

"Kathy, stop. I've soundproofed the room." Samantha did look upset. Tears were welling up in her eyes. Her voice broke when she said, "This is for your own good."

Chapter Twenty-Three

Kathy remained alone for the rest of the night. She was unable to break free from the binds, and the amulet hanging around her neck blocked her magic. She was stuck.

Sleep was difficult to manage in the hard chair, leaving her to replay her whole turbulent relationship with Will. She had been through this a hundred times, but now that she was finally alone with her thoughts without the distraction of her sister, husband, or a demonic attack, she could finally think for herself.

She started with the basics: she and Will certainly had chemistry. That much was obvious. Before Will even had a chance to cast any sort of spell or hex on her, she had found herself attracted to him. But the next time she saw him, he had delivered the earring that she lost—which, in effect, placed the infatuation hex on her—and that's where it got fuzzy.

As a result of the hex, their courtship and subsequent marriage sped up. But she wondered if she would have married him eventually if she hadn't been hexed. That was the ultimate question. If she would have, there was a chance she and Will had a future together. There was no way to tell.

The fact that she turned against her sister and nephews and joined Will's side in a quest to organize the demonic underworld, that was what she was left with. She didn't want to believe she had voluntarily gone to the dark side, but the only spell Will had placed on her—that she knew of—was the infatuation spell. That wouldn't make her turn evil. It only enhanced her desire for him.

No. Deep down Kathy knew that she became the big, bad witch all on her own. She gave in to the temptation of the dark side. It may have been a side effect of the infatuation spell, but the choice had ultimately been hers. She'd let her inhibitions go as a result of the infatuation spell. Maybe the draw of the dark side had been too enticing for her to pass up when she was already under the influence of lust?

She shook her head. Will was not to blame for that. Sure, he did lie to her and placed a spell on her without her knowing, but she had been the one to suggest they take the Queen's throne. She had started their descent into the darkness. Will had been the hesitant one. He only wanted Kathy as his wife.

But all that didn't change anything about her feelings for Will. Even after she rejoined her sister, Will was still on her mind. Surely that wasn't the work of his little infatuation spell, was it? She didn't even know if the spell had officially been broken, or if she was just aware of it now. She wasn't sure how strong that spell had been, and she feared that the blood bond they now shared would haunt her forever. Will was satisfied with having Kathy as his wife, but once she'd suggested they take over the demonic world, he took full advantage.

Kathy's thoughts were interrupted when Samantha entered the room. She was dressed in a pair of sweatpants and an old hoodie. She'd pulled her hair back in a ponytail.

"Are you going to let me go?" Kathy asked.

"Not yet. I told the boys I was going for a run," Samantha said. "Told them you had to work early."

That stung Kathy. Samantha believed that Kathy had betrayed her again, and yet she was still lying to the boys to cover it up so they would keep their faith in their aunt. Despite all the doubt running through Samantha's mind, she was still determined not to tarnish the boys' image of Kathy.

"So what do you expect to happen?"

"I want to get inside your mind," Samantha responded. "Unfortunately, the amulet I put on you prevents me from probing through your head like I did when you had me tied up at Will's apartment. So we'll have to do this the old-fashioned way."

"So why can't you untie me if you just want to talk? Why do you have to look at me like I'm some kind of criminal?"

"Because you've shown that you can't make decisions on your own!" Samantha was angry now. "Kathy, that man is poison! He's already proved that he can't be trusted, and yet you think you still have a future with him. Look at what he's already done to you. To your family!"

"That doesn't justify you tying me up! Right now, you're no better than him!" Kathy bit her bottom lip, wishing she hadn't said that.

Samantha closed her eyes and looked away. When she finally looked back at her sister, she said, "What other choice do I have? You lied to me last night."

"Why did you let me go, then?" Kathy knew it was nearly impossible to lie to Samantha. Either she'd have to be distracted or too tired to see through the thin veil of a lie.

Samantha crossed her arms but didn't respond.

"What, were you testing me?"

"I thought I could trust you. I wanted to trust you."

"So you thought you could gain my trust by barging into Will's place like a maniac?" Kathy's voice was even and calm. She could see a difference in her attitude. Her previous fights with Samantha over Will had seemed to quickly escalate and get out of hand. She wondered if the blood bond or the spell he had placed on her was responsible. Either way, the amulet she wore seemed to protect her from the magic. At least when she wasn't in his presence.

Samantha sighed. "Okay, maybe that was a little extreme." Kathy knew Samantha well enough to know that it pained her to admit defeat. "But you never came home. What was I supposed to think? Nobody knew anything about going out, so that only left one other person."

Kathy took a deep breath. She needed to approach this

delicately. She needed to make Samantha understand what she had been feeling, even if Kathy wasn't sure herself. Too bad Samantha wasn't an empath.

"I'm not positive that the spell he placed on me is completely lifted yet. And now that our blood is bound together, that connection might never go away. But right now, under the protections you put on me and the amulet, I still feel the same about him as I've always felt." She shrugged—the extent of her movement in the restraints. "That emotion might be heightened when I'm around him, but even when I'm not..." Her voice trailed off.

Samantha studied her sister for a moment and then looked at the digital clock on the nightstand. "I have to get downstairs before the boys notice I'm gone too long." She stepped past Kathy and shut the door behind her.

* * *

The soundproofing Samantha put on the room prevented Kathy from hearing the boys getting ready for school downstairs. By now, she figured everyone had already left. She was pissed at being tied up so long. After being held hostage most of the night, she was starving.

Samantha's screams pierced Kathy's thoughts. She muttered spells to herself to try to break free of the binds, but the amulet around her neck prevented any of them from taking shape.

Before Kathy had any success with the ropes, Samantha burst through the door, breathless.

"What is it?" Kathy asked.

Samantha shut the door and fumbled with the rope around Kathy's left wrist. "Hellhounds."

Kathy gulped. She hadn't known they were real, but from the sound of the snarling coming from the opposite side of the door, she didn't want to meet them.

"Call Will," Kathy said.

"No." Samantha kept her eyes on the ropes. "Damn it, why did I tie these so tight?"

"Sam, you can't rely on the boys to handle this. Will knows what to do. Call him," Kathy pleaded. "Send a text from my phone if you want."

"Your phone's at Will's," Samantha said.

The door burst open and the hound—wiry black hair and foaming at the mouth as he bared his teeth—lunged at Samantha, but Will appeared in front of her, blocking the beast with a large shield. He passed a sword to Samantha and bellowed, "Aim for the throat!"

In one swift swing, Samantha sliced open the beast's throat and it collapsed on the floor. His black blood puddled on the hardwood.

Together, Samantha and Will fought off the hounds, but they continued coming, more and more appearing in the doorway.

"They're not going to stop!" Will shouted, pushing one of the beasts off him with his shield. "There's an endless number of them."

"So what are we supposed to do?" Samantha lopped off the

head of another one, and his blood splattered along the wall. The black blood from the hounds was all over everything. This was going to be a hard mess to hide from the boys. Luckily, the bodies of the hounds disintegrated shortly after they died.

"We need Kathy to freeze them." He swung his sword and delivered another deadly blow. "That'll give us some time to use the—" A hound tackled him to the floor and bit at his neck.

Samantha yanked the amulet from Kathy's neck, breaking the chain that held it. She swung the sword and sliced the neck of the hound attacking Will. When she turned around, Kathy had already teleported out of the ropes and frozen the rest of the lot.

"Will!" Kathy shrieked, falling to her husband's side. "Will, wake up!" Tears welled up in her eyes. He wasn't moving and had a mix of red and black blood splattered across him. It was much worse than the Dhampir attack from the night before.

"Kathy, we need to get rid of these hounds before they unfreeze!" Samantha said but knew it was no use. Kathy was too distraught over Will.

She thought for a moment. She only had a minute or two to think of a spell to banish the hounds. Kathy was usually the one to craft the spells.

Back to the place from which you were sent,
I sentence you to banishment!

The floor opened up and swallowed the remaining beasts, leaving the only sound in the room Kathy's sobs. She was holding

Will's hand and wiping the blood away from his face.

"Will, sweetie, wake up," she muttered, kissing his hand and smearing his and the hellhounds' blood on her lips.

"Kathy, that was a nasty bite," Samantha said, gently placing her hand on her sister's shoulder. "I don't—"

"No! I don't care if you don't like him. He just saved our lives!" Kathy shouted, cutting Samantha off. "The least we can do is try to save his!"

"We don't have any healing spells or potions powerful enough for this," Samantha said. "Besides, I'm not even sure our white magic will work on him."

"Then we have to find someone who can heal him!"

"At what cost? There are evil leaders who have a grudge against you already. I don't think it's smart for us to give them another reason to hate you," Samantha protested.

"Just go look in the book," Kathy said. "I'm not leaving him."

* * *

"I found someone who might be able to heal him." Samantha held the magic book in her hands and returned to the bedroom. She glanced down at Will. His skin was turning gray, and she wasn't sure if he was already dead. The puddle of his blood had grown significantly bigger.

"Hurry, his pulse is so weak," Kathy said.

"There's an enchantress we can call. She specializes in demonic healing."

"Is there a spell to summon her, or do we have to write one?"

"There's a spell, but, Kathy—this is dangerous. We're willingly calling evil into our home," Samantha said.

"We have to save him! I owe it to him." Kathy ran her bloody thumb across Will's lifeless cheek. "Where's the spell?"

"We just need a few things," Samantha said. Kathy sighed. "I'll hurry," she added.

She ran to her bedroom and snatched up three black candles and a box of matches. They needed an altar rug, but she figured she could substitute an old towel in its place.

When Samantha returned, Kathy stood and watched her light the candles and place them on the floor in the shape of a triangle.

> *I call upon my inner power,*
> *to send my plea within this hour.*
> *Before Will succumbs to the fall,*
> *the power of Valerie we will call.*

The air began to stir inside the room and rapidly picked up pace. Objects in the room—pillows, lamps, knickknacks along the windowsill—crashed into the walls. The girls' hair whipped in their faces. In an instant, the wind stopped and a woman stood in the center of the candles, their flames still burning brightly despite the wind.

"Good morning, ladies," the enchantress said with a smile. "My name's Valerie. To what do I owe this pleasure?"

Kathy pointed to Will. She couldn't bring herself to look at him again. If the enchantress couldn't save him, she didn't want to remember him like this.

"Please heal my husband."

Valerie flashed another smile. "Aw, sweetie. I see girls like you all the time. Desperate for any help they can get, so they call me as a last resort."

"Cut the bullshit," Kathy spat. "We've already wasted enough time. Can you fix him or not?"

"I only deal in the dark arts."

"That's exactly what he is!" Kathy shouted. She could feel the bond she shared with Will weakening with every passing second.

"He's a Dark Knight," Samantha added quietly.

Valerie looked perplexed, but then her eyebrows arched as she let out an elongated, "Oh!" She smiled and continued, "So you're the witch everyone's talking about! The one who joined us, promised to lead us, and then betrayed us." Her smile faded. "Tell me, why should I help you? What do you have to offer me?"

"I…" Kathy's voice was small. She hadn't thought this through. She should have known that any demonic creature wouldn't do a favor for free.

"I suppose I could help you out." The enchantress held up a single painted finger. "On one condition. You need to promise to rejoin your husband and lead us out of the chaos the underworld has slipped into since the last ruler died."

"That's ridiculous!" Samantha shouted.

Valerie kept her eyes locked on Kathy. "What do you say,

sweetie? Do we have a deal?"

Kathy squinted. "Why do you want me to lead? Wouldn't it make more sense for you or someone with more loyalty to lead?"

"I don't have that kind of power, dear."

"Neither do I!"

"But you have the potential to," Valerie shot back. "Among all things magical, witches have the most potential for power. It's a shame not many of them realize it all. If you rejoined the Dark Knight, you would be unstoppable."

Kathy still wasn't convinced.

"Look, I'm not one of the movers and shakers of the underworld. I can't lead a whole army and rest comfortably on the confidence of my powers. That's beyond my capabilities," Valerie explained. "But, that doesn't mean that I can't recognize an opportunity when it arises. Besides, if word gets out that I played a part in restoring order to the underworld, it'd be great for business."

Kathy studied the enchantress, weighing her options. This woman was the only chance of saving Will. She still didn't know if she wanted to be with him, but she couldn't hide her feelings. She loved him. That meant she needed to protect him.

"You can't seriously be considering this!" Samantha shouted, breaking Kathy's concentration.

"You could be great. It wouldn't take long to re-gather the troops," Valerie pressed. "Many of them are simply desperate for someone to follow, to look up to. You could be that person. What do you say?"

Kathy chanced one last glance at Will. She looked up at

Valerie—avoiding Samantha's stricken expression—and said, "I'll do it." She extended her hand, and they shook on it.

Valerie smiled. "Long live the queen."

Chapter Twenty-Four

"How could you agree to that?" Samantha asked, disgusted.

"It was the only way she'd save Will," Kathy said. She was on her hands and knees rolling up the bloodstained carpet. "Give me a hand with this." The room would take weeks to clean up properly. She hoped that the hellhounds' blood didn't stain anything. Not that that was the first thing on her mind.

Samantha grabbed one end of the rolled-up carpet. "Are you thinking this through? Just because you love him doesn't make it right." She slowly backed down the stairs, watching her feet to make sure she didn't trip.

"It doesn't matter. We'll find a way to take out the enchantress before she demands that I hold up my end of the bargain," Kathy explained. "Will still doesn't know, so we just have to make sure he doesn't find out. I don't want him to get the wrong idea."

"I still think it's a slippery slope." Samantha backed into the door and stepped into the backyard. She and Kathy dropped the soiled carpet behind the garage.

"I'll have to take it somewhere to dump tomorrow. I don't want anyone questioning it and finding Will's blood on it," Kathy said. She walked back into the kitchen with Samantha following. "I want to talk to you about something, though. And I don't want you to get mad."

Samantha scoffed. "That's not giving me a good feeling."

"Just hear me out," Kathy started. She took a deep breath before continuing. She knew Samantha wouldn't be happy. "I think we should tell the boys. About everything."

"What!?"

"Will's hex, my demonic marriage, my conversion," Kathy finished. "I think it's a good way to show them just how easy it is to slip to the dark side. Eventually they will be on the front lines, and they'll be faced with the same temptations."

"That's ridiculous! That'll only confuse them, and I don't want to add that stress to their lives."

"No, what's ridiculous is the fact that you can't accept that Will is not completely to blame for everything. *I* was the one who suggested the dark wedding. *I* was the one who wanted to organize dark magic. *I* was the one who plotted to kill you and the boys!"

Samantha's mouth dropped open, and she stared at her sister for a long time, speechless. Kathy knew she had overstepped and that Samantha would have been better off not knowing the extent of her betrayal.

Finally, Samantha regained her composure. She snatched her keys from the hook and walked to the front door.

"I need to get some air."

"Sammy," Kathy started, but she knew there was nothing she could say that would make the situation any better. Learning that Kathy had plotted to kill Samantha and the boys had hit her sister like a ton of bricks.

* * *

The next few days were filled with tension. The sisters barely saw each other, and when they did, they only spoke to keep up appearances for Josh and Chris. Kathy could tell the boys weren't buying it, but they never said anything, so she didn't ask.

She continued to see Will, although not as much as before. Samantha's words churned in her head. *Just because you love him doesn't make it right.* As much as Kathy didn't want to, she always came back to those words. She was so sick of questioning everything in her life that she wanted to confidently declare something good and happy, like the love of her life. But she knew deep down that wanting Will to be good for her wouldn't change the fact that he wasn't.

The enchantress was still on her mind, too. She had no idea how to kill her, or even find her. She had the summoning spell, but that wouldn't help them if they didn't have a way to take her out. It didn't help that Kathy was basically riding solo for this enemy.

Valerie was brought into their lives to heal Will, and, in effect, she had brought a death sentence on their family—especially since Kathy had no intention of going to the dark side again. Samantha wouldn't be up for that fight. She probably still wondered what Kathy's intentions were.

The day care was under-enrolled the following week, so Kathy had a day off. She wanted to try to find a way to make amends with her sister. She couldn't stand their constant disagreements and wanted things to go back to the way they used to be. Before Will. She didn't know if they could return to that if Will was still in her life.

Samantha had been going into work early to avoid any encounter with Kathy. She woke the boys up and then went on her way out the door hours before she normally would. So now it was up to Kathy, even on her day off, to wake up early and make sure the boys had breakfast and were ready for the day.

She wanted to complain and say that it wasn't her job, but she knew it wouldn't last forever. Even if Samantha never forgave her, she couldn't last long without spending more time with Josh and Chris.

After her alarm sounded, Kathy tossed the covers off and placed her feet on the cold hardwood floor. Immediately, a vision struck her.

Sitting behind a large metal desk, a man busily tapped away at his keyboard. Kathy didn't recognize him, but she figured he must work downtown. He was wearing a suit, and the neighboring buildings were visible through one of the large windows behind him. On the wall between the windows was a large clock that read 12:55 p.m.

The man's head snapped to the door of his office when another man entered. He was obviously supernatural, sporting a sword for an arm and black leathery wings on his back. He had tribal tattoos up his opposite arm that continued onto his face. His ears were lined with an assortment of piercings, and he had a metal bar running through his nose.

He stepped closer, and the man in the suit looked startled; fear was displayed across his face. Still, as Sword-arm approached, Suit-man stayed in his chair, gripping the armrests tightly.

Sword-arm was now standing over the man in the suit. He raised the sword and swung, slicing Suit-man's head off.

Kathy snapped back to reality. She clutched at her chest and tried to put out the image that greeted her upon waking. What a way to start the day.

She reached for her phone and texted Samantha. This wasn't Will related, and Kathy must've had the vision for a reason.

Before she even made it down the stairs, Samantha was calling her name.

"Kathy! Get the boys and the book and meet me in the kitchen!"

Rounding up the boys from their bedroom, Kathy asked Chris to grab the book from under Samantha's bed, and the three of them shuffled down the stairs.

"You guys ready to use your magic?" Samantha asked the boys. She still wouldn't look Kathy in the eyes.

Asking the boys to use their magic was rare for Samantha. Kathy wondered if her sister was letting her guard down about that as a way to avoid asking for help from Will.

"But, Mom, I don't have powers yet," Chris whined. He placed the magic book on the kitchen table and slid it to the center.

Samantha placed a hand on her son's shoulder and smiled at him. "It'll happen soon enough, Chris. I can sense it."

"What's up, Mom?" asked Josh. He glanced at the clock. No doubt he was worried about getting to school on time.

"Aunt Kathy had a vision," Samantha started, opening the book, still not looking in Kathy's direction. After flipping through a few pages, Samantha finally looked to Kathy and said, "I don't know exactly what I'm looking for." She passed the book to her sister and turned to the pot of water already boiling on the stove.

Kathy skimmed through the pages of *The Art of Magic* and explained her vision further: "A man will be murdered by some creature with a giant sword for an arm. The creature has a lot of piercings and tattoos on his face. He..." she glanced up at her nephews, unsure of how descriptive to be with them, "uh... decapitates the man."

"Did you see when it is supposed to happen?" Samantha asked, throwing some ingredients into the pot while keeping her back to Kathy.

Kathy nodded. "Luckily, there was a clock in my vision. It will be about one this afternoon."

The Full Moon

"Does this mean we don't have to go to school?" Chris asked with a smile on his face.

Samantha chuckled lightly. "You're still going. Just be prepared to leave early." She looked back at Kathy briefly. "What am I putting in this potion?"

"I'll pick them up," Kathy offered. Samantha was the best one to make the potion, and once Kathy found the creature in the magic book, the extent of her knowledge would be reached.

"Thanks, but I'll pass," Samantha snapped.

Kathy rolled her eyes and continued flipping through the book. Her sister could be so stubborn. Not that Kathy could blame her. She had displayed her own stubbornness recently. Finally, she stopped and turned the book to her sister. "Here he is."

"Josh, sweetie, can you reach me the rosemary from the top shelf?" Samantha asked. When he handed it to her, she sprinkled a dash into the mix. "I'll have to pick up more when I take the boys to school."

Kathy was increasingly overwhelmed with the cold shoulder Samantha was giving her. She just wanted Samantha to finally look at her so she didn't feel invisible. "Sammy, we're going to have to talk about this sooner or later."

"Boys." Samantha turned on her heels to face her children. "Why don't you brush your teeth and finish getting ready for school? I'll be ready in ten minutes."

Josh and Chris shuffled out of the kitchen. As the door swung shut, Samantha glared at Kathy. "You need to be more careful."

"They need to know," Kathy pressed. "Yes, I screwed up. Of course I'm sorry, but I don't think hiding it from them is going to do them any good."

"They don't need to know that their aunt, their own flesh and blood, offered them up as sacrifices for her demonic marriage to a Dark Knight," Samantha spat, straining to keep her voice down even as her anger rose. She had one hand on her hip and the other on the kitchen table.

Kathy sighed. "Don't tell them all the details, then. But don't you think they suspected something was up when I virtually disappeared for a month, and then when I suddenly returned, you have a grudge against me?"

Samantha waved her hand and busied herself with the magic book. "They don't notice that."

Kathy's voice rose. "You're not that good of an actress, Samantha. I'm not saying that you should make an excuse for me, but I think it's important that they know how easily and how deeply you can slip into the darkness." She shrugged. "I don't want them to hate me for what I did, but it is what it is."

Samantha kept her eyes down, her fingers curled around the page of the open magic book. She didn't say anything for a long time. Finally, she looked up at Kathy and said, "You stay here and make the potion, and I'll take them to school." She stomped out of the room before Kathy could respond.

* * *

"Hey, did you get my text about the sage and juniper berries?" Kathy asked as Samantha walked in with a brown paper bag of herbs and spices.

Kathy had been studying the creature since Samantha left with the boys. Unfortunately, she still didn't know his name. She wasn't sure how Samantha explained her absence from work, but up until recently, the woman had never missed a day. She probably had loads of time off built up.

"Yeah," Samantha said, hauling the bag onto the kitchen table. She pulled out items and attempted to put them away, but Kathy tugged on the bag, drawing it to her.

"I can get those," Kathy offered.

"No, it's fine." Samantha pulled the bag back, but it started to tear. She threw up her hands. "Fine. Did you finish the potion?"

"Mm-hmm," Kathy hummed, stretching to put away the ingredients on the top shelf, away from the prying eyes of visitors.

"I told the boys I'd pick them up at noon—" A knock on the back door cut Samantha off.

Kathy froze. Samantha hadn't seen Will since they had summoned the enchantress to heal him.

"I swear, I didn't know he was coming. I told him to stay away from you and the boys," Kathy said. She got up to greet her husband.

"Are you still seeing him?" Samantha was disgusted.

Will stepped in the door and smiled at Kathy.

"What the hell are you doing here?" Samantha demanded.

"I heard that you were going to be attacked by one of the Queen's best men," Will explained. "I thought I'd drop by and offer my expertise."

Samantha snapped, "We don't work with evil, and we don't want word to spread that we do."

Kathy cringed. She wanted all this to be over. The hatred between Will and Samantha had only escalated as time went on, and them being in the same room wasn't helping.

"No, I get it," he started, then added, "Well, not really..."

Samantha rolled her eyes. "That's a surprise." She crossed her arms and stared him down.

Will groaned, letting his frustration get the better of him. "I don't understand why you're refusing help! Sure, you say I'm evil, but I'll be of help to you, so what does it matter?"

Samantha burned with anger as she shouted, "Get out of my house! I don't want to see you near my sister, near my children, or near this house ever again!"

"Will, sweetie," Kathy cooed, reaching for his arm. She tried her best to diffuse the situation, but it was too late. He was ignoring her, his eyes locked on Samantha.

"You'd better change that attitude, because if you don't focus on the task at hand, then Garmond will destroy you," he warned.

"Garmond? That's his name?" Kathy tried to get his attention away from Samantha.

"If you really want to help us, just give us his location," Samantha said, caving. Kathy bit her bottom lip. She wished Samantha hadn't said anything.

"I thought you wanted me to leave?" Will asked.

"Leave or stay, I don't give a damn. But if you stay, you're going to help us."

"I'll help you in my own way, on my own terms. I'm not sure where he is, but I do know that he's not very well protected at the moment. We can find him," Will said.

"I want you to look me in the eye and tell me that you're not going to screw us like you have in the past," Samantha said. Her arms were still folded, and Kathy knew she was trying to find a way inside Will's mind. "If you help, you follow *our* terms. Do you understand me?"

The two had a standoff, sizing each other up. Finally, Will spoke up. "I will try to find out his plan of attack." He kissed Kathy on the cheek. "I'll see you later, babe." Kathy cringed again, wishing he hadn't done that in front of Samantha.

Once he was gone, Samantha said, "I don't understand why you just don't break up with him. After all he put you and our family though. Kathy, this is serious."

Kathy bit her lip. "I know." She shrugged. "But I can't help it, I love him. I just want to be with him."

Samantha closed her eyes and shook her head. When she opened them, she kept her head down and said, "I can't even look at you. I really hope whatever spell he has on you gets broken soon." She grabbed her keys out of her purse and headed toward the front door. "I'm going to pick up the boys. Call me if anything happens."

* * *

Just as Kathy was pulling the pot off the stove and placing it on a cooling rack, she heard a crash at the front of the house. She pulled a knife from its holder against the wall and crept to the kitchen door.

She peered around the corner and was suddenly face-to-face with Garmond. Screaming, she jumped back.

He let out a growl and lunged for her, but Kathy managed to shove the knife right in his chest. He stumbled backward and looked down at the knife piercing his chest. With a tattooed hand, he reached down and slowly pulled it out, tossing it to the side.

Kathy slid around the other side of the kitchen table, trying to put as many barricades between her and Garmond as possible. As he stepped closer, Kathy eyed the potion. If she could get to it and throw it on him, he would be a goner. Of course, she would burn her hands severely in the process, but that was the price of saving lives—even her own. She just needed to distract him so that she could get to it. He was within an arm's reach of the potion as well.

"I thought you had a job downtown?" Kathy asked. It was nearly twelve thirty, and the clock in her vision had shown Garmond killing that man in just twenty minutes. Even with his wings, it wasn't enough time.

She wondered if she had the day wrong. Nothing in the vision said the attack occurred today. But wouldn't a vision showing a threat to her life be more significant? Especially if he was supposed to kill her before he killed the man downtown. She couldn't think of that now, face-to-face with the enemy.

She braved a step closer to the potion, but Garmond anticipated her move and swung his arm across the counter, knocking the pot to the floor, spilling the contents all over.

Kathy turned and ran up the stairs. She went to her bedroom, slamming the door shut and locking it. She cursed herself afterward. The sound of the door gave away her location.

Pressing her back against the side of her dresser, she tried to push it in front of the door. She managed to cover part of it, but the dresser hit the doorknob and wouldn't budge. She deemed it good enough and searched her room for any kind of weapon.

Stabbing him didn't work, so she needed to think of another plan. She wondered if he could be knocked out. That would buy her some time for Samantha to come home. Or to call Will.

The sound of Garmond's fist on the door kicked her into action. She dropped to the floor and swung her arm under her bed, looking for anything she could use. Her hand clasped a baseball bat she'd hidden under her bed after Steven moved out. She'd never had to use it, but it used to help her sleep at night. She'd since forgotten about it and was glad that she never got around to cleaning out the junk under her bed.

Garmond's sword-arm broke through the door as Kathy jumped to her feet, gripping the bat. He continued swinging, breaking off pieces of the door until he was able to kick his way through. The dresser toppled to the floor as he entered.

"You're dead, witch!" he grunted.

Kathy waited until he stepped closer before swinging. The bat collided perfectly along the side of his neck, delivering a satisfying crunch. He dropped to the floor, unmoving.

She let out a deep breath and carefully stepped around him and through the shattered door. Once she was back in the kitchen, she heard Samantha calling her name from the front door.

"Be quiet!" Kathy hushed, following the sound of her sister's voice to the front foyer. Josh and Chris were with her. "He's knocked out in my bedroom."

Samantha looked quizzical. "How did he end up in your bedroom?" She held up her hand. "Never mind. Are you okay?"

Kathy nodded. "Yeah, but he must've known what kind of potion we were making. He threw it on the floor, so that's gone."

"Damn," Samantha muttered. "Okay, we need another plan. Maybe a spell or something. He seems midlevel, right?"

Shrugging, Kathy said, "I thought so, but maybe somebody supercharged him or something. He was going for the kill, that's for sure."

There was a crash upstairs. They heard some murmurs, as if two people were talking.

"It's just Garmond up there, right?" Samantha asked. Her eyes were fixed on the ceiling.

Kathy wondered how long the second intruder had been in the house. "It was…" Garmond had left the front door wide open, so there was no telling who'd strolled in unnoticed.

"Let's go get him!" Chris shouted, running toward the stairs.

The Full Moon

Samantha pulled on the back of his shirt. "I don't think so. You boys stay back."

Garmond appeared at the top of the stairs and smiled as he sauntered down.

"That's Garmond?" Samantha asked.

Chris lost his enthusiasm and stepped back. "Mom, kill him!"

Samantha shot a quick glance to Kathy. "Any ideas?"

In her mind, Kathy ran through everything she knew about the creature. "Stabbing him doesn't work. He'll just heal himself."

Josh spoke up. "So we need to do a quick kill and make sure it sticks."

Will ran through the ruins of the front door. "Stand back!" He put out his hand and ushered Samantha, Kathy, and the boys back farther into the next room as he conjured a sword.

Garmond leaped from the stairs and swung his sword-arm, aiming for Will's chest. Conjuring a shield, Will was able to evade the attack.

"Stupid knight!" Garmond shouted. "You will pay for your betrayal!" He turned his attention to the witches, swinging his sword-arm at them. Kathy dove out of the way, and Josh and Chris ran to the living room.

Samantha held her ground. She jumped in the air and threw her foot against Garmond's chest, kicking him to the floor.

"Will, pass me the sword!" she called. She circled Garmond and watched as he struggled to get up off the floor.

Kathy saw Will hesitate. She shouted, "Give her the sword!"

She couldn't believe that even in a situation like this, he was still holding his grudge. Samantha seemed to ignore it for the time being, so why couldn't he?

Will tossed the sword in the air, and Samantha caught it one-handed and swung it in front of her. Even as an adult, Kathy admired her big sister and the skills she possessed.

Although she knew Samantha could handle herself, Kathy didn't want to run the risk of Garmond getting the upper hand.

"Will, watch the boys," she said before joining her sister.

Garmond was standing now, and he and Samantha sparred in the foyer. Kathy jumped and grabbed hold of the light fixture on the ceiling. She brought her feet up and kicked Garmond in the back.

He staggered but didn't fall. He swung around behind him in Kathy's direction. She only had a second to jump back, but still he sliced the front of her blouse.

"No!" Will hollered. He was at Kathy's side in an instant, pulling her to the floor. He knelt in front of her and blocked her view of Samantha and Garmond.

She pushed him away. "Will, it's fine. I'm all right."

"Let me see," Will urged, lifting her shirt to examine her stomach.

Kathy pushed his hands away. She could hear Samantha beckoning Garmond closer but couldn't make out what was happening. She heard Samantha's sword sliding across the floor, and she moved to stand, but Will pushed her back down.

"I'll take care of it." He stood and shouted to Garmond. The demon turned toward Will.

Kathy saw her sister reaching for the sword, but Will conjured it into his hands just as Samantha was about to grab it.

"Why don't you pick on someone who is a little more skilled at swordfighting, huh?" Will asked.

Garmond went on another attack against Will, and they squared off. The room was silent, save for clanging swords. Kathy moved to the boys and stood in front of them, holding an arm out to the side protectively. Samantha joined them and took a similar stance.

"Do you think we can come up with a spell?" Kathy asked. She was the one to craft the spells usually, but Samantha knew more about whether a spell could replace a potion or not.

"I don't know; do you think you could freeze him so we could recreate the potion?" Samantha asked.

Kathy shook her head. "It wouldn't be enough time. My magic would wear off before the potion was done."

Will and Garmond disappeared into the next room, and the crash of furniture filled the air.

"Maybe we should just run?" Josh suggested.

"No," Samantha said sternly. "He came here for a reason." She looked at Kathy. "I don't get it, your vision showed that he was killing someone else at this time. How did he end up here?"

Kathy shrugged. "I don't know! Maybe he got different orders? These things can change."

There was a loud thud, and the four witches turned to see Garmond turn on them. Will lay still in the corner.

Images of the last time Will had nearly died flooded Kathy's thoughts. "Oh, Will!" She ran to his side.

He appeared to have only been knocked out. She turned him on his back and smacked his face a little. "Wake up!" It didn't seem to be working. Kathy could hear Samantha and Garmond fighting once more.

"Will, honey, wake up!" Kathy cried, grabbing hold of Will's jacket and shaking him. She looked over her shoulder to see how Samantha was doing and saw her on the floor with blood on her face and Garmond delivering a kick to her side.

The reoccurring nightmares came rushing back to Kathy. How could she not have known that she was having visions in her sleep? She had been warned about this attack a long time ago, and she'd still failed to prevent it.

She stood, determined to correct her oversight.

"Leave her alone!" Kathy warned, sending another kick at Garmond. He caught it and twisted. Her ankle cracked as she felt searing pain up her leg. She cried out and crumpled to the floor.

When Garmond turned back to Samantha, it wasn't Kathy's broken ankle that kept her in place, but fear. She watched as Garmond delivered kick after kick into Samantha's side. She hated to see her sister so defeated but didn't know what she could do to stop him.

Samantha coughed up blood and grumbled, "What do you want?"

"Not so tough anymore, huh?" Garmond sneered. He drew back his foot to send another kick into Samantha's side, but a gust of wind stopped him. Everyone looked to the direction of the wind and saw Josh standing with his palms out.

He turned to Chris. "I told you it wouldn't work!"

Garmond stepped closer to Josh, but stopped when a vase crashed near his feet. Kathy snapped her head back and saw Samantha crawling toward the boys. Even in this state, she was still on a mission to protect her kids.

"Get the hell away from them," Samantha said in ragged breaths. "Run, boys!"

The boys took off, and Garmond turned his attention back to Samantha. Kathy heard rustling from behind her and saw Will starting to stir.

"Will, wake up! Samantha needs your help!" Kathy knew it wasn't the best motivator, but she hoped that he would step up and do what was right. Her ankle was throbbing with blinding pain. There was no way she could move.

Kathy was hopeful when Will started to rise. She turned back to Garmond, who took Will's rising as a threat and delivered the final blow to Samantha, driving his sword-arm into her back.

Watching her sister crumple to the floor dead pushed Kathy over the edge. She shrieked as the tears poured down her face. She didn't care about anything—Garmond seeing her as weak, Will's survival, or even her own safety. She was completely focused on her sister, who lay in a bloody, crumpled mess across the room. An image she had seen many times in her sleep.

When one of Garmond's wings burst into flames, Kathy finally snapped out of her hysterics. She turned and saw Chris staring at his hands. Kathy suddenly felt guilty. The pain and loss she felt was immensely worse for Josh and Chris.

Chris threw his hands in Garmond's direction and blew up his other wing. The creature fell to his knees but pointed his sword-arm at Chris.

Kathy suddenly worried that her nephew was going to be his next target, but Will's voice roared behind her as he charged the demon.

The Dark Knight swung his blade down on Garmond's sword-arm, severing it. The creature screamed in pain, but Kathy didn't pay attention. She was silently cheering on her nephew. If this was his specialty, he was now able to defeat Garmond.

"Chris," Josh said, "you have the power to kill him. Focus."

Kathy watched as her youngest nephew took a deep breath and once again waved his hands in the direction of the monster. In an instant, Garmond was obliterated; the only sign of him being the sword-arm that Will had cut off.

"Whoa," Kathy said, gaping. Her attention again snapped to her sister, and she crawled across the floor to Samantha's side. Her ankle was on fire, but she ignored it. She reached for her wrist, feeling for a pulse that wasn't there. Tears once again filled her eyes as she kissed the back of Samantha's hand.

Josh and Chris were a mess as well, both boys sobbing. Kathy put her arm around Josh, refusing to let go of Samantha's hand, and drew him in close.

"Aunt Kathy, can't you go back in time and stop this?" Josh asked in between sobs.

She shook her head. "I don't have that kind of power, sweetie."

Chris reached for Samantha's other hand, covered in blood. He brought it to his face and cradled it, smearing her blood on his cheek. Finally, Kathy let go of her hold of Samantha and slung her arm around Chris, pulling both boys close to her.

They only had each other now.

Chapter Twenty-Five

W hy won't you let me find someone to heal that for you?" Will asked, driving Kathy home from the hospital. Her ankle was wrapped in a pink cast. She had a set of crutches propped up next to her.

"Because, Will, I need a break."

"From what, exactly?" he asked, turning onto Route 19. "Just because Samantha's de—gone," he corrected himself before the word could come out, "doesn't mean there are any fewer threats against you. If anything, it means there are more. They know you're vulnerable, and they'll use this opportunity to attack."

"I need a break from everything!" Kathy shouted. "From work, from magic, from life…from you. Everything that happened these past few months has happened so quickly. I never really got a chance to stop and process anything before something else came in. Give me a while to grieve."

It had been two days since Samantha had died and she tried to pretend it hadn't happened, tried to act like her sister was just working late. After all, the last week or so she had kept her distance from Kathy, so she and the boys had grown used to her absence. But that didn't hide the fact that Samantha wasn't working late. She was never coming back.

Kathy lost her big sister. Her best friend. Josh and Chris lost their mother. The only true parent who hadn't abandoned them. Even Kathy—who had acted as a parent once Steven was gone—betrayed them when she married Will.

That was another pressure resting on Kathy's shoulders. She knew that she had renounced any affiliation with the dark side—especially now that Samantha was gone and she needed to look after the boys—but what else would spring up as a result of her brief conversion?

Although it would be a challenge to shift from the fun aunt to a parental figure, she knew she could step up to the plate and take on the responsibilities. The question was, could Will? If she had a future with him, she needed to make sure he would be there for the boys.

They rode home the rest of the way in silence. Kathy tried to think of anything else besides Samantha. She thought about work and how gracious they were for giving her as much time off as she needed. She was still a new employee and knew they didn't have to do that. She wondered, though, if their generosity wasn't tied to the under-enrollment they were experiencing at the day care.

Both Josh and Chris wanted to go to school. They didn't want to sit around the house, reminding themselves of everything that was their mother. Her favorite spot to sit on the couch. The way she was always bustling over the stove, whether it was working on dinner or a potion.

The boys couldn't even bring themselves to enter the front foyer yet. Kathy had used a spell to clean up the area. She tried to stay away from using magic for housework, but this was different. Scrubbing her sister's blood off the floor was a chore she didn't want to partake in.

When they pulled up to the house, Will turned off the car but neither of them got out.

"You going to be okay?" he asked, breaking the silence.

Kathy nodded.

"Do you want me to walk you in?" He pulled back his sleeve to look at the watch on his left wrist. He had taken the morning off to take her to the hospital.

"I should be fine," Kathy said. She reached for her crutches that were propped up against the door. Will leaned in and kissed her, but she turned her head and he kissed her cheek instead.

"I love you," he said, his voice uneasy.

She gave him a tight smile and hopped out of the car. She positioned the crutches under her arms before closing the door. "Thanks for taking me."

"No problem. I'll be back after work. If you need anything, call me."

Kathy gave a slight nod and shut the door. She hobbled up

the driveway, working around to the back door. She didn't want to go into the front foyer either. That would change today. She needed to get ready for Samantha's memorial.

By the time the boys came home, she had already been visited by several neighbors. With the catering company dropping off the food for the memorial the next day, she figured she wouldn't have to cook for a week. That would give her time to learn how to cook.

She filled the garbage can to the brim with tissues. She cried most of the day. The kitchen was Samantha's domain, and trying to put together a meal somehow felt like she was intruding in her space. Everything about that room reminded her of her sister.

When Kathy heard the boys, she pulled herself together. They didn't need to see her like that.

"Hey, boys, how was school?" She flashed a smile to try to lift their spirits.

"Fine. How'd the hospital go?" Chris placed his backpack on the stairs.

Kathy stuck out her foot brandishing the cast. "I'm laid up for a bit, but I think we could use some time off anyway."

Josh cleared his throat and changed the subject. "Where are the tables?"

"Out in the garage. I think we're going to need all three," Kathy responded. "Will should be here in an hour or two to help."

"You should sit," Chris said. "How long have you been standing?"

She reached for her crutches and moved over to the table and lowered herself into the chair.

"I've been on my feet—foot, all day." She shook her crutches. "These things are going to take some getting used to." She rubbed at her armpits.

"You should just use magic," Chris suggested.

Kathy gave a tight smile but didn't respond. She wasn't ready to use her magic yet. It hadn't been able to save Samantha, so she couldn't see the value in it anymore. She knew that would pass, but for the time being she was content living simply. Without magic.

"C'mon, Chris. Let's go get those tables," Josh said. He and Chris disappeared out the back door.

* * *

"You need to get to bed," Will said, leaning against the kitchen table across from Kathy. "You look exhausted."

"I am exhausted," Kathy said. She was folding napkins. "There's so much stuff to do." She didn't want to admit that she was afraid of reliving the attack in her sleep—something she was prone to do with her time specialty. The attack had been haunting her the past two nights.

"Let me take care of it," he insisted, taking the stack of napkins from Kathy.

She gave him a look and was about to snatch the napkins back from him, but Valerie appeared in a puff of black smoke.

"Miss me?" she asked with a sneer.

"What are you doing here?" Kathy demanded. She picked up a

knife she had been using to cut cucumbers earlier. She didn't want to give away the fact that she was on crutches, even though they were perched right next to her. She was glad Will was between her and the enchantress.

"I noticed that your husband here is alive and kicking, yet you're still playing white witch," Valerie said. She casually opened the cupboards and read the labels of a few jars. She replaced them and wiped her hands together, as if knocking off dust. "What gives? I held up my end of the bargain, now it's your turn."

"What bargain?" Will asked, his head bobbing back and forth between Kathy and Valerie.

Kathy didn't want to tell him. She tried to will Valerie into silence but knew it was no use.

"You were dead," Valerie said. "Or nearly dead. I healed you on the condition that your wife rejoin you as the leader of the demonic world."

"Why would you want us to lead?" he asked Valerie. "You should be ecstatic that we're no longer your competition."

The enchantress gestured to Kathy. "As I told your wife, if you two take over and word spreads that I helped put you there, I will see more customers as a result. It's all business, really."

Will shook his head. "No. I don't buy it. What you want is for us to continue our plot, and you will continue to make demands, studying us, learning our weaknesses. Then, after you've gained our trust, you'll kill us and take over yourself. I've seen it happen a hundred times. I know your kind. You're all the same."

Before Valerie had a chance to protest, Will had conjured a

sword and drove it right through her stomach. The woman fell to the floor dead.

"Will!" Kathy blurted, frozen to her spot behind the table.

"I'll take care of her, don't worry," he said. "But I need you to promise me that you won't make any more deals like that. Understand?"

A familiar anger bubbled up inside Kathy. She hadn't felt this way since she'd been bound and determined to become the queen of the underworld. She took a deep breath and reached for her crutches. She couldn't believe Will would kill Valerie when Kathy was so emotional. Two deaths in the house in a matter of days.

"Get rid of her and leave," she said before slowly hobbling up the steps.

* * *

Kathy sat at the end of her bed the next day brushing her hair before the memorial. She was regretting the decision for a pink cast since it clashed so much with her black dress. Samantha's dress. Kathy didn't own anything that fit the occasion. Despite her line of work, she rarely went to funerals or memorials.

There was a knock on her door and Will stepped in. She hadn't seen him since the night before when he killed Valerie. She was relieved he had listened to her and not come back after disposing of the enchantress. She needed time away from him to think.

The Full Moon

"Are you almost ready?"

She nodded. "Are the boys ready?"

"They're downstairs and all suited up," Will said. "Just waiting on you." He was dressed in a black suit—one of the many he wore to work. He took a seat next to Kathy on the bed. "Are you going to use the crutches today, or do you want me to find you a wheel-chair?"

"The crutches are fine." She didn't want to think of how he would obtain the wheelchair. Probably steal it from an old woman.

As much as she tried to see the good in him, she couldn't push certain things from her mind. Like how he hesitated to help Samantha in battle and how he was suddenly so concerned about Kathy being shoved to the ground when Samantha had been toe-to-toe with Garmond. Whether or not he had a grudge, he wasn't putting forth an honest effort to save them. She wondered if he had really been knocked out for so long or if he had just been acting.

She pinched the bridge of her nose. She needed to stop thinking like that. She was depressed and it made her angry with everyone—especially with Will's inherit evil influence because of their blood bond. This was also not the time to be getting involved in any sort of spats.

This day was for Samantha.

* * *

The guests filling the living room were a perfect icebreaker for

Kathy and the boys' reentry into the front of the house. Kathy knew how fast the boys had set up the front foyer the night before so they could spend as little time as possible there. The crowd of people helped to erase the painful memories that had taken place there. It would still be a while before the three of them were comfortable being in that room alone, though.

Will had noticed how distant Kathy was being and wouldn't accept her grief as an excuse. The crutches prevented her from sneaking away from him quickly.

"C'mon, Kathy. Don't give me some half-ass answer," Will urged, frustrated. "What's wrong? Do you have a problem with me?"

"Not now, Will," Kathy said, hopping into the kitchen to ask the boys to refill the sandwich platter.

Mrs. Kors from across the street stopped Kathy. "Why don't you sit? You poor thing. The boys will take care of everything!" She never hesitated to volunteer Josh and Chris for any task. Even at their mother's memorial. After a few more people suggested she sit, Kathy finally parked herself in the living room.

Even with people surrounding her, buzzing about how sweet Samantha had been and how strong of a woman she was, Will was still in Kathy's ear.

Finally, Kathy couldn't hold it any longer and froze the room.

"Will, stop it!" she shouted. It was a burst of energy she had been trying to rein in and control all day.

"Tell me what's going on," he insisted, an edge to his voice.

She glared at him. She hated him for ruining Samantha's

memorial for her. Now, whenever she thought of this day, she would think of Will's insecurities and overall annoyance. Not of peacefully laying her sister to rest.

"Fine. I wanted to wait until after this was all over, but I guess you're too impatient," she started. "I need some time."

"I can give you time. I just need to know what's going on."

"No, Will. I need time away from you," she clarified. "I told you before. I need to figure everything out. You're not helping. A lot of the factions that were attacking us are either dead, or they have backed off. Now I need to sort us out." She waved her hand between them. "You haven't given me any space to think."

"I've been more than patient with you, Kathy. I allowed you to have your sister back in your life, and I'm cleaning up the mess you made when you reneged on our deal."

Kathy cocked an eyebrow. "You *allowed* me to have Samantha back in my life? I shouldn't have had to choose to begin with!" She put her fingers to her temples and gaped at him. "How can you not see that?"

"Your sister put you in the same spot."

"She's my family, it's a little different with her."

Will paused for a moment. "I thought *we* were a family?"

She didn't respond and focused on her nails, running the thumbnail along the other, chipping off the black paint she'd applied the night before.

"What brought this on? I thought we were doing well. That we've moved past all the nonsense from the beginning of our marriage."

Now it was Kathy's turn to look confused. "What made you think that? What, now that my sister's dead and there's no one warning me about you?"

"No, that's not it at all," he protested. "We were moving forward. I thought you had your space and we were ready to restart."

"Listen to me: I need to make some changes in my life. Obviously, things aren't working for us the way they are. I need to simplify. Right now the boys need me more than anyone else in the world. They're my responsibility now. They're the reason I wake up in the morning."

"I know! I don't have a problem taking on the boys—they're my nephews, too," Will said.

Kathy cringed. Even though she considered Will her husband, she didn't think about the effects it had on her family. By marrying him, she'd introduced an uncle and a brother-in-law. An addition to the family that she hadn't received anyone's blessing for. Yet another thing she felt guilty for.

"I need to focus on them right now," Kathy continued. "I don't want to deal with a tarnished marriage while learning how to act as a parent."

"We don't—"

"We *do* have a tarnished marriage. It was cursed from the beginning," Kathy declared. She shrugged her shoulders. "Maybe we do have a future together. But if that's the case, it can wait until I take care of the boys—my boys."

Will studied her face. "I'll always be here for you."

She kept her gaze down on her hands. She had successfully

scraped off the paint from three whole nails.

"I need you to leave, Will."

He hesitated, trying to catch her eyes, but she refused to look at him. Finally, he stood and meandered through the frozen crowd. She didn't look up until she heard the front door close.

Chapter Twenty-Six

Kathy sat at the dining room table and held the trigger of the lighter, igniting the three candles in front of her. Each was a different color: white, silver, and black. They were supposed to help her cleanse herself of any spell that might be lingering over her. She wanted to free herself from her temptations once and for all.

Once they were lit, she closed her eyes and focused. She tried her best to clear her head but she couldn't. It was filled with worries about her nephews, questions about her husband, and memories of her sister—they were all she had left of Samantha now.

She let out a deep breath and recited:

For those who wish to interfere;

THE FULL MOON

to their power I won't adhere.
The magic has taken its toll.
Banish their power from my soul.

The air in the room began to stir, but it soon dissipated and Kathy felt no different.

After referring to the magic book, she decided to strengthen the power of the spell with a few herbs. She grabbed a rusted old pot from the kitchen and the few ingredients she needed and hobbled back to the table.

Once she was back in her chair, she tried to clear her head again. It still didn't work. Especially now that she was frustrated that the first spell hadn't worked. That and her limited mobility were testing her patience.

She recited the spell once more. At the end of each line, she lit a bit of each herb: lavender, sage, rosemary, and valerian. The valerian usually had a horrible smell to it, so she burned it first. Luckily, the scent of the other herbs hid its potent smell. After the spell was complete, the air stirred once again, but still Kathy felt no different.

Frustrated, she blew out the candles and consulted the book again. She flipped through the cleansing chapter several times and still came up short. There were loads of spells and rituals to cleanse a house or a room. Plenty of protection spells. No spells to lift an unidentified spell on a witch.

She wondered if she could craft one herself, but she knew the only way she could really get it right was if she asked Will exactly how he'd done the first spell. She knew she couldn't do that—especially after she told him to leave Samantha's memorial. It had been four days since the memorial and Kathy hadn't spoken to Will yet. She figured that was about to change now that her emotions were in better check. She owed him a better explanation, one that wasn't supercharged by intense emotions and supernatural influences. She hadn't changed her mind about their marriage, but she hoped that she could better express her thoughts with a clear head.

* * *

"He just finished up a meeting, so he should be free," Debbie told Kathy upon her arrival at his office. It being the middle of the day on a Tuesday, she knew this was the best place to catch him. Plus, she wanted the security of a public place so any arguing wouldn't escalate too much.

Despite her anger with Will, she couldn't help but cast side-long glances at Debbie, comparing her to herself. What did she have that Kathy didn't? How was Debbie better as Will's secretary than she would have been? Still, she was glad she never got the job. That would mean she'd be out of one now, when she so desperately needed one. It would've been yet another tie to Will.

Debbie excused herself to run down to the lobby for some coffee and offered to have Kathy sit, but she decided to stay on her crutches. She still wasn't used to them. Getting up and down from the chair would take too long, and her visit wouldn't have the same effect if she needed Will's help up.

Outside his office door, Kathy leaned on one of her crutches and her good foot and dug through her purse. She pulled out the medallion Samantha had placed on her after her and Will's date at the club.

Before she could pull it on over her head, she heard voices coming from his office. They were speaking softly, trying not to have any eavesdroppers, but their deep voices carried out of the room anyway.

"...I'm not worried about the Queen's advances. She's a minor threat to me. But we need to make her think she still has power. Pull together your weakest men and attack her. Once she kills them, she'll have a false sense of security."

"Aren't you worried about depleting our forces?"

"No. It'll be a good distraction for her. It'll keep her out of our hair while I focus on recruiting my wife."

Kathy's ears perked up, and she clutched the medallion hard in her right hand.

"Do you really think that's wise?"

There was a pause before Will responded. "To rule with my wife?"

"To infiltrate our forces with a white witch."

Will's voice remained quiet, but stern. "I didn't go through the trouble of arranging Garmond's attack to not bring my wife along. Now that her sister's not chirping in her ear, she can be by my side once again. I just need some time."

Kathy froze. How could she be so stupid? Will was evil. He had shown that time and time again. He had successfully managed to hide it behind Kathy's obsession with her brief conversion to the dark side.

Samantha had been right all along. And it had cost her life. If Kathy hadn't been so adamant about salvaging her marriage, Samantha would still be alive. Kathy was the one to blame for her own sister's death.

She let go of the medallion, and it dropped to the ground with a clang. Both voices in the office stopped.

Fighting back tears, she picked up her head and tried to regain her composure. She grabbed the handles on the crutches and strode into Will's office. It wasn't the dramatic entrance she wanted to make, but he still wasn't expecting to see her.

"You bastard," Kathy started, slamming Will's office door behind her. "I trusted you! I fought for you!"

Will was alone now, his accomplice having taken off when he heard the medallion drop.

"Kathy, sweetie," he started, but she greeted him with a slap across the face. He touched his cheek briefly before finishing with, "what a surprise."

"Cut the shit, Will. I heard everything. You murdered my sister!" She tried to keep her voice steady, but it wavered. Her anger was rising.

"No. That was Garmond," he countered. "And guess who killed him? Little Chris. Talk a little louder and I'm not going to be the only one answering questions."

Kathy was satisfied that Will's face was turning red from

her slap. Still, she narrowed her eyes and forced herself to lower her voice. "And who sent Garmond? You said he worked for the Queen. You lied to me."

He tried to pull her into an embrace, but she pushed him away. She hopped back a step to put distance between them. "Baby, I think you're overreacting."

"Don't call me that." She hadn't been this angry since she'd lived with Will. She stopped dead, remembering the night they fused their blood together. She and Will were connected magically. No cleansing spell could erase that. The fusion was irreplaceable unless one of them died.

"You're still emotional about your sister," Will said. "I don't blame you. You're entitled to irrational anger."

"Irrational ang—" She stopped herself. There was no sense in continuing the argument. His presence was only multiplying her anger. She turned on her good heel and hobbled out as fast as she could.

* * *

The boys were already home when she pulled into the driveway. She knew she could've just used her magic, but she was still uneasy about it. Plus, she liked using Samantha's car. It made her feel closer to her, like her sister was still with her.

"Where were you?" Chris asked when she came through the door. He was at the table doing homework with his brother.

"I went to talk to Will," she said, regretting it immediately.

She knew they didn't know much about her relationship with Will, but they at least knew that he wasn't a good influence on her. "What are you guys thinking about for dinner?" She wanted to distract them, and herself. It had barely been a week since Samantha had passed, and she didn't need to bring any other worries into their lives.

"Pizza?" Chris asked, hopeful.

Kathy wanted to agree, because it would be easy, but she needed to start acting more like a parent. Healthier meals were part of the package. Plus, it wouldn't buy her any time to calm down from her ordeal with Will. The only lines with spells she came up with on her way home would cause serious harm to Will. She wasn't sure if she was ready to kill him yet, but she was close.

"How about..." She opened a few of the cupboard doors and peered in each. Samantha used to prepare most of the food. Kathy grabbed a couple of blue boxes from the cupboard and asked, "Mac and cheese?"

The response was lukewarm, but at least it was a hot meal.

After dinner, she was too tired from using the crutches all day to worry about the dinner cleanup and left the dirty dishes in the sink. She perched herself in the living room with her cast propped up on the coffee table and brainstormed a solution to the bond she still shared with Will.

She was interrupted when Chris came down and clicked on the TV.

"What are you working on?" he asked.

"Oh, just," she waved her hand in the air, "stuff."

That didn't pacify him and he pressed on. "Josh says Will is evil."

Kathy looked up at him. She debated how much she wanted to tell him, if she wanted to tell him anything at all. She ultimately decided that they were safer knowing more than they did. Both boys had active powers to protect themselves. It was her job now to teach them how to use them and prepare them for any threats. That was one thing Samantha had lacked as a parent of two witches. She knew Samantha wouldn't have been happy about it, but their lives were getting more dangerous. Thanks to Kathy.

"Get your brother. I need to talk with both of you."

Once Josh and Chris were both seated on the couch, Kathy set her pad of paper aside and considered where to start.

"Chris told me that you think Will is evil." She looked at Josh.

He was stunned, his eyes wide as if he was in trouble. "I—uh, Mom was never very happy with him. So I just sort of figured…" He shrugged.

"You're right," Kathy said with a nod. "He's a Dark Knight. A demonic bodyguard for the bad guys."

"Did you know that?" Chris asked.

She closed her eyes and confessed, "Yes. It was stupid and reckless and I regret it immensely."

"Were you evil?" Josh asked.

Kathy was silent for a long time. She didn't know whether or not to tell him the truth. Samantha didn't want them to know about her betrayal, so she needed to protect her wish. But still, she didn't like lying to them.

Finally, she answered, "I did a lot of bad things. Things I'm not proud of. I hurt a lot of people. It's not so easy to make amends after everything I did, but I'm trying." She looked up at them. "The first thing I need to do is get away from Will."

"So are you guys getting divorced?" Chris pressed.

"It's not that simple, Chris," Josh said before Kathy could answer.

"No, it's not," she reiterated. "We're married. A legal separation isn't going to change the magical bond we share." She gave a sideways smile. "That's where I'm stumped. I don't know how to cut ties with him magically. If we're still connected, he will forever be influencing me and my decisions." She raised her hands. "I'm stuck."

"Did he put a spell on you or something?" Josh asked.

She nodded. "At first, yeah. An infatuation spell. But I think I've come out of that influence. Your mother was able to erase the bond we share temporarily, but it also bound my magic in the process."

"Oh," was all Chris could muster. He was more interested in making stuff happen with his bare hands than studying the magic book. His brother, on the other hand, was always looking to learn something new.

"But our connection goes deeper than that. By blood." That was the extent of information she was willing to share with the boys. They didn't need to know how she had originally drained Samantha's blood in order to steal her power.

THE FULL MOON

"What about a cleansing or healing spell?" Josh suggested.

"Tried them this afternoon. Nothing."

They fell silent as they all considered their options.

"I'm afraid Will is going to kill us," Chris said.

Kathy's heart sank. Her teenaged nephew was fearing for his life, and she was the one who had brought it upon him. She waved her hands at them and said, "Come here." Both boys squeezed next to her on the couch, and she wrapped her arms around them and kissed the tops of their heads.

"I would never let that happen." She squeezed tightly. "You boys mean the world to me. Will knows that. He's not going to attack you if he wants me to do anything willingly."

She knew that in order for anything to go as he had planned, Will would need Kathy to operate on her own. No spell was strong enough to completely wipe away someone's free will forever. Those spells were too easy to break.

"Why don't you remove your powers?" Josh suggested.

Kathy loosened her hold on them and looked him in the eyes. "What?"

"You said Mom did it when she bound your powers temporarily," he said. "Maybe whatever magic he has on you is linked to your powers?"

"I couldn't do that. I need my powers to protect you boys." Although, she had to admit, lately she was doing more harm than good with her magic.

"We have our own powers now," Chris said happily. "You could teach us how to use them."

She looked at him. He was the one who had been able to kill Garmond. And she had been boycotting her powers since Samantha's death and nothing major had happened. Still, it made her uneasy.

"I'm not even sure it would work," she said, fishing for excuses.

"I read in the magic book that when a witch is infected magically—whether by a poison or by a spell—that the best way to clear the infection is to remove the thing that it's feeding on: their magic," Josh explained. "It's not a quick fix, like when Mom was sick, but it'd work." His voice grew more somber. This was the first time they had really talked candidly about Samantha since she died.

"Would I need a spell or a potion?" Kathy asked.

Josh shrugged. "The book didn't have one. I would think a power-stripping potion would be too dangerous. What if someone accidentally slipped it to you and left you defenseless?"

Kathy smiled. He had a point. "Okay, do you guys want to help me write the spell?"

* * *

"No candles or incense or anything. I need to be able to call them back wherever I am if I ever need them," Kathy said.

"Just don't call them back too soon," Josh added. "I would at least double the time you were infected. Maybe even triple, just to be safe."

She took a deep breath and nodded. This was her future:

trusting her nephews with the magical responsibility while she corrected the mistakes she'd made with her own magic.

"I'll still be able to say spells, right?" she asked for the thousandth time.

"You should. A witch always has that ability," Chris said. "I was able to say spells before I got my power."

Kathy took a deep breath and looked at the two spells in her hands. One was to remove her powers, and the other was to call them back. She needed to do it soon. She kept asking the same questions to stall the inevitable.

"Here it goes."

> *I call upon the power of the skies,*
> *to help me see through this evil disguise.*
> *Rid my magic for its protection;*
> *to help clear this wild infection.*

Kathy's skin was illuminated brightly, and the boys turned and covered their eyes. She closed her eyes and tilted her head up, her body lifting an inch off the ground. The illumination exited her body and floated above her head momentarily. Her body slumped back on the couch as her magic left her. When Josh and Chris ran to her side, the light had disappeared into the night.

Chapter Twenty-Seven

Kathy's first day back to work after Samantha's funeral was rough. The kids weren't behaving at all. They loved the sub so much that they weren't happy to see Kathy return.

Nap time, which was usually Kathy's downtime during the day, was filled with constant berating. A group of boys refused to lay down. Their protests woke the kids who were complying, and the afternoon was even worse than the morning because most of the kids didn't get a nap and were therefore cranky.

Being on crutches didn't help the situation at all, either. She even tried to get sympathy from them by saying she was hurt, but most of the kids didn't seem to care.

By the time the parents started arriving, Kathy was about ready to quit. She was not in the mood to deal with any more crying three-year-olds. But she knew that she couldn't quit.

Especially now that Samantha was gone and the day care was their only income.

When the last kid finally left and the classroom had been picked up, Kathy was exhausted. It was way past her normal quitting time, and she was anxious to get home.

In the parking lot, Will waited for her by her car.

"What are you doing here?" Kathy asked as she hopped to her car with the help of her crutches. She tried to ignore him and unlocked the car door, throwing her purse on the passenger seat. She still didn't want to talk to him after her discovery that he had ordered the attack on Samantha.

"I'm surprised you drove," he said.

Kathy got in the car and pulled her crutches in, slapping him in the legs with the ends. He held the door before she could close it. "The car's mine now. Why wouldn't I drive it? Beats taking the bus. Especially with this." She indicated her foot.

"I want to apologize for what you think you heard the other day—" he started, but Kathy cut him off.

"I know what I heard, Will. You sent Garmond after Samantha to kill her. Seems pretty clear to me." She tugged at the door, but his grip was strong.

"How is that different from what you were trying to do a few months ago?" His words froze her anger. It brought up inner demons that she tried her hardest to keep down.

She took longer than she wanted to respond. Her voice betrayed her at first, too. "That's different." She knew Will picked up on the pause. She cleared her throat and pressed on: "I was under the influence of evil. Thanks to you." She looked down at the steering wheel and muttered, "I've taken care of that."

"Thanks to me?" Will said, his anger building. "I thought we decided that our whole affair—the one I'm still cleaning up—is your fault?"

Kathy's eyes flashed with anger. "That whole affair that I supposedly started is what killed my sister. Don't lie to me and tell me that you're still cleaning it up! You're taking advantage of the army we started to build together. You're continuing our quest despite me leaving you."

She yanked the door from his grip, fired up the engine, and sped out of the parking lot before he could say anything.

* * *

After dinner, all Kathy wanted to do was lay in front of the TV and forget about the world for a few hours. But she had promised the boys—mostly Chris—that she would start their training.

It was a routine they were going to practice again and again until she felt confident enough that they had a firm grasp on their powers. She wasn't sure if that day would ever come—she could already feel the change in her from aunt to parent. Now she was worrying whether she was corrupting them with their exposure to magic and all the negativity that came with it. But that's what made their training even more critical. She needed to show them that magic also had a good side. She needed to remind herself of that, too.

"What are we starting with? What can I blow up?" Chris was jumping up and down, bursting with excitement.

"Chris, relax," Josh said, laughing. "I'm sure we're not going to jump into using our powers right away anyway."

"Actually, I think that's the best place to start," Kathy started. "You need to have a handle on your powers first and foremost. Your powers are uniquely yours—part of the reason why whenever someone steals someone else's, the results are usually pretty bad."

"So I can blow things up whenever I want!" Chris cheered.

"Not so fast! You need to be able to protect yourself first. The other stuff—writing spells, making potions, attacking," she shot a look at Chris, "that all comes later. Fortunately, your mom had already worked with you guys a bit on that stuff, so it's not new. That's why I think it's best to start with practicing."

"I've known my specialty for a while now, but it's not very powerful," Josh said.

"The wind? Josh, think of tornadoes," Kathy said. "That could be you some day. Not right now, but you'll get there. My powers are still evolving—well, they were..." Her voice trailed off. She missed her powers and the security they provided. But she was feeling better, freer, without them. Josh had been right; the spell Will cast was connected to her magic.

Outside, Chris was amped to start using his powers. Josh was a little more apprehensive.

"Each power has a trigger. You have to learn what that trigger is to activate your magic." Kathy leaned on her crutches in front of them and instructed. She felt like she was back in the classroom, except her nephews were more tolerable than the whiny three-year-olds surrounding her all day. "Chris, I'm willing to bet that yours is anger or fear. Right now, that's what you need to focus on to use them. As you get more intuitive with your powers, it'll be like second nature."

"What about me?" Josh asked eagerly.

Kathy thought back to the few times Josh had used his magic. Fear was certainly not his trigger. He tended to underperform whenever he was put in a situation that relied on him to use his magic. That worried her, but she kept it to herself.

"I don't know. What were you feeling the last time you used them?"

He grew quiet. When he eventually spoke, his voice was low. "Well, it was when Garmond attacked and Mom…you know…"

Kathy's heart sank. "Oh. Well, don't think about that. Sadness is not a trigger for anyone—that I know of, at least. Just close your eyes and try to focus on the wind. You'll learn."

"Can I start?" Chris asked.

Kathy wanted them to know how to use their powers, but she didn't want them to make any mistakes while learning. Allowing them to use their magic was a big step, but she knew she was going to have to let them do it eventually. Better teach them while she still could—Samantha certainly hadn't gotten the chance.

"Just be careful. No live animals and nothing expensive. If it gets too loud, we're going to have to stop for the day," Kathy said.

"We don't want to draw the neighbors."

Chris focused on the cluster of rocks in the corner by the fence. He made several waves of his hands but nothing happened. "What gives? Did I lose them?"

"Focus, Chris," Kathy said. "You certainly didn't lose them. Right now your powers are foreign to you. After a while they'll become more natural, a part of you that you won't even have to think about to use. Like walking. It's a part of you now, but it wasn't always that way. You had to learn how to walk."

They practiced for most of the night. The boys were both discouraged that they didn't see much magic, although Josh had a few better results than his brother. Kathy assured them that it would get easier. She also racked her brain for the best way to recreate Chris's trigger and how to find Josh's. They needed to feel like they were experiencing the emotion without it being fabricated. At least until they could call upon the powers on their own.

* * *

"Go to hell, Will!" Kathy shouted into her phone after he tried calling her for the fourth time that morning. She was only scheduled for the afternoon at work. The shortened hours would be a cut to her paycheck, but she was grateful to have the morning off to relax without any responsibilities.

Of course, Will ruined that.

She wanted to go for a long run to clear her mind, but she

couldn't. It was a beautiful day to go, too. Early October was unseasonably warm, yet the leaves had already started to turn. It was one of those "looks like fall, feels like summer" days and she didn't want to spend it inside.

Since she'd started at the day care, she hadn't had time to really run like she used to. She missed it. It helped her sort through everything in her life by giving her a small piece of her morning to lose herself in. She could focus only on her breathing and the way her feet hit the ground, and let her mind be clear.

But it would be a while before she had clearance to run like she used to. Instead, she pulled a lawn chair out onto the sidewalk leading to the front door and read a magazine in the sun.

After she had finished reading the glossy, she sat with her eyes closed and soaked up the sun. If she couldn't get endorphins from running, she wanted to try for some vitamin D.

"You look beautiful."

Kathy's head jerked. She hadn't heard Will walk up.

"Stalking me now?" she asked, trying to sit up in the chair. She reached for her crutches on the ground next to her.

"It's the only way to get through to you," he responded, stepping closer but still keeping his distance. "You won't answer my calls—not politely, at least."

"What do you want? Clearly, I want to be left alone."

"I actually came here to help you. This involves both of us," he started. "About a week or so ago, I felt different. Weaker."

Kathy raised her eyebrows. "Then go to the gym."

"You know what I mean," he said sternly. He managed to keep his voice low so the neighbors wouldn't hear him. "Magically, I wasn't up to full strength. Not the strength we shared after our blood bond. I think someone might have done something to us—put a spell on us or something. Something that feeds on our magic and weakens us. I thought I'd come and warn you."

Kathy rolled her eyes as she lifted herself up onto her crutches. "There isn't anyone feeding off our powers, Will. I gave mine up. They're gone." She wondered if it was the best idea to tell him that she was suddenly defenseless, but she figured this was the perfect way to show him how much she wanted to end their relationship and move on.

He looked surprised. "You gave them up? Why?"

"Because of our blood bond. Because of the love spell you put on me. Because I felt like I was feeding an infection in my own mind," Kathy blurted. "Now that they're gone, I'm free."

"But how are you going to protect yourself against the factions?"

"Let's be honest, Will. You've rounded up the factions under your lead. Any attack by them is an order from you."

Despite everything, she still knew that he wouldn't hurt her—at least not yet. He still loved her, of that much she was sure. She couldn't say whether he would hurt her nephews, but she was preparing them for that. Once she and Will had some more distance between them and he had time to fall out of love with her, he might be a threat again in the future. She was hoping by then that she would have her powers back.

He was silent for a long time, and then he asked, "So now that you're free from my magic, what are your feelings toward me?"

Kathy considered for a minute. She hadn't thought too much about it. She knew for certain that her head was cleared of any influence: she had finally stomped out that headache. But her feelings for Will hadn't changed. It seemed the spell he'd cast ignited and sped up a true love. But that didn't change the danger it put her and her family in.

"I do still love you," she confessed. "But that has to change. I can't keep doing this. The last few months were the worst thing I've ever been through and it cost me a sister—cost the boys their mother."

"I can change. I mean it this time," he pleaded. "We deserve a fresh start. You've given up your powers, I can give up mine. We'll be like a normal couple. No magic. No threats. Just us."

Kathy was shaking her head as he spoke. "No, Will. I'm done. My love for you doesn't change anything. You are responsible for Samantha's death. Whenever I look at you, I see everything I want to forget. All the things my sister is going to miss in her children's lives. I see the sad look in my nephews' eyes. I can't ever forgive you for that."

"But you were the one who—"

She held up her hand to cut him off. "I know what I've done. It's a regret I'm living with. Sure, it'd be easy to say yes and give in to you. But I can't keep lying to myself by thinking that this relationship has a future." She sighed. "I need you to leave me alone so that I can get over you."

"You're wrong. I may have used magic, but even without it you feel the same way about me that you've always felt," he declared. "I'll show you we're worth it, Kathy."

"Please don't."

He was walking away now. Kathy hurt him, which was upsetting, but she knew it was the only way to get through to him. She hoped that he wouldn't use it to retaliate.

"I still love you, Kathy!"

She gave him a sad smile. The love from their marriage still lingered, but the passion she had for him was gone. She knew Will didn't feel the same way, and as much as she wanted the relationship to be over, she knew she hadn't seen the last of Will Brown.

KEEP READING

The Harvest Moon

A legacy of magic and danger.

All Danielle Bowen wants is a normal life: white picket fence, kids in the nursery, and peace and quiet with her husband Simon. But she can't escape the fate her family has wrought for her. Born into a tradition of witchcraft, she has also inherited a deadly enemy: Toxanna, a dark witch who will stop at nothing to destroy the last of the Bowen line.

But will Danielle's powers be enough to save her family—or even herself? And when Toxanna sets her sights on Holly, Danielle's only daughter, will anyone have the strength to rescue the newly fledged witch? The darkness is closing around the last of the Bowens. In a world of wizards and powerful demons, how can one family of witches survive?

Leave a Review

If you enjoyed this book please consider leaving a review online. This helps future readers determine whether or not this book is something they might want to immerse themselves in as well. If you really liked this book, feel free to sign up for my mailing list and follow me online. Thank you for your support!

Stay in the Loop

Help out an indie author and subscribe to my newsletter! Subscribers will be the first to receive information on upcoming releases. What are you waiting for? Head over to www.davidnethbooks.com to sign up!

About the Author

David Neth is the author of *The Blood Moon*, the first in the Under the Moon series. He lives in Batavia, NY, where he dreams of a successful writing career and opening his own bookstore.

Follow the Author

www.davidnethbooks.com
www.facebook.com/davidnethbooks
www.twitter.com/davidnethbooks
www.instagram.com/dneth13

ACKNOWLEDGEMENTS

I feel very lucky to be sitting here putting on the finishing touches of my second book. This novel has been my favorite thing to write so far. The dynamic between Kathy, Will, and Samantha was so much fun to write. Kathy is my favorite character I've ever written and I can't wait to see where she goes later on in the series.

Like *The Blood Moon*, the ideas for *The Full Moon* have been circling in my head since I was a teenager. Through that time, there have been so many influential people in my life who have shaped the way this book came together without them even realizing.

I am forever grateful for the work my copy editor, Tammy Salyer, did polishing the manuscript to make it publishable. I look forward to working with her on future books.

My cover designers, Slobodan Cedic and Jelena Gajic, have also been a tremendous help with this book. They gave it a face—and a remarkable one at that—that is something I can be proud of.

I dedicated *The Full Moon* to my mother because her strengths and imperfections remind me of Kathy. It wasn't until I was in the final edits of this book that I realized I was drawing from her for inspiration. Along with the rest of my family and friends, she listened to me ramble about story lines and word counts and marketing ideas and encouraged me the whole time. Without her, I wouldn't have had the inspiration to complete this novel. Thank you, Mama!